Dear Lindsay,
I hope you real...

NO IDEA

SI PAGE

with my best wishes,

Si Page
x

All rights reserved

Copyright © Si Page, 2016

The right of Si Page to be identified as the author of this work has been asserted by him in accordance with Section 78 of the Copyright, Designs and Patents Act 1988

The book cover picture is copyright to David Hall. The Masterplan font is copyright to Billy Argel Fonts.

This book is sold subject to the conditions that it shall not, by way of trade or otherwise, be lent, resold, hired out or otherwise circulated without the author's or publisher's prior consent in any form of binding or cover other than that in which it is published and without a similar condition including this condition being imposed on the subsequent purchaser.

This is a work of fiction. Names, characters, businesses, places, events and incidents are either the products of the author's imagination or used in a fictitious manner. Any resemblance to actual persons, living or dead, or actual events is purely coincidental and unintentional.

A CIP record for this book is available from the British Library.

No Idea is also available as an e-book via Amazon.

www.sipage.co.uk

Other works by Si Page
Missing Gretyl: You Only Love Twice
The Inside Scoop: The Secret Journal of a Prime Minister

Si Page was born in Romford, Essex in 1970 and grew up with a love of football, films, frolicking and females (the priority of the four 'F's reversed during his late teens).

After attending three different secondary schools, Si decided it was a waste of time taking his GCE exams and bunked off to head for the workplace via the YTS scheme. Earning little more than twenty-something quid a week and a clip round the ear for cutting carpet 'very wonky', Si set off in search of new horizons.

He describes the next ten years of his working life in grim fashion: 'I worked as a telesales 'thingy' (ew), vending machine salesman (spit), insurance clerk (snore), debt collector (ouch), recruitment consultant (liked that one) and a mortgage broker (worked for sharks and didn't last long).'

Things drastically changed in 1996, when Si decided to study for a B.A. Hons. Theology Degree somewhere outside of Essex, in a strange land called 'The North'. Things were reportedly so bad 'oop North', Si fully expected to be living among whippet-racing peasants dressed in shell suits and living off a diet of mushy peas.

Si heard about something called the North-South divide and mistook it for the Northern and Southern Hemispheres. He reasoned that pollution due to population density must have been the reason for the shorter lifestyle amongst the race of Northerners, and not just the peas.

After a car journey up the M6 motorway to a grassy dwelling called Cheshire, Si survived three years of student life, avoiding Sudden Death Syndrome by refusing to eat the carcasses cruelly served up in the college canteen. He finished his degree in 1999 and until 2007 he worked as a Reverend in the North West of England – Merseyside and Lancashire. Among more sophisticated company, he would like to point out that he resided a few miles away from two world class golfing resorts – the first near Royal Birkdale, and the second, a few cosy miles from Royal Lytham.

Si has since been involved in a number of creative projects, including an Oscar-nominated short film called 'Most'. He has of course, written several hilarious books. First, the comedy novel, 'Missing Gretyl' (also a screenplay) and the second, a parody and satirical work on David Cameron, called 'The Inside Scoop: The Secret Journal of a Prime Minister.'

Totally dedicated to writing, Si has taken his classroom humour, workplace banter and on a more serious note, life skills from the pastorate, to write funny, challenging and original drama.

Si has two lovely boys called Ruben and Freddie and has been married for eighteen years to a beautiful lady called Solana, who prior to meeting Si, enjoyed the full use of her mental faculties.

Si hopes to make a decent living from his books, sooner, rather than later.

You can keep up to speed with Si's latest news via his website at www.sipage.co.uk, www.facebook.com/SiPageauthor or twitter.com/Siberpasta

Contents

Chapter 1: Floppy Memories	11
Chapter 2: Guru Rob	37
Chapter 3: Bottle of Coke	47
Chapter 4: Brat Doll	57
Chapter 5: Pound Wise	63
Chapter 6: Captain America	67
Chapter 7: Accident and Emergency	71
Chapter 8: Judgment Day	75
Chapter 9: Conflict/Resolution	79
Chapter 10: The Prodigal Son	85
Chapter 11: Milking It	95
Chapter 12: Wake Up and Smell the Coffee	123
Chapter 13: Doing God	127
Chapter 14: The Adventure Begins	135
Chapter 15: Chat Show	143
Chapter 16: Wi-Fi Boost	155
Chapter 17: Old Wounds	169
Chapter 18: The Daily Telegraph	177
Chapter 19: Official Business	183
Chapter 20: Cover Story	189
Chapter 21: Game Changer	193
Chapter 22: Saving Grace	207
Chapter 23: The Disguise	215

Chapter 24: Farewell	225
Chapter 25: Tel Aviv	239
Chapter 26: Bombshell	251
Chapter 27: Decisions	259
Chapter 28: Poetic Licence	271
Chapter 29: Faith and Mortality	277
Chapter 30: Robots Do It Best	291
Chapter 31: Too Little, too Late	299
Chapter 32: Pierce Morgan It Is	309
Chapter 33: Breaking Good	321

Thank you

I wish to add my sincere thanks to the many friends who have encouraged me and offered helpful feedback for NO IDEA. By way of thank you and with permission, some of you are named characters in this story. As a work of fiction, any likeness to the characters named in this book is most likely, coincidental.

Special thanks go to The Book Club and Author Chat Forum members on Facebook, along with Kate Irwin and Kath Middleton for their careful editing, David Hall for the front cover artwork and Jo Roderick for his formatting.

To my precious wife, Solana, and my two darling boys, Ruben and Freddie: You are engraved upon my heart.

No Idea

"Tis strange -- but true; for truth is always strange;
Stranger than fiction; if it could be told,
How much would novels gain by the exchange!
How differently the world would men behold!
How oft would vice and virtue places change!
The new world would be nothing to the old,
If some Columbus of the moral seas
Would show mankind their souls' antipodes."

George Gordon Byron (Lord Byron), Don Juan,
Canto the Fourteenth, Verse 101

Chapter 1

Floppy Memories

I fumbled through my flat mate Rupert's pants and socks drawer. Wearing a pair of surgical gloves would have been the smart idea, but I braved it and pressed on in the sure and certain hope I'd find a pair of my own and importantly, 'clean' underpants. I had no worries about waking him up as his nasal grunts indicated there would be a good few hours before he got his backside out of bed.

The two lads who shared my flat were always nicking my stuff and never bothered to wash their own clothes. Rupert nabbed any item of clothing I'd left drying on the radiator, his bizarre colour coordination and lack of dress sense only measured by how much skin he decided to cover. Martin rarely removed his Scotland footy shirt and shorts, but when reluctantly forced to do so, he would wear his girlfriend Pit Bull's charity shop purchases.

At the back of the drawer I was surprised to find an old floppy disk of mine, labelled, 'Rob Wise notes,' entwined in the thread of a pair of Rupert's faded Union Jack print boxer shorts. What the heck it was doing in Rupert's room, I had no idea.

Intrigued by the discovery of the disk I unwound the cotton string from the black 1.44MB floppy disk and searched the room for my old Windows 95 laptop I'd given Rupert after upgrading mine. Maybe he'd

No Idea

found the disk in my old laptop bag? Anyway, I gave him the laptop on the understanding he'd look for a job online or do some study or Open University course – basically anything to get him away from the booze. Five years later, his drinking problem hasn't gone away and his bank balance is non-existent, but I haven't had the heart to kick him out and replace him with a rent paying tenant.

I looked under his bed and found my old silver laptop covered in dust, fluff and god-knows-what else, surprised he hadn't pawned it. Only a few months ago, the muppet swapped an expensive Swiss movement watch for a crate of beer with one of the Burberry-clad chavs across the road. I tried to use some calm negotiation to get his watch back, but my Jedi mind trick failed to work on a ferocious Doberman. I returned empty handed and with a black eye gifted to me by one of the hoodies. When my feisty flat mate, Martin, learned of the incident he marched across the road shouting, 'Ye dinnae touch ma mate! Ye'll be dealin' with me now.' Despite hearing endless tales from Martin of the famed Glasgow kiss (head butt), I ran out to stop him, and I'm glad I did.

My other flat mate, the scantily clad Rupert, was far from the fighting type (A pillow fight would probably be his limit), unlike the forty year old ginger-haired and tattooed Martin, who, while being game for anything (and quite mental) was only 5ft 2" and wiry like a pipe cleaner. He wouldn't have lasted a minute with the zombies across the street.

I gritted my teeth before wiping the crud off the laptop and plugging the old beast in. I remembered replacing the Windows 3.1 operating system and its opening tune of, 'ta-da,' with Windows 95 and its six second piece of composed music. Though the upgrade was a vast improvement on 3.1, if you couldn't afford an Apple Mac, you had to put up with the dreaded 'blue screen of death,' that crashed more times than Kurt Cobain.

I recall reading that Bill Gates paid Mick Jagger millions to secure the rights to use his song, 'Start Me Up,' for Microsoft's TV advertising campaign. The song choice was ironic considering Windows 95 was more bug-ridden than the mattresses in our flat. It was no surprise then why Microsoft never used the bridge in the song, 'You make a grown man cry.'

After a few minutes booting up, the Win 95 logo appeared on the dull aqua green background, so I inserted the floppy disk into the machine. The laptop whirred as the computer read the saved information on the disk. I stared at the list of file names that were displayed on the screen:

1. The Millennium Lover
2. The Collar (Little Rev)
3. Jo Walsh letter

Scenes from my teenage years came flooding back at the sight of the filenames.

I had just turned eighteen when I entered a competition for aspiring young authors, sponsored by the Radio Times. My 3500 word short story, 'The Millennium Lover,' was a sci-fi/fantasy blend of the best traditions of Star Wars and the worst type of Hollywood romance - a kind of spoof/parody of popular film back in the 90s. It resembled something closer to a screenplay than a novel, and I wanted to impress the panel of reviewers with something original and hoped the cheesy dialogue would set it apart as something quite different. However, my short story bombed. It wasn't to be, and it was the last time I'd sent anything off to a publisher, more than fifteen years ago.

The second file on the disk, The Collar (or as I first called the story, Little Rev,) was inspired after listening to my granddad talk about his childhood and watching the Billy Elliott movie. The last file on the disk was a love letter to my first girlfriend, Jo Walsh. Cute with curly brown hair and freckles, she had agreed to go on a date with me, so I wrote her an over-enthusiastic, (fanatical) letter and handed it to her at school. She read it, cancelled the date and we never spoke again.

I didn't want to read my story, the Millennium Lover, for reasons I will explain soon, and reading my letter to Jo Walsh might do me more harm than good at the moment, but I was fascinated by the discovery of my unfinished story, The Collar.

I double-clicked on the file name and waited for Microsoft Word to open my story. This is what loaded onto my screen:

THE COLLAR – Chapter One

'Buried deep within the undergrowth, I lifted my chin a few inches above the sodden ground and squinted with my perfectly trained right eye through the crosshair of the rifle.

I'd been lying in wait for what seemed like hours, when my eyelids began to feel heavy. My camouflaged cover had lulled me into a false sense of security and my concentration was waning - a luxury no professional soldier dared accommodate while his index finger was wrapped around the trigger, waiting for the target to appear.

My heart banged loudly and my lungs took deep inhales of breath, before exhaling CO_2 into the cold night air.

A cloud of cigarette smoke rose from the bunker and escaped like a phantom into the night. 'It has to be him,' I told myself, squeezing my finger a few extra millimetres around the trigger and fixing the rifle butt firmly into my shoulder. It was him. I'd recognise that balding, grey matted scalp anywhere, and I was ready to fire a large calibre 7.92-mm bullet into it.

BANG!

My brother, Mike (I am fostered, so neither my foster parents or their children are biologically related to me), slapped my head several times, snatching his Army Men comic from my grip, before pushing me off my bed and onto the floor. My perfect moment may have been squandered for now, but the great thing about living inside my head was I knew I'd soon return to the same scene, and the bullets would still have HIS name etched on them.

To avoid any further slaps from Mike, I walked down the stairs and grabbed my coat.

No Idea

My foster mum yelled from the kitchen, 'It's raining bloody cats and dogs out there and I don't want you coming in like a drowned rat. If you're going out, stay out until you get yourself dry, you hear me?' I wasn't sure how I was supposed to get dry in the rain, but I had learned never to question her and I was already on my way out of the door.

The grey sky crackled and then a rumble of thunder rolled through the clouds. I conjured up a whole plethora of Alsatian and Dachshund dogs chasing Persian and Siamese cats as they fell from the sky, to the musical backdrop of a Tom and Jerry cartoon. I wanted to believe that pets could actually fall from the sky. Sometimes I loved being a child.

A child's imagination can be both a frightening world and a wonderful playmate. I was happiest when away from the house and my daydreaming served me like a childhood friend, but I didn't want my imaginary friend around when things were bad at home, where my thoughts always seemed murky and dark. Though I believed reading comics would help me escape reality, I've decided to stay away from my brother's ones. They always gave me the worst nightmares, and I think they must fuel the rising anger inside of me.

I opened my garden gate. The street was awash with water, glistening like a crystal lake in sun-soaked showers, and the roads looked like someone had stretched cling film over them. I smiled at the sight of copper-bronzed and crimson red leaves as they floated like miniature sailboats en-route to the nearest drain.

My foster parents wanted me out of the house as often as possible, and especially during school holidays, though I doubt they knew or cared where I was. I'd leave about ten in the morning, and after borrowing my neighbour Bill's shampoo, bucket and sponge, I'd walk the streets and knock on doors offering car washes. My price was negotiable depending on their willingness to pay. If I was short of cash or they simply didn't want it done, I'd offer to clean their car for a quid, but there were other generous neighbours who paid twice that and more, depending on how much they admired a ten year old's work ethic.

I'd seen the Oliver Twist movie so many times, I'd mastered the, 'Please sir, may I-?' look of innocence. One lady always fell for it and ended up helping me wash her own car. She still paid me the full amount. I wondered if she was as lonely as me.

If it wasn't loneliness, I reckon she helped because of the dried soapy suds I always left on her new pride and joy. Bill's cheap Halfords Car Shampoo was no match for the Wonder-Wax Super Care Total Wash and Polish at the petrol garage a few minutes away. Mind you, I reckon theirs cost at least a fiver more than I charged.

Though the afternoon was incredibly wet, I'd made my way to St. Stephen's to kick my football against the large bricked wall of the church. It was perfect - even if it was raining.

No Idea

There was no one to shout at me, no chores to do and no one giving me nipple twists or dead legs. It was just me and my imagination.

Lately I've been particularly successful with my football, picking out a particular spot next to the stained glass window of the Virgin Mary (a few bricks away from her nose, to be precise). I pretended it was the top corner of the goal, I was the centre forward and this was the sudden death penalty that would seal a World Cup Final victory against the ruthless Germans. Over and over I practised my side foot technique - confident that if I was ever called upon to take such a penalty, I wouldn't let my country down.

The heavy rain lasted most of the afternoon, only giving reprieve in the last half hour. I was now drying out in the sun like a prune, and my wrinkled shirt gave ample proof I had taken it off, dried my hair with it, and like a shammy leather, wrung every last drop of water from it.

It was nearly tea time, and if I wanted to eat I needed to get a move on. Leftovers at my house were not an option when you had two teenage brothers who: 1. Ate everything they saw; and 2. Didn't care whose plate it was on.

I was moving briskly toward my house at the end of the street and bouncing the ball on the pavement when I was distracted by a sharp pain piercing my calf muscle.

'Orphan, Orphan, Gypo, Gypo scum!' rallied from across the street. I turned to make eye contact with the chants and recognised a few

boys from school, their faces snarling like a pack of hyenas.

Barely seconds passed, and I was struck again, this time in the head, with a jagged stone. The blood trickled down my forehead and into my mouth, its salty taste following a loud voice booming in my head: 'Run you idiot, run!' I took off like an Olympic athlete, barely 400 yards or so from my home, to the taunts of 'Come here you pussy,' as they chased hard after me. I turned my head to see if they were gaining on me but I had managed to keep my distance as one of the boys stuck up his middle finger at me while the others threw more stones.

'I'll head for the alleyway and over my garden fence,' I thought. 'That way they won't stone me while I wait for Mum to answer the door.' I turned into the alleyway and rolled myself over the fence and into my garden.

I was sobbing as I lifted the rim of the kitchen window before climbing inside, and extended my arm onto the kitchen counter to balance myself. I froze, half suspended, as I accidentally nudged my foster dad's whisky bottle and watched it smash on the tiled floor.

Paralysed by fear, I couldn't move an inch, and the pain in my head intensified as blood from my wound dripped onto the white kitchen counter. The next thing I remember was being dragged by my shirt collar across the counter by my dad as he uttered words I have found so hard to forget: 'My drink... you little git!'

No Idea

Like a fisheye lens closing inward, the room became deepest black.'

***

I wiped my wet eyes as I remembered being so excited as I wrote, The Collar. Reading my story again I could see something of the little boy that I was, and importantly, the need he had for love and acceptance.

I felt so alive and hopeful when I typed those words more than fifteen years ago, but everything changed in the space of a few weeks. I received a rejection letter, and my best friend, Tom, received a publishing contract.

Tom and I were only eighteen years old when we entered a competition sponsored by the Radio Times with a tagline that said something about a search for a New Young Romance Novelist of the Year.

We never stopped dreaming about seeing our books in the stores, and spent hundreds of hours together writing and discussing ideas for plots and characters. Now one of us had hit the jackpot, Tom and I were ecstatic. No mean feat for my best friend who had just earned himself a two book deal.

However, the rollercoaster ride soon ended for me. I didn't get off the ride - I was thrown off. Barely a fortnight after Tom's win, his phone calls and visits stopped. I had been cut out of his life without a single word or reason why. He never replied to my calls or letters I'd sent by recorded delivery. Ten years of friendship had gone, like an apparition in the desert, and the memories of our time together, desecrated.

I tried hard to stop the feelings of bitterness I had, and made up excuses for why he never kept in touch. But each one was lame and I knew it. I had to face up to the truth that whether it was fame, money or success, my best friend had moved on and become an arsehole, my sense of loss had been replaced by resentment.

Tom's first best-seller, 'The Trouble with Marilyn,' was all the talk in the media: 'How could a teenager dream up such an erotic fantasy about a student and his teacher?' they asked. I'd put that down to the porno films he watched when his parents were out, but I noticed this small detail wasn't mentioned in his interviews.

They say trouble comes in threes, and though the bitterness slowly dissipated over the years, I'd always been haunted by his betrayal. I forever looked back and foolishly blamed Tom for the domino effect on my life after his abrupt departure.

I had allowed the past to determine my future for far too long.

I was no longer the prolific teenage writer churning out thousands of words every day. I'd become the stereotypical yet largely false depiction of the Hollywood writer - hunched over my keyboard for days or weeks on end and staring at a blank screen while agonising over the next paragraph of my novel.

After the publisher rejected my story, The Millennium Lover, I had plans to continue writing The Collar into a larger novella or full size novel, but following Tom's betrayal and barely a few chapters in, I allowed his actions to put a stop to that.

Tom's lift had gone all the way to the top floor. Mine had plummeted into the basement... and oblivion.

***

Twelve years later I was celebrating my 30th birthday at the O2 Academy Brixton in London.

The upper half of my body jolted under the strobe lights as each thud shuddered through my body. If it wasn't for the drum n' bass, you might have thought I was being tasered and succumbing to an epileptic seizure. Wedged between multitudes of ravers, my feet shuffled awkwardly to the beat and fought to keep me upright as I moved in a dance space not much larger than the standing room on an underground train during rush hour.

After three hours I was knackered, off my face, and my movements had become all the more spasmodic... not that I cared. When the speakers banged, I raged harder and didn't give care what anyone thought about my lack of coordination while I offered my body to the orchestra of musical demons.

'Do you want to get out of here?' said a blonde haired and partially clothed girl dancing in front of me. Stomping in her purple Dr Martens boots, she jerked away in her tight ripped jean shorts and a third of a t-shirt that finished a few inches below where her bra would have been, had she been wearing one.

'Did I want to get out of here?' It wasn't quite the pick-up line I'd imagined or hoped for, but then, I was being pretty unrealistic looking for love in a nightclub – especially when I'd just sweated half of my body weight and replaced it with alcohol.

The girl's arms waved in the air and showed off her perfectly shaved arm pits while she waited for my reply.

'What did you say?' I yelled back, making sure I understood her European accent. I could hardly hear her voice above the thud of the grime meets electro dance track, 'Wearing My Rolex,' by Wiley.

Her hot breath entered my earlobe again. 'Let's get out of here. We can go to my place.'

The sweat on this girl's face had smudged the black eye shadow and orange makeup around her eyes, while the mascara from her eyelashes had run down her cheeks. Yet, despite her Rocky Horror show look and after throwing far too many Snake Bites down my gullet, I agreed to her suggestion and followed her to the exit.

I wondered if lurking beneath the heavy makeup and brazen debonaire was, on a sober occasion, a kind and intelligent girl also looking for a relationship.

I nodded over to my mates, Pit Bull, Martin and Rupert, and shouted, 'See ya later!'

Rupert and Martin high-fived each other and thrust their hips back and forward in childish fashion, believing that my night of Drum n' Bass promised to finish with a different kind of bang. Their faces suggested they knew far more about my date than they were letting on.

After a few minutes in the taxi, we arrived at her flat in Electric Avenue. She fumbled with her keys and giggled while struggling to find the keyhole.

'So what did you say your name was again? Where are you from?' I asked. We'd only been dancing together for about ten minutes before she invited me back to her place.

I closed the door behind me and followed her up the stairs.

'I'm Astrid,' she replied all too abruptly, before taking me by the hand into her flat and sitting me down on the edge of her bed. 'I'm Scandinavian. My mother is from Norway and my dad is from Sweden.'

'I love all things Viking,' I replied. 'And you gotta love Braveheart!'

'Erm, I don't think Mel Gibson played a Viking?' she replied with a sexy, Nordic accent that replaced her w's with v's and o's with an oo sound.

I've always been fascinated by accents and the way people's mouths performed different actions as they spoke. Her mouth had a tension in the corner of her lips, and as she replied her jaw hardly moved and was closed a little, like she was chewing gum between her canine and molar teeth.

'Ah you're right about Mel not playing a Viking. That's the drink talking,' I replied.

'Yes, we need less talk and more action, English boy.'

'My name is Rob,' I muttered, shocked by her boldness and frankly, a bit put off.

Astrid was clearly NOT in the mood for chit chat, as she lifted my white Fred Perry Polo shirt over my head.

'I hope you won't disappoint me,' she whispered in my ear, nibbling it before shoving me back on the bed.

'I'll do my best,' I replied in a less than convincing manner.

She reached over to her bedside table and opened a drawer that was crammed full of condoms. 'Choose whatever you like. I must go shower first!'

It was clear that Astrid had no problem sleeping with a total stranger. I was having second thoughts. Call me old-fashioned, but even a drunk can have a few principles and I felt uncomfortable at just how direct this girl was. On one hand, I wasn't a virgin, but on the other, I didn't consider myself a male slapper either, even if I was bewitched by the combination of far too much alcohol and a 'Norwegian' accent.

'Tell me about yourself, Astrid,' I asked, as she walked toward the bathroom.

'First, you give me what I need and then we talk!' she replied, before adding, 'Check the magazines in the corner. That is all you need to know for now.'

I heard the shower switch followed by the spray of water, so I got up from the bed to take a nervous walk around the room and noticed a sizeable pile of hardcore porn magazines on top of an Ottoman.

I wanted out. Even in my drunken stupor, I didn't want a one-night stand with someone I couldn't look in the eye the following morning. I closed the bedroom door gently behind me, and walked down the steps to the front door.

Having a good time was one thing; Leaving with some self respect and wanting a girlfriend I genuinely cared for... entirely another.

***

Present Day

Three unforgettable years had passed since my visit to Astrid's flat.

I opened my eyes and returned to the surroundings of my freezing bedroom, gazing up from my bed at the grey Artex ceiling that may have been Dulux white a few decades ago.

Apparently the colour grey inspires knowledge, wisdom and intellect. The 'prison cell' grey surroundings in this flat were only inspired by the palette of cigarette smoke, mould and dirt - something akin to Tracy Emin's famed Turner Prize entry, 'My Bed'. In all of its shameless panache, the contemporary artist's empty booze bottles, fag butts, soiled sheets and worn knickers gained a notoriety that took the question, 'What is art?' to comical and farcical dimensions.

I had considered asking my 'arty' flat mate, Rupert, to paint a depiction of his room and try to sell it to raise some rent money. I figured that his dirty underpants, empty beer cans and half-finished take away boxes decorating his Marihuana plants might make a fetching piece of art on someone's wall or even a book or album cover. Never mind.

If I had a girlfriend, I wouldn't dare invite her to this flat. For starters, it begged for more than a paint brush, clean, hoover and tidy. Most of our possessions needed bagging up and taking to the refuse tip.

Considering myself the creative type, I've always wanted to finish writing a book, but in my malaise, I foolishly waited for a bolt of inspiration - the kind that forced my fingers to hit letters in the hope they formed into words, sentences, paragraphs and chapters worthy of someone's attention.

Restless, I dragged myself out of bed and over to the small sink in my room to throw some cold water onto my face. I glanced at the mirror and was startled at just how thin my face appeared. Gone was the round, healthy face of my youth. Now I looked like a cadaverous guy who suffered from poor nutrition. At 5ft 10, my natural weight is about 140lbs, but the last time I weighed myself, I was 30lb lighter.

I glanced out of the window for a change of scenery and noticed a huge Alsatian squatting outside my front gate. The rising plume of methane announced that the bowels of this canine beast had opened.

I had no idea where my ex-mate and mega-famous author, Tom, lived these days, but I doubt he was gazing out of his window at a heap of poop (unless gazing admiringly at a pile of his own paperbacks). He was probably sitting in some swanky apartment overlooking the Manhattan skyline or daydreaming out of a charming study window that opened out to a ten acre, perfectly landscaped garden.

I glared at the dog owner in her onesie and fake Ugg boots as she walked away from the steaming pile at my gate.

My breath made clouds on the inside of my window as I tried to prise open the frame to shout some carefully chosen obscenities, but it was painted shut. I guess that's probably a good idea for two reasons: First, Rupert is an alcoholic and would have probably fallen out of the window by now. Second, if the windows were opened, Environmental Health would be beating at our door.

I'm sitting on a stained and odorous mattress (probably fourth generation), in my biodegradable and frayed cotton underpants that held little in and would serve better for composting. I need to state for the record this is Rupert's mattress and this is the second time this week he's swapped my odour-free mattress with his.

I'm not only cold, but starving and find myself ogling a bowl of concrete porridge that's been sitting on my bedside table for several days. Though it closely resembled the sealant paste PolyFilla, I picked up the bowl and bit down on the hardened oats, but they provided no relief for my arid mouth.

I'm grateful Rupert has left his Canesten Oral tablets and cream lying around, even if they were an unpleasant reminder of his frequent, ungodly visits to Zara Flores across the road. It would be shameful to talk about what they get up to in secret. A man had to be worse than drunk and mentally deranged to go near that woman. Rupert was that man.

If you've seen the black comedy, Withnail and I, then picture Withnail (Richard E. Grant) in your head and that's Rupert. He spent his university years wasting an Art degree while taking drugs with other disgruntled students who ended up becoming anarchists with him. His anti-everything ideas (establishment, capitalism, war and globalisation) led him down a path of disillusionment and alcoholism.

I met the now twenty-eight year old art student while taking a stroll in Wandsworth Park. We got chatting and after hearing he was homeless, I invited him to stay with Martin and me, over five years ago. I don't regret giving him a roof over his head, but I wasn't fooled by his posh 'plum in mouth' accent. He had become a drunk who was wasting his life in this squalid flat.

When Rupert ran out of alcohol, that's when he would visit Zara. Sadly, he's not the only one who visited her, and for similar reasons. But I don't judge Zara, and I feel sad that blokes like Rupert take cruel advantage of her. It's a sobering thought she was once someone's little girl, but now she's older and chosen her own path, and I keep well away from it.

I am grateful my community-acquired pneumonia followed by five nights' stay in hospital (and three different courses of strong antibiotics) was the sole reason for the destruction of my immune system and Candida fungus.

My burning palate was only outdone by the thrush that had spread to my nether region like an army of red ants. I scratched myself for some temporary relief before exhaling deeply and staring out of my window again, watching the raindrops slither with the speckled bacteria spores and Pigeon guano coated on my window.

The flat made me feel like a stowaway who, unaware of how long he'd be trapped inside his container, began to panic and hyperventilate, succumbing to a slow, horrible and lonely death.

My alarm clock told me it was 11.35am, so I reclined on the bed and folded my hands behind my head and closed my eyes, thinking. I was usually comatose until early afternoon, but I'd been working up to this moment for a while. I needed to move on, look life in the face and fight back. I needed to get out of this flat and start writing again.

A wise person once said, 'If you always do what you've always done, you'll always get what you've always got.' I get that. I may have felt safer in my cage, but I couldn't expect anything to change if I just sat on my backside and waited for stuff to happen.

I drifted off to sleep and imagined I was heading for the front door with my few belongings and yelling, 'Bon voyage'. I had no idea where I'd go, but I was hoping it beat eating rotten porridge and freezing to death in the flat.

※ ※ ※

I woke to the sound of an aerosol can before feeling its wet and puffy lather cover my face.

Martin laughed hysterically as he waved the can of shaving foam at me. I jumped up out of bed and chased him out of the front door, but Rupert was lying in wait for me. A sharp, cold pain shot from my neck and down my back as he emptied a bucket of ice cold water over my head. I was drenched, standing in nothing but my birthday suit and rotten underpants and in full view of several dozen highly amused people at the bus stop. One girl pointed her camera phone in my direction so I took a bow, as if playing for an audience yet secretly humiliated that strangers were laughing at my partial nakedness and rotten underpants.

Martin ran back to our ground floor flat and locked himself in the toilet, still laughing uncontrollably. Wet through and shivering, I resisted the urge to kick the door down and returned to the kitchen to grab a few tea towels to dry myself, before stepping over the sleeping Michaela (aka, Pit Bull - Martin's girlfriend) to reach the remains of last night's congealed shavings of reformed Donner kebab meat drenched in chilli sauce. It's frightening what a man can be reduced to when he's starving and the food cupboard is empty.

As the electricity was off, I couldn't reheat it in the microwave so I dared myself to eat the kebab cold and dived in, grateful for the yellow polystyrene box that kept the fly larvae away. Those determined little buggers had recently moved out of Rupert's room and taken up residence around the kitchen bin.

There was a loud knock on the door, so I answered it while drying my hair with a tea towel. It was Mrs Popov, my Russian next door neighbour and the only outsider who has visited our flat more than once. Actually, all four feet ten inches of her visited two to three times each week, and always with the same request. We called her Yoda.

'Hi, Mrs Popov,' I answered the door, my mouth stuffed with kebab meat and a rogue onion hanging out of the side of my mouth. I muffled a half-cocked apology while covering up my unmentionables.

'Zat little theeeng, don't vorry hiding,' she chuckled. 'Cocktail sticks, bigger ones have!'

'What can I do for you this morning?' I replied, smiling at her accent and the use of her vs.

'Young man, very direct, you are. Blush at your inviting I vould, but I'm vorldly voman. Anyway, any sugar I have not, my dear.'

My neighbour walked in and stepped over the sleeping Michaela who was curled up in a foetal position on the floor.

'So it's the usual then, Mrs Popov? Tea, four sugars? Oh wait. Hang on a sec. We don't have any electricity, so I can't boil the kettle.'

'I'll have glass vater and chat, ve must, you and I.'

Since I'd told my charismatic neighbour I had a GCSE in Computer Studies and I was interested in social media and the internet, she wanted to chat about her missing grandson, Alexei. He disappeared at the age of eighteen having bought a one-way ticket to London, over three years ago, and sounded like a strange guy who collected Nazi memorabilia including rifles, WW2 helmets and uniforms amongst other paraphernalia. His main interest was computer programming and according to my neighbour, he was a genius who, part of a gifted and talented government scheme, loved solving puzzles and won many prizes for his mathematics during his childhood in Russia.

Mrs Popov handed me a sheet of paper and said, 'Rob, fallen from shelf, this book vith inside note. It's Alexei. He's dead, I'm thinking! Messaging me, he is!'

'Aw, don't be silly. I'm sure he's alive. And anyway, I doubt he'd be knocking books off your shelf, Mrs Popov. Let me take a look.'

Inside the book, 'Cybersecurity and Cyberwar: What Everyone Needs to Know,' was a folded A4 sheet of paper Alexei must have printed off before he disappeared. I figured this, because Mrs Popov didn't know how to turn a computer on, and I'd put her down as more of a Mills and Boon reader, rather than a computer security expert.

Apart from a cartoon drawing, some random words and unrelated sentences on the paper, there were references to bitcoins. I knew they were an online, cryptographic digital currency that cut out the middle man (banks and governments) thus creating a platform for undetectable transactions - an almost perfect way for criminal organisations to hide their movement.

There was also a reference to the Tor Browser on Alexei's notes, so I figured he may have been dabbling on the Dark Web, the hidden world behind the Internet. It was thought to be at least 500 times larger than the surface internet we see, and some

No Idea

likened it to an iceberg lying beneath the surface, hidden from view, its websites untraceable.

I'd watched a documentary on YouTube about the murky world of the Internet and I remembered that the Deep Web referred to content that wasn't indexed (recorded) by search engines. The Dark Web took things a step further – you needed a special browser like Tor to access it. It offered anonymity to its users and provided the perfect opportunity for criminal activities to take place, largely untraced.

I passed Mrs Popov a glass of water before continuing. 'I'll take a read of this and let you know what I think.' If Alexei was into computer programming, this dangerous and murky digital world may have proved too much of a temptation for him to stay away from.

Mrs Popov wiped her eyes and took my hand. 'Rob, help find my Alexei, you must. Alone, I am alvays, and, missing him, I do, so much.'

'Mrs Popov, I will do everything I can. I'll set up a Facebook page for him and circulate it around the internet, if that would help?'

'Yes, you must. I'm hearing Facelift, many people go into.'

I try hard not to chuckle at her reference to Facebook.

'Can you put me in touch with any of Alexei's friends?' I asked.

'My boy, his friends, I don't know. Internet, they must live in.'

I took another look at the sheet of paper. From what I could surmise, the world Alexei was interested in was totally out of my depth.

I had only known my neighbour for about a year, since she moved in next door. Alexei (she raised him like her own son after his mum died giving birth to him) went missing from Wolverhampton, after bunking college one Friday morning and buying a one-way ticket, arriving at London Euston station several hours later. Since that day he hasn't been seen or heard from again, and the only sighting was one recorded on CCTV as he left the station entrance. The police took nearly a month to call up the recordings, and by then, the camera footage in the area was either wiped clean or of no help at all.

Apart from putting up posters with the caption, 'REWARD' with a photo of Alexei underneath, I have always tried to make time for my neighbour. I took care of any telephone calls she had to make, as her muddled English caused her further distress on the phone, not to mention the operators who tried to decipher it.

My world was pretty small - two dossers (Martin and Rupert), Martin's girlfriend, Pit Bull, and a lonely, broken-hearted neighbour, Mrs Popov.

Martin shouted to me from the bathroom, 'We recorded th' whole foam-face, ice buckit prank oan mah mobile phone an' we're puttin' it oan YouTube.'

'Rob, famous, it could make you? Happy then, you must be!' Chuckled Mrs Popov.

Could today get any worse?

No Idea

Chapter 2

Guru Rob

I'm thirty three, single, and I haven't had a night out since the O2 Academy Brixton and my escape from the clutches of Astrid, three years ago.

When the summer months pass and the winter draws in, I feel all out of hope - at least until spring the following year. I should explain I suffer from SAD (Seasonal Affective Disorder). I know it isn't particularly brave saying it with a keyboard, but my vocal chords are far shyer. I haven't told anyone about it, because if you haven't suffered from depression, it's hard enough to explain it, let alone understand it, and my mates are hardly the sympathetic type anyway.

Whenever I've made the effort to leave the flat, the fresh air, exercise and whatever daylight I can get does help somewhat, but trapped inside the four walls of this flat and with just a few working light bulbs, I feel dreadful and don't want to leave my room. I've also been feeling quite agoraphobic lately, like I'm serving out my sentence in my own, custom-made cell.

I've been thinking a lot about my childhood and how I watched my mum, Sally, suffer with her mental health. She had difficulty getting up in the morning and always complained about a lack of energy which led her to oversleep, eat too much and put weight on.

She soon replaced the gluttony with alcohol and medication and relied on her friend Caroline, to help out. If it wasn't for her kindness ferrying me to and from school, I would have missed most of my education.

Her misery was exacerbated by the regular absence of my father, non-existent family time and barely having enough to make ends meet. Dad said her irritability was just 'women's hormonal stuff,' and her mood swings were better left alone. He constantly undermined and belittled my mother at every given opportunity. Some say SAD can be brought on by some kind of trauma. I think that might be true for my mother and me.

Before she made some life-changing choices, her response to her failing marriage was to drink. I can recall her stumbling around and swigging from a bottle of cheap wine while strangling the lyrics to Bonny Tyler's song, I need a Hero. I recall how often she would belt out the words, 'Where have all the good men gone?'

The husky voiced, chart-topping singer might have been singing about men who were heroes and were up for a fight... but even then I knew Mum wasn't interested in that sort of hero. All she wanted was a man who would pay her some attention. I can hear her say, 'Son, if only your father loved me more than his visits to the pub!' Not one to keep a secret of her miserable marriage, I was privy to all of my dad's failings. I wondered if she wanted me to hate him so she had an ally, someone to sympathise with her, but she'd begun drinking heavily before my father left us.

I wanted a dad. Not the one I had, but the one I hoped he could be.

My idea of a hero was someone who would gift me with his time and attention and importantly, without the influence of alcohol; nothing more. Our lives might have been different if my parents hadn't drunk themselves out of a marriage.

Growing up a keen reader, I used to think the protagonists and heroes in the novels I read were nothing like your average Joe, but now I'm not so sure. Hollywood seems to cheer the anti-hero these days. Look at characters like Bruce Wayne in Batman, James Bond, Clark Kent in Superman, or a more recent fictional character like Walter White in the hugely popular TV series, Breaking Bad, and you'll find your antihero.

Heroes aren't what they used to be, perfect men and women with muscles of steel and minds unstained by sin. A true (human) hero is a flawed character who makes more right choices than wrong ones and finds courage when it matters most. Take a look at Batman – he isn't a twenty-first century cartoon caricature anymore. He's a Dark Knight with some dark deeds and even darker thoughts. And then, James Bond's gone all tortured, and Walter White's turned a motorhome into a meth lab. How do we feel about heroes now?

Could it be that great protagonists are also your average Joes?

Maybe there is light at the end of the tunnel after all?

No Idea

***

When the winter months kick in, I'm like a hedgehog that's entered a state of stupor and hibernation, dropping its body temperature to match the environment and slowing down its bodily functions.

I know I'm not going to see much sunlight trapped inside the flat, but writing these words have helped me to unravel my head and get something down on the laptop. Since reading my story, The Collar, from the floppy disk and writing my thoughts down, I'm finding it therapeutic and I feel like getting stuck into some writing again.

I've wanted to be an author for as long as I can remember, but the insurmountable challenge of finding a publisher or agent has been a huge deterrent. The alternative is to self-publish a book and sell them on Amazon or another online retailer, but after reading that many authors earned royalties of less than a few hundred quid a year, it doesn't seem much of a good career move - not that I have a career at the moment.

Most writers aren't deterred by the minuscule income writing brings, because 'storytelling is in their blood.' I'm not sure what's been in mine for more than a decade. I've been positively anaemic and feeling like the constipated writer that's taken strong laxatives in the hope the end result isn't crap.

I've been listening to an online podcast from my ex-mate and world sensation that is Tom Davey. I know - why I do it to myself? It's called, 'Ten Tips for Writing Raunchy Fiction for Bored Housewives'. He always seems to patronize women with his sexist, belittling remarks, but it hasn't stopped him selling millions of copies.

Tom's next sound bite stopped me in my tracks as his smarmy voice changed pitch. He could barely hide his squeal of delight as he giggled like a pre-pubescent school girl boasting how superstores needed extra security at the launch of his latest book, 'Fast Love on the School Run,' the follow up to his best seller, 'Housewives Come First'.

In scenes that resembled Black Friday amongst other shopping riots, Tom told his podcast listeners, 'My fans have been amazing! My book trailer has three million hits in the last few hours, and YouTube almost crashed when it showed my readers fighting to the bitter death, and the victors holding my book aloft like an Olympic torch.'

My experience with girls has turned out pretty naff over the years, and I've struggled with how I viewed romance 'in the real world'. But the bad times have never made me feel like belittling women, unlike Tom who does this often. I can't understand how anyone falls for his kind of crap? He has an army of readers the size of China and millions of sales every year, but to me he still sounds like the same nasty piece of work that walked out of our friendship.

I tried writing romance once, but gave up after my last girlfriend, Jeannie Schofield, read a few pages and yelled something about her inner feminist screaming. She followed it up with, 'You... write romance? I don't think so. You don't have a romantic bone in your body.'

It's fair to say Jeannie never brought out the best in me.

Here is a sample of the short story I wrote that Jeannie hated:

"Noire Bistro, Chancery Lane, London. Sunday 6:40pm.

'From the moment she looked in my direction, her hazel brown eyes beguiled me. I wished they'd stayed on me for just a few seconds longer. Never before had I been so intoxicated with someone's eyes, not to mention, the cute brown freckles that playfully danced for me on the bridge of her nose. She sipped from her wine glass and smiled, her smooth, voluptuous pink lips engaging my vivid imagination. I stopped breathing.

I took another breath as Barry White's classic soul tune, 'Never, Never Gonna Give You Up' played softly in the background.

Fate had selected the perfect tune for the perfect moment.

The soft bistro lighting made her wavy brown and autumn red hair shimmer with a copper tint, while her statuesque figure was perfectly wrapped in a stylish blue suit jacket, pink silk scarf, white-collared shirt and slim fitting denim jeans. I looked down at her smooth, tanned feet and her bronze-coloured sandals revealed sun-kissed toes and polished nails that were beautifully decorated with painted flowers. A silver ring sat upon her left big toe. This girl was gorgeous.

I knew if I didn't pluck up the courage to speak to her, I'd regret it.

I tried to stop staring, afraid my gawping mouth would start to dribble and someone might think I was having a stroke. One more glance, and I might be robbed of the remaining oxygen in my lungs.

My attention was distracted by a table to the left of me. Two women were laughing and mouthing what sounded like insults in her direction. She readjusted her scarf around her neck, trying to deflect the unwanted attention. Incensed, I stood up, ready to say something to the women.

I once read that women displayed their survival instincts when in the presence of other female competition. I knew sod all about women but I thought that's precisely what's happening here.

I walked towards her, rehearsing in my head, 'Hi, my name is Rob. Can I buy you a drink?'

Before I opened my mouth she stood up from her table to address the women.

'I heard what you Jeremy Kyle-watching donuts were saying. You trash-talk others to make yourselves feel better about your pig-ugly boyfriends and crappy lives. Now why don't you go supersize yourselves on some fancy-arsed cupcakes and swig it all down with some cheap Lambrini before you cry yourselves to sleep.'

I stood there, stunned, sandwiched between the two shocked women and my feisty dream date with her deep, husky voice.

No Idea

Her silk scarf fell to the floor, so I bent down to retrieve it and rose, ready to place it around her neck, before I was halted by a prominent protrusion.

My dream girl's larynx was so large it looked like she'd swallowed a pick axe. The Adam's apple was a dead giveaway.'

I was seriously trying to be romantic, but my romcom days were ended by Jeannie before they had begun, so I changed the story by adding the Adam's apple twist at the end.

These days you can find my ex, Jeannie, in a bottle. Rub her up the wrong way and you'll wish you never had.

Jeannie definitely belongs in my top five worst girlfriends list and I'll tell you why. First, I've only had five girlfriends. Second, she was one of the few 'steady' girlfriends I'd had, and third, I imagined most girls are an awful lot nicer than her. After all, how many girls would argue every day about how you look, smell, breathe, think, talk or walk or even make a cup of tea? We only lasted a few months, but the effect of her negative comments lasted far longer.

I can hear myself as a kid say, 'Sticks and stones will break my bones, but words will never hurt me.' Utter crap. Hurtful words, left untreated, get buried deep inside a person and grow into unforgiveness or self-loathing. I know. I've lived with both.

I have racked my brain time and time again, wondering if I should have done anything different with Jeannie. Now I've come to the conclusion that it's impossible to make to incompatible people, compatible.

How many of my failed relationships have been good for me? Maybe all of them are, if I can learn something from them. But I need to do more than learn. I need intuition.

If it is true that most women are remarkably intuitive, I'll take my failed relationships as a twisted kind of compliment: My girlfriends saw qualities in me that I never did.

I had called this chapter, 'Jeannie', but this time she won't be having the last word. I've decided to call it something far more positive: 'Guru Rob'.

Ooh Ra!

No Idea

Chapter 3

Bottle of Coke

Being lonely is a bummer, but I can't expect to bag a girlfriend and move on with my life if I never leave the house; especially when my personal grooming looks like it's at the bottom of my crumpled To-Do list.

I can't remember the last time I had a haircut, there are purple bags under my eyes and my skin is dried out from late nights and a poor diet. My lack of finance means I have to make my razors last, so I only shave my cheeks and let my beard grow like a half-cocked impression of Brian Blessed and Emperor Ming.

The greasy stains on my navy blue shirt have morphed into a slug-like white paste and the kebab grease is proving impossible to budge as I scrape away with my fingernails. The unsightly clumps will have to stay until I have some money for washing powder.

I reach down and pull up the Levi's hanging off my 32 inch waist and thanks to Pit Bull leaving my Nike trainers at her work, I've seconded her lime green Crocs decorated with flowers. We have the same size feet, except my toes are hairier and she paints hers.

No Idea

Though we call Michaela 'Pit Bull', she certainly doesn't look like one: far from it. She earned the nickname after a Pit Bull ran at her friend's daughter and Michaela managed to jump in the way of the dog before it attacked the little girl. The dog mauled Michaela's arm right through to the bone. Miraculously, she never lost her limb after her friend beat the dog off with a guitar and then used a tourniquet to stop Michaela's blood while they waited for an ambulance.

Pit Bull is like family to us and works part-time at the local Chinese takeaway. I think she must be paid in food parcels, because most days the only food we eat is the leftovers that come from Wong's kitchen.

My stomach is churning like it's auditioning for a voiceover part in the Exorcist. Eating meals after midnight has played havoc with my innards so I'm hoping whatever is being strangled in my intestines doesn't reach my bowels too soon, as we are out of toilet rolls.

The flat always stinks of Rupert and Martin and their unwashed clothes, not to mention Pit Bull's heady scent of frying oil, garlic and onions that saturates her clothing, poorly masked with knock-off perfume. Apart from Pit Bull, I'm pretty sure I am the only one who takes regular showers.

Smells have always been a problem in the flat, highlighted by a recent visit from two Jehovah's Witnesses. The old ladies seemed delighted to be invited in until they saw Rupert sprawled across the sofa, swearing profusely with his public school boy accent while playing Grand Theft Auto on the Xbox and wearing nothing but underpants that looked tighter than a camp man's Speedos.

One of the ladies held a handkerchief to her nose and said they would have to leave because she'd left her bible at a house up the street. I offered to lend her my own which my mother sent me, but she said, walking toward the front door, 'That version is wrong and will only lead you astray. Here, take one of these magazines. It's nothing but the truth, and if you'd like a visit, do call the telephone number on the back.'

My granddad was a committed church goer, but he had nothing good to say about JWs. His best friend Jim was one and when he was critically ill, his religious group told him that he must refuse a blood transfusion because it was forbidden in the bible. Jim died because he believed a lie.

I miss my granddad. I'd only been living with him for a month or so when he died. He left his house to Mum and me so we sold it and split the money. I was eighteen with a lot of cash blowing a hole in my pocket. Within a few weeks, I was down five grand and had little to show for it, so I set up an account where I couldn't withdraw more than two hundred quid a week.

Fifteen years later, my granddad's money has dried up and I am faced with the uncomfortable prospect of having to move out of the flat, find a job and ask myself questions like, 'Where the heck is my life going?'

I grabbed my cap and contemplated heading for the door before I realised I'd unwittingly emptied Martin's fag butts on my head. I shouted a few obscenities in his direction and Martin groaned something from his room, but he was comatose as usual.

It was nearly two o'clock in the afternoon and Father Time had been messing with my body clock. I wondered if he was trying to tell me something. Could this be the day I dared to walk away from the flat? Carpe Diem, seize the moment, kind of thing?

I walked to the front door and opened it a few inches. The fresh air felt good on my face, so I opened it a few more inches to take a peep outside. It was bright and the sky didn't look as grey as it did from inside the flat. 'That'll be the filthy windows,' I deduced.

'Sod it!' I muttered, before putting on my long parka coat and taking a step outside. Thanks to my self-diagnosed SAD, I hadn't left the flat in over a month, but now I was marching down the path in defiant mood. 'Sod the depression! Sod the cage I've been living in! Sod everything that's been stopping me from getting off my backside and having a life! Sod the voices in my head! Long live Rob Wise!'

It was freezing outside, and in no time at all the cold fresh air in my lungs told my dodgy bladder I needed to pee and pee quickly, so I took a cheeky glance and made sure no-one was around and headed out of sight for the nearest bush.

I started relieving myself and just my luck - an elderly neighbour was hobbling down the path! I commanded my bladder to empty faster but I was running out of time. Thankfully I spotted an empty Coke bottle a few feet away, so I bent over to grab it off the floor (while trying not to pee on my shoe), and voila! I finished off inside the bottle while holding the plastic tube underneath my long coat. The feeling of relief was palpable.

The poor luv had reached her front gate and hurried past me, so I offered an apologetic grin and smiled awkwardly. The sight of my hand shoved up my coat and in front of my nether region must have frightened her half to death.

I scanned the floor for a plastic cap for the half-filled bottle, but couldn't find one. Now I had a different urge this time - one that shouted at me to return to the flat, back into my little cage, but I resisted and decided to walk toward the shops with the bottle and in search of a bin.

Before I reached a waste basket Martin approached me, holding hands with Pit Bull.

'Whit yur doing outside? Has th' flat burned doon ur somethin?' asked the thin-lipped Martin sucking hard on a rolled joint.

'I needed some fresh air to think,' I replied.

Martin dragged the joint out of his mouth with the tips of his two fingers and handed it to Pit Bull for a drag. 'Ye... think? Loove it! Gezz some ay that,' asked Martin pointing to my Coke bottle.

'No, It's my-'

He grabbed my bottle and lifted it toward his mouth. I panicked and tried to wrestle it from his grip, but the contents splashed over my coat.

A bleary-eyed Martin cried out, 'Man! That's honkin'!'

No Idea

I swallowed hard and tried to think of something to say.

Martin laughed. 'Lest time Ah ask ye fur a bevy! I'm oot here. See ye later.'

Feeling a deep sense of embarrassment I looked around to see if anyone was staring at me, and crossed the road toward the nearest bin, before reaching McDonald's restaurant less than ten minutes later.

I decided to park my backside on the pavement against the fast food joint. The American description seemed far more apt, than calling it a restaurant.

I removed my cap and placed it on the floor before running my nails through my hair and massaging my scalp. I inhaled deep breaths of cold air through my nostrils and tried to relax.

The ants were playing around the weeds next to my foot when a foreboding presence surrounded me, like the sky had become heavy, pushing down upon my shoulders. I didn't want to look up. I wanted to be alone and was reminded that this bear was safer in its cage.

I heard a chink and noticed a pound coin in my cap. A guy in shades and a grey pin-striped suit nodded at me and walked away. It's a kind act, but he couldn't have made me feel any worse. Did I look like a homeless person? After the coke bottle incident, I must have smelt like one.

I placed my head in my hands, frightened to open my eyes or look up and pretended I was invisible - even if I was sitting against a shop window in the middle of a busy high street.

I thought back to my neighbour, Mrs Popov and her missing Grandson, Alexei. Was he living rough on the streets somewhere? Was he in danger? Does he feel like he has no-one to turn to for help? What kind of relationship did he have with his Mrs Popov? Clearly, a warm room and two hot meals a day wasn't enough to stop him running away. And that reminds me. I promised to help her look for Alexei, but apart from looking at social media and using Google to search for any possible clues, I've been at a loss where to start.

A few minutes passed, and I could hear the rustle of plastic, before someone tapped me on my shoulder. I opened my eyes to find a white-haired old lady smiling at me.

'There you are dear. I hope you don't mind, but you look like you've fallen on hard times.'

She handed me a carrier bag full of toiletries, a loaf of bread and some tins of tomato soup. Her kind face looked three times my age and full of compassion.

'Thank you. Erm, I don't know what to say. You see, I'm not...'

I stopped myself saying, 'I'm not homeless.' Who would believe me? I looked a mess. Sure, I may have had a roof over my head, but I'd been without a real home for too long.

'God bless you, young man. I hope you find some good fortune in your life. Goodbye.'

Tears rolled down my cheeks as I sobbed outside MacDonald's. I had no idea if anyone could see or hear me. I didn't care. A dam had broken inside of me – one that needed to break for a long time. The warm salty tears trickled down into the corner of my lip. My chest tightened as I sobbed again, so I tried to distract myself and looked inside the carrier bag. I couldn't remember the last time I was the recipient of such underserved kindness. Rupert and Martin hardly bothered to fill the cupboards with anything at the flat. They had relied on my charity and Pit Bull's food parcels from Wong's Chinese, for far too long.

I was sobbing as I recalled scenes from my wasted life, while one particular memory pierced me. It was a note Mum left on her dining table.

She had been writing to me for a few years, but I never replied. She didn't have my current address, just an old flat I used to rent, and the landlord had been forwarding any post addressed to me. I phoned them last week and asked them to stop redirecting it.

I felt an aching inside of me that was either a dodgy takeaway tapeworm or my conscience speaking? One thing I was sure of though: This old life had to go and do one.

I guessed life was like the basic three act structure of storytelling, with a beginning, middle and end. The problem was I had foolishly viewed my life like the second act was one long, predetermined and dreary disappointment before I bowed out in the third and final act. That kind of lame thinking had stunted my growth as a human being. It was time to wake up and smell the coffee. There are arcs in every well told story, and obstacles as well as opportunities. My life needed to take shape and only I could write the pages, one at a time.

I lifted my head. Something was nagging me. 'Crap! I had to be at an appointment at the Job Centre in five minutes.'

No Idea

Chapter 4

Brat Doll

I arrived five minutes late at the Job Centre and was ordered to take a seat.

The girl's manner was frosty and suited a miserable Monday, the grim kind of day that confronted a jobless bozo like me with the impossible task of facing the week ahead like an ill-prepared rookie climber gazing up at Mount Everest.

The gods had decided I needed to sign on at the Job Centre today; the perfect day I'd discover whether the system would finish me off with the endless, complicated forms, or I'd be sanctioned again for turning up late.

I could hear Bob Geldof singing something on the radio about not liking Mondays and he wanted to know why? I sympathised with him.

I was sitting at a table waiting to be seen by a Job Advisor who was unashamedly scrolling through Facebook on her pink diamante smartphone and not giving a damn about my future.

'Let's see... right.' The girl screwed her face up and huffed several times. I hoped it wasn't my coat she could smell, because her expression matched the gloomy ambience of the room. She looked so miserable I decided to name her, Miss Monday.

No Idea

'So what skills do you have?' she asked abruptly, with more than a hint of sarcasm. She was holding the palm of her hand over her face and hadn't looked up at me once.

'Erm, I guess you'd call me a writer?'

'Don't guess. Let's start again shall we? What... skills... do... you... have?'

'Like I said, I'm a writer, YOU SARCASTIC COW!'

Okay, I didn't say those last three words, but I felt good typing them, and especially with the CAPS LOCK on.

'So what have you written then?' Her left eyebrow was raised while the right one was dead still. I wondered if Miss Monday was having a strange reaction to Botox, as I hadn't seen any skin move on her forehead.

Back to her question, 'What have I written?' I could see from her deadpan face that she expected me to announce I was the author of the life and works of some uninteresting, dead bloke. She still hadn't looked up at me.

I replied, 'What have I written? Now let's see... nothing yet.'

'So you're a writer who hasn't written anything?' Her monotone voice was getting to me. I knew I was being mocked.

'I'm a writer. I didn't say I'd written anything or I'm actually writing at the moment.'

'So you're a writer that hasn't written anything and doesn't write?'

Admittedly, if I was sitting in front of a bloke I might have chinned him by now, but I backed down from her jibe, realising the futility of my defence. Sure, I might have owed the universe an apology for my wasted life thus far, but definitely not 'Miss Monday'.

'Well, I live in a dingy flat with a bunch of dossers, so it's not the best place for writing, if you know what I mean?'

Miss Monday looked up at me, having saved her best scornful look for this moment. 'How would I know what you mean? Do I look like I live with dossers?'

'Far from it,' I replied. I imagined Miss Monday lived on a supermarket aisle inside a glossy, pink cardboard box labelled, 'Brat Doll'. I couldn't see her 'real' name anywhere, but I guessed it was Chelsea, Britney, Jordan or Paige. I went with Brat Doll.

So Brat Doll (aka Miss Monday) looked as plastic as her false, dagger-like nails and paper thin like a coat hanger. Her glued on eyelashes, Sharpie-inked eyebrows, inflated boobs and smudged orange tan made her a perfect candidate for a 'Hugh Hefner house bunny,' or contestant for the TV show, 'Take me Out'. If she failed to get a date there (opening her mouth would do the trick), there were always roles for Brat Dolls in TV shows like, 'The Only Way is Essex,' or 'Made in Chelsea'.

Brat Doll sighed loudly and told me to wait a moment. I straightened up in my chair and looked down to see what she was typing on her phone:

No Idea

'Sitting with a total loser who stinks, says he's a writer but he's never written anything, and wait for it... he doesn't write!?! Kill me now! Next pleeeeeeease!'

I had let myself go. Back in my youthful, Livin' la Vida Loca days, Mum was into everything Latino, and said I looked like a young Ricky Martin. But these days my unkempt beard and mop of unruly hair wasn't doing me any favours.

Brat doll was still distracted by her phone and shook her head with all the demeanour of an SS guard who'd just won the 'nastiest bitch in the camp' award.

'I can't see anything on the system that's suitable for you,' she barked.

'Is it because you're still on Facebook?' I replied.

Brat Doll hid her phone under some papers and wiggled her mouse, pretending to do something on the computer screen. I thought I'd seen her best scornful look, but I was wrong. This had to be her best Halloween face, because she was so wound up her pasted tangerine forehead had cracked like a fault line. I pointed at her head and motioned with my finger from left to right, signalling the need for her to fill the crack with some Fake Bake or trowel on some orange Plasticine.

Brat Doll extended an eerie grin that belonged to a Chuckie Doll.

'Mr Wise, your benefits sanction is still in place since you failed to turn up for your last appointment. You're welcome to challenge this decision, but I wouldn't bother, as you were more than five minutes late for this appointment!'

I stood up to leave, before Brat Doll continued,' Oh, and I'd suggest you go back to college or something. I doubt you'll find any vacancies for writers who have never written anything and don't write anymore. You have a nice day now, won't you? Byeeee!'

No Idea

Chapter 5

Pound Wise

The last job I had was at Pound Wise, a place so grim you could get employee of the week for turning up on two consecutive days and staff sickness was so prevalent it should have been reported as a local pandemic. News of staff who failed to turn up for work was frequently met with, 'Aw, it was my turn to go off sick!' by the deputy store manager.

I was eighteen, still living at home with Mum, and the only person thrilled with my new job was Granddad. He loved a bargain. One of his favourite mottos was, 'penny wise, pound foolish,' so you can imagine how pleased he was when I began working in retail. He said:

'The trick, son, is to make customers think they'll only spend a quid or two, but once they've seen how much crap they can buy, they'll end up leaving with half a dozen carrier bags on each arm. You mark my words.'

My last day at Pound Wise was memorable.

A heavily tattooed young mum conveniently ignored her screaming spawn while it kicked lumps out of my shin. Totally unfazed, she proceeded to thrust a box into my face: 'If this is only a quid, how do I know it'll work? Boots wants nearly a tenner for theirs?'

No Idea

I assured her everything in the store was a pound.

'So how much if I buy three?' she asked. 'Will £1.80 cover it?'

If I had a pound for every time I was asked how much something was, I'd have more pounds than the fattest man in Britain.

Our conversation had been interrupted by the ring of her mobile phone and the torrent of abuse that resulted. Barely five minutes passed before the same angry mother returned to my till, waving the stick in my face.

'I won't be needing this tester for the next nine months so I want my quid back!'

She must have sneaked into the staff toilet and peed on the stick. Before I had a chance to say I couldn't give a refund if she'd already used the pregnancy testing kit, she interrupted.

'I want a refund - this stick doesn't work!'

I smiled awkwardly. How could I possibly respond to that? 'I'd be foolish to cross this Black Widow,' I thought. She looked like she ate her men after mating. Maybe the tear drops tattooed on her cheeks were keeping tally of her prey?'

The Black Widow was interrupted by Mrs Fowler's poodle as it jumped the queue and mounted my leg, humping my shin.

The aged and eccentric Mrs Fowler (who was rumoured to be on her third pacemaker and fifth husband) chuckled loudly.

'Oh Smithy, you are a randy little thing! Let's get you home.'

I kicked out at Smithy, more in reflex than a vindictive act of violence, and knocked the dog flying as it skidded across the newly mopped surface, yelping. Mrs Fowler screamed and swung her handbag at my head, knocking me from my stool onto the floor.

The Black Widow stepped in as I rubbed my head. I wondered if her face would be the last I'd see before I closed my eyes.

''Excuse me luv! Before your mutt was bonking his leg, I was getting my refund so wait your turn. I want my quid back!'

I stood to my feet, grabbed my jacket off the back of the chair and walked out of the store.

I hated the job and was glad to leave, but I did hurry back and give the girl a quid out of my own pocket. I didn't want to be another tear drop on the Black Widow's face.

No Idea

Chapter 6

Captain America

After walking out of my job at Pound Wise, I arrived home and turned the key in the door of my red-bricked porch. It was already unlocked.

'Mum would never leave it like that,' I told myself. 'Something seems different?'

I double-checked to see if I'd entered the wrong house, but it was definitely my home. I panicked, fearing we'd been burgled, but what I discovered inside was far worse.

Gone were the endless pairs of high heels, boots and polka dot umbrellas that were always piled high on the porch shelves. I moved quietly toward the inner front door and noticed it was open. My heart raced and I tried to stop coughing nervously, not wanting to alert an intruder and lose the element of surprise.

In stealthy fashion I opened the door, and was shocked by what I discovered. I grabbed my mobile phone from my pocket and hit the number nine key three times while my thumb hovered over the green dial button, ready to press at any moment.

It looked like they'd taken everything. Several rectangles of picture-framed dirt surrounded each hook on the wall and the awful Camelia flower print was gone, along with the chintzy vases, the poodle draft excluder and the three tiered macramé plant holder. I pressed the dial button on my phone and whispered to the Emergency Operator a report of burglary at my home in Garratt Lane, Wandsworth.

I preferred to wait outside for the police before going back into the house, and told myself it was probably just a couple of jobless dossers who had broken in and filled their van with our tat to sell at the car boot. I don't remember us having anything of value in the house that my dad hadn't pawned before he walked out on us.

Thirty minutes passed and I was still waiting for the police to arrive. I was also worried why Mum wasn't answering her brick mobile phone. The thought dawned on me, 'What if she's injured and lying unconscious on the floor?'

I rang my Mum's friend, Aunty Caroline, to see if she was there, but the number just rang out, so I grabbed a metal dustbin lid handle, thrust it forward like a shield in front of me and walked cautiously back inside the house. I'd moved no further than the entrance to the lounge before I heard a police siren outside. Relieved, I rushed toward the front door with my dustbin lid in hand, not realising I must have looked like Captain America without the mask. Before I had time to say a word to the officers, I was wrestled to the ground and my arms were cuffed behind my back.

'I'm arresting you on suspicion of burglary. You have the right to remain silent blah blah blah,' said an intimidating copper.

I screamed as my shoulder blades felt like they were about to pop out of their sockets.

Ten minutes later after I'd been thrown in the back of the police van, the officers had done their checks so I was released and allowed to follow them back into the house. What I discovered lying on the table was about to change my life.

I lifted the pink-lined notepaper from the table and recognised Mum's handwriting. In a split second, a multitude of scenarios presented themselves to me. Was it a suicide letter? I quickly surmised that unless she'd bagged up her belongings from the house and jumped in the river Thames with them, suicide was highly unlikely.

The note said:

'Dear Rob,

I don't know how to say this, but since your dad left us, you know I've not been coping. As you can see, I've taken my belongings and left you this note, which your granddad must be reading to you now. I've had a word with him and he's promised to take good care of you.

I need to move on with my life, Rob. I hope you understand. Trevor has been so good to me since your dad left, so I'll be moving in with him. And guess what? He's taking me on holiday to Magaluf tomorrow! I think it's somewhere in Spain, and that's abroad, son! All inclusive as well, and Trevor said that means free grub and drink!

I wanted you to come with us, but Trevor said I needed a break, a real honeymoon, and I agreed. He's such a romantic!

No Idea

Anyway, I think you're ready to move out and find your own way. I've raised you the best I could under the circumstances. Let's chat about stuff when I get back home.

I'll be in touch - after I've caught some sun, of course! I'll send a postcard to granddads.

Love, mum x

PS. I've packed your suitcase and put some Jammie Dodgers in the front zipper of your suitcase! X'

Nearly fifteen years ago I stood in the lounge, holding her letter and crying my eyes out. A female officer stayed with me until Granddad arrived, but he'd fallen asleep and turned his hearing aid off, so I sat in my bedroom holding my suitcase for nearly an hour, neatly packed with my belongings, waiting for him to collect me.

I was eighteen years old. I was scared. I was angry. And I made a tough decision that day - I had no one to call mum.

Chapter 7

Accident and Emergency

After my breakdown in town and subsequent humiliation with Brat Doll at the Job Centre, I decided to spend the rest of the day shut away in my room.

Rupert shouted out from the lounge, 'Rob, ol' chap, we're watching, "Babs Does Blackpool – The Movie." Fancy it?'

'I'll pass, if you don't mind. I've got a banging headache,' I replied.

The lads always liked watching this tack when Pit Bull left for work, but I didn't want to watch porn. After growing up reading my dad's stash of magazines poorly hidden under his bed, looking at that stuff again would cause me more trouble than it's worth, and anyway, I wanted to think differently about women.

I remembered Granddad saying to me, 'Men love boobs, but only a tit marries for them.' He always taught me to look at life differently and was never short of cheeky banter. He instilled in me a desire to love and respect women. It's a shame my own father never learned the lesson, because my life would have been very different. Beauty is fleeting, but loving someone for who they are – that was attractive to me.

No Idea

Granddad took me to lunch once and pointed at the desserts in the glass cabinet. 'Son,' he said. 'A cake can look enticing, but remember, it's what's inside that really matters. Don't be fooled by its appearance.'

Apart from paying frequent and depraved visits to our neighbour, Zara Flores, Rupert's idea of finding love was limited to looking at dating websites. I'd often find him on my laptop scrolling through one of his favourite sites, Chicks Galore, saying, 'No, no, no, no, no,' hundreds of times, until he'd shout eureka and tell us he'd found the love of his life. All of this came down to how the girl looked. He never bothered to read their profiles.

I've always had a fantastic memory for names, and especially difficult ones. Rupert last professed his undying love for a girl called Sapna Chamaria he found on the website, but his attempt at pronunciation sounded like Sarah Chambers! He had an annoying habit of always anglicising names, and when I repeated Sapna's name back to him correctly, he replied, 'Oh fiddlesticks! She's a gorgeous bit of totty for sure, but damn it man, I'd get tongue-tied pronouncing her name. So I think I'll just keep looking, ol' chap.'

Admittedly, my efforts to find a girlfriend were worse than Rupert's. I looked for love through the lens of a screen and preferred to stay in my bedroom watching romcoms on my laptop. The lads said that was precisely why I had no success with women and put my dislike of dating websites and anti-porn stance down to some psychological illness.

Anyway, who needed porn when you could watch Sandra Bullock in a chick flick like, 'The Proposal'. She played the typical boss-bitch in the office to Ryan Reynolds, her assistant, who was expected to run at her beckon call. As you can guess, there's a reason why she was so hard, and it's a battle of the sexes all the way, until Ryan wins her over.

My ex-girlfriends went to war with me on such a regular basis that on reflection, I should have changed my name to Private Ryan. And I don't remember winning any of the battles either. It's a wonder I have any romantic inclinations at all.

I put my Sandra on hold and pressed pause on my laptop after hearing several loud thuds on my door.

'Rob, I've got a few painkillers for your head, mate.'

I opened the door to find Rupert holding a glass of water and a few pills.

'Thanks Rupert. I appreciate it,' I replied, swallowing the two blue pills before returning to my movie.

I was less than an hour into my film, when Sandra Bullock stepped out of the shower. The experience had a profound effect on me and my headache was replaced by a different kind of throbbing elsewhere.

My movie was interrupted by another advert on YouTube. This time, Nigella Lawson was advertising her cooking programme leaning over a bowl of whipped cream and peeling a banana. Now I had a rush of blood and a huge, uncomfortable erection that wouldn't go away.

No Idea

I closed my laptop lid and began to panic as my chest tightened. Sharp pains shot through my rib cage so I stood up, wondering if I had trapped wind or something.

'Rupert, what were those pain killers you gave me earlier?'

Rupert and Martin laughed hysterically. 'Nothing to worry about, dearie... just a double dose of Viagra.'

Had I been watching Panorama or an interview with the host Jeremy Vine or guest Ann Widdecombe, the tablets may not have worked, but this bad boy didn't look like he was giving up any time soon, and the thumps and sharp twinges in my chest were causing me a great deal of worry. I was soon clutching my chest and finding it difficult to breathe.

Next Stop: King's College Hospital.

Chapter 8

Judgment Day

After the escapades at A&E, I was still fuming and ready to kick off when Rupert and Martin woke up.

Pit Bull was up first from Martin's bed and walked into the kitchen to flick the kettle on, wearing nothing but his union jack boxer shorts and a red bra so tiny, you could barely fit two cup cakes inside them (I know, Martin tried it once). Seeing Pit Bull walking around semi-clad was a familiar sight and far from weird, though I had to ask the window cleaner to stop coming after I caught him taking photos of her on his mobile phone.

Now my money had evaporated like a dried up well, judgment day had finally arrived. Apart from Pit Bull, none of us were employed, which meant the landlord wasn't getting next month's rent. Hard to believe I'd never put a deposit down on a flat with Granddad's money, but I had other plans. I was supposed to travel the world, buy a nice car, do stuff - another reason to loathe myself - but I was trying hard not to throw a pity party. That wasn't the way forward for me, even though I felt like crap.

The last postcard I received from my mother, read, 'Hope deferred makes the heart sick, but a longing fulfilled is like a tree of life...' Proverbs, the Bible.

No Idea

I thought of tearing up the religious postcard, but something stopped me from doing it. The words made some kind of sense.

It's not just SAD that's tried to rob me of hope. Crush a writer's dreams and you squeeze the life out of his creative soul. I guess a heart that's all out of hope is a sick one?

I wondered if Mrs Popov had any real hope that she would see Alexei again? Maybe he was still alive, or he ran off to join some strange cult. Maybe he just gave up on life and was lying at the bottom of the river Thames or he was living in a mud hut, thousands of miles away? Actually, the last idea made no sense, because Mrs Popov said he practically lived on his laptop, and the only friends he had were his gadgets. He trusted no one and never gave any indication that he was leaving.

She tried to hide the pain, but I could see it. Behind every request she made for a cup of sugar, there was a longing to talk to someone, to talk to me, and I gladly obliged.

My mother has wanted to talk these past few years. She's become quite the prolific writer. Not in the writing books sense, but scribbling letters. Ever since she 'found Jesus' at some happy-clappy church, she'd been pouring her soul to me out via the postman. I've been so angry and even envied the postman because envelopes can't talk and he doesn't have to hear it all.

Mum wrote incessantly about how sorry she was about the past, but what grated on me was that even though we haven't seen each other since she'd walked out on me fifteen years ago, she was still giving me advice. 'Rob, I've been praying you will find your soul mate,' and 'If I could undo the past, I would.' Mum had found her soul mate at church and within six months, they were married.

The last letter I received from mum suggested I pray about my future. It was the first time I felt like writing back and tell her to go take a long walk off a short pier. She may have meant well now she's a church goer, but most of what she wrote about God n' stuff just flew over my head.

She tried to explain away my crappy childhood in another letter and said I was always a pearl in the making. Well, I'd certainly been rubbed up by all kinds of crud in my life, but deep down, I knew I couldn't blame her for everything.

There was one big positive in all of this: writing this stuff down on the laptop was therapeutic, so maybe my trials could be good for something?

No Idea

Chapter 9

Conflict/Resolution

Martin and Rupert were still sleeping in bed, so I flicked the kettle on to make a cuppa. Yep. No electricity.

I knew I could be waiting a while for this lot to get up so I shouted, 'Pitt Bull, be a darlin' and get the sleeping beauties up, will you?' There was no answer. I figured she'd gone back to bed and wondered, God only knows, how any of us would manage to keep down a full-time job?

Rupert was the first to make a guest appearance in his hideous purple onesie and dumped a huge stack of white serviettes on the kitchen table. 'Here you are, Rob. That should take care of your bottom,' he said as he winked and bowed with an ostentatious flourish.

I did the face-palm thing. 'Did you go out in that onesie? You look like one of the Teletubbies.'

Rupert gyrated in hideous fashion. 'Why, of course! The ladies can't get enough of this Tinky Winky.'

'The dippy ones more like,' I replied. 'Have you been nicking serviettes from McDonalds again?'

'I haven't stolen anything. You do know that customers get them for free?'

No Idea

'Rupert, the key word is 'customer'. They aren't like you. They buy things.'

Martin walked in and snatched a handful of the tissues. 'Ah nae th' Maccy D ones. KFC's ur better. these ones ur like wipin' yer butt wi' sandpaper.' He walked off towards the toilet with a wad of tissues, while Rupert joined me at the table with Pit Bull.

I cleared my throat. 'Martin, can't you just hold it in for a minute? We need to talk.'

Martin gritted his teeth. 'Sorry mate. I've got th' ol' tortoise-head-thin' gonnae on.'

Repulsed, I was mercifully glad I hadn't eaten anything yet.

Pit Bull snapped. 'You're so gross! And Rob... can't you just wait a minute while he goes and does his business? I can't bear looking at his poo face.'

'I'll tell you why I can't wait,' I replied. 'If his mushroom cloud escapes from the bathroom...'

Martin walked back to the table and sat on Pit Bull's lap. 'It's okay. Ah think th' tortoise has gain back in its sheel fur noo. Anyway... what's sae important 'at Ah cannae tak' a jobby?'

Pit Bull glared at Martin. 'Enough of the tortoise and jobbies please. I'm a visual learner!'

Every eyeball was staring at me. The room was unusually quiet and for the first time in ages I could hear the clock on the wall ticking. I took a deep breath before Rupert interrupted my thought.

'What's up, old chap? Has that dastardly doctor given you 24 hours to live?'

'It's serious and it involves us all,' I replied.

Martin looked at Rupert. Rupert looked at me and I glanced at Pit Bull.

'There's no money. It's all gone,' I announced.

'We wondered wa th' elecy wasnae oan. who's nicked yer money? Ye bin mugged ur somethin'?' asked Martin.

'In a manner of speaking, yeah. Apart from Pit Bull's food parcels, none of you contribute to the bills in this flat, and in case you lot have forgotten, I have to find over two grand a month for bills and rent! And now my money has dried up.'

'I hardly have enough for a swift pint these days,' replied Rupert.

Martin stood up from the table. 'Since ah dain mah back in, I've nae bin able tae wark.'

'You work with computers, Martin. All you have to do is sit down.'

'Exactly. An' mah back cannae tak' it. Ah hae tae lie doon flat ur go fur a walk.'

'But that's it, Martin. There's always an excuse! Look at us. We're a disgrace. Sorry Pit Bull, not you love. If it weren't for you, this flat, along with us, would have been condemned years ago.'

'I knew this would happen,' cried Pit Bull. 'I've tried so hard to get Martin up from his lazy arse, but he never listens to me.'

Martin nudged Pit Bull off his lap and walked over to the kitchen counter to roll a Rizla.

'This is a wake-up call for all of us,' I replied. 'It's just like the Titanic! There was nothing gonna stop that ship from sinking and basically, because you lot are unemployable, we have to jump ship! I can't keep bailing us out with my granddad's money. And anyway, it's all gone now.'

The room fell quiet again while every eye gazed at the floor.

I continued. 'We've brought this upon ourselves. Have any of you got any ideas?'

Rupert was the first to reply. 'I could trot over to Kelvin's place and stay on his sofa?'

'For cryin' out loud, I mean any ideas to get some cash in. Not ideas for accommodation!'

Pit Bull spoke up. 'Is anyone gonna go out and try and get a job? Don't you want to stay together?'

The silence continued.

Martin turned to Pit Bull. 'Cannae we stay at yer mum's place, darlin'? I'm nae bein' funny', but she coods probably dae wi' th' company? Didn't ye say 'at she felt lonely?'

'She lives in a care home, you idiot!' snapped Pit Bull.

'Och aye. Ah forgot abit 'at. 'At woods explain 'er boredom 'en.'

Pit Bull left the room crying while Martin followed after her.

'Look what you've jolly well started,' said Rupert. 'We were one big happy family until you brought this up.'

I lashed out, 'I can't listen to this anymore,' and left the room disappointed and angry that no-one other than Pit Bull wanted to make an effort for us to stay together.

I returned to my bedroom and grabbed my small black sports bag from underneath my bed and placed my laptop inside, along with my mobile phone, a few loose clothes, alarm clock and a small collection of my favourite books: Catch-22, Pilgrim's Progress, Nineteen Eighty-Four, The Art of Staying Dead, Aeonosphere, Brighton Rock and some handwritten notes.

Pit Bull ran toward me as I approached the front door.

'Rob, what are you doing? You can't just up and leave? Please don't go.'

'I'm sorry but I can't take this anymore. My head is done in! Maybe this is the kick up the arse we all need? Besides, I don't think the boys are willing to lift a finger to help?'

I opened the front door, and before leaving, turned around to say my last goodbye. Pit Bull was crying. It was nothing like I imagined. No bravado or 'Bon voyage' - far from it. I had no idea where I was going, but something had to change and it had to start with me.

No Idea

Chapter 10

The Prodigal Son

I hadn't used public transport for some considerable time, so I was shocked when the bus driver said I couldn't pay for my ticket with cash. I needed an Oyster Card, so I crossed the road to the ticket office in Brixton Station to pick one up and boarded the number 59 bus to Streatham Hill.

Mum had been writing and asking if we could meet up. Her timing was if anything, apt, and recent events had forced me to look at stuff. Yes, I knew I had nowhere else to live, but I was surprised I was taking this journey. I hadn't seen her for fifteen years and like I'd said before, she abandoned me to go and live with her boyfriend, Trevor, while I had to move in with my granddad. Barely a month later he died of a heart attack, so I embarked on a year of sleeping on a few mates' couches before I rented my own flat in Brixton.

My mother's departure took place barely a year after my dad left us for a younger woman. I haven't a clue exactly where he went, but the truth was, I barely knew him. He was rarely at home and preferred to spend his time out drinking, among other things.

Fifteen minutes into my journey I was ready to step off the bus just a few minutes away from the

No Idea

address on Mum's letters. I panicked and gripped the guard rail by the exit.

'Pathetic. You can't even get off!'

I yelled back at the mocking voice inside my head, 'Yeh? We'll see!'

In determined fashion and ignoring every impulse to stay on the bus, I jumped off the steps and onto the pavement to make my way toward Telford Avenue.

I was trying hard not to think about what I was going to do or say when I saw my mother. I'd been angry every time I had read and reread her apologies. Maybe it was her guilty conscience talking, but how could walking out on your teenage son be undone with a letter? It wasn't easy when my dad left, but a year later, my mother as well? Did she think her words would magically undo the past?

Despite my anger, I had kept all of her correspondence. Maybe there was a part of me that still wanted my mum, but I had no idea how my visit was going to play out. Would she want to see me as I was now? I'm not the eighteen year old lad that she left. How would I react when I saw her again? What about her new bloke?

She had written to me about life with her new husband, Vince (I don't know what happened to Trevor?). The new man in her life was by all accounts, an astrophysicist - hardly the supernova I'd imagined her wishing for, but then she was always interested in the stars.

I remember doing my homework and asking her if she could name any of the Constellations. She said, 'I've not heard of them, but I could name every one of the Beatles.' She was a stargazer of the celebrity kind.

Astrophysics and Cosmology interested me though, and I enjoyed watching Professor Brian Cox on the BBC wax lyrical about the origins of the universe. With his rock star 'boyish' looks and his black leather jacket, jeans and boots, he'd made black holes and dark matter sexy to a younger audience than Patrick Moore and his Sky At Night BBC series that ran for over fifty years.

From the picture my mother painted in her letters of her new hubby, I imagine he was a pipe and slippers man, not dissimilar from the now deceased, Patrick Moore. Vince might be the younger of the two and without a monocle, but I expect he made the latest insights of the formation of the galaxy about as alluring as watching your hairy-chinned, denture-less grandma suck on a Rich Tea biscuit.

I was walking down Telford Avenue and asking myself, 'What do I want out of this visit?' A warm bed and working light bulbs would be a good start, until I can work out what I'm going to do with my life. The past will have to wait. If I drag stuff up, who knows where that will take me? For now, I need to calm down, take a deep breath and make sure I don't kick off.

In the distance a woman was pushing a wheelie bin onto the path. She stopped and stared at me. Then she walked briskly and then ran toward me. She was crying. Crap. It was Mum! I froze and then quickly turned around and walked in the opposite direction. My heart was racing, totally unprepared for the encounter.

No Idea

'I knew it was you. I knew it was my Rob,' she shouted, weeping as I heard her voice draw closer. I stopped to face her and then turned my back again, unsure of what to do. She embraced me from behind and hugged me tight. I turned around again and she kissed my cheek repeatedly.

Far from any rage, I was overwhelmed and something broke inside of me, just like it did in town outside McDonalds. The tears were streaming down my face and my legs gave way before I knelt on the floor. Whatever I'd bottled up over the years was coming out now. This wasn't what I had planned at all, not that I had a plan.

I wailed as she held me tighter and I couldn't stop the words welling up from deep inside of me, 'Mum, why did you leave me?'

'Rob, I'm so sorry I hurt you. I love you. I made a huge mistake. Please forgive me, son. I've dreamt of the day I would see you again.'

We were kneeling on the pavement, both of us in tears, and embracing each other. I didn't understand where my anger had gone. Maybe it will come later, but all I wanted now was Mum to hold on to me. I wiped away a huge trail of leaking snot from my nose before burying my head in her chest again.

'Come on, love. Let's get ourselves inside. I'll make you some cocoa the way you used to like it.'

Mum wiped her smudged mascara tears away as we rose to our feet and walked back to the house. Several of the neighbours were peeping out of their curtains and staring at me. I looked back down at the floor, self conscious. What did Mum think about me now? Did I look a failure? Was she ashamed of me? What would I say if she asked me what I'd been doing for the past fifteen years?

Seeing Mum again, I was afraid of what SAD might do to my mental state, but I knew I needed to hold it together. I certainly hadn't planned on showing such teary emotion, and especially so early on in my visit. I wondered if my tears were the sole result of my depression or if the love I once had for my mother hadn't dried up?

Mum's large red-bricked Victorian house was three stories tall with several large plum trees and a meticulously mown front lawn. There was no way she could afford this, so I presumed her new husband must have been minted. Mum opened the navy blue door and I was greeted by a hall with red and white tiled flooring that looked the length of a landing strip.

'Vince, you'll never guess who's here with me now,' she yelled up the stairs.

Before Vince had time to reply, Mum shouted, 'It's my Rob! The prodigal son has returned!'

'Mum, I never left. You did.'

'You're right son, but I've been waiting for you to come home. I want to make things up to you.'

Mum grabbed my hand and led me toward a woman in the kitchen who was wearing a bandana on her head and more paint on her face than an Amazon Warrior. Her appearance was all the more comical, given the fact she must have been all of eighty years old.

'Rob, this is my neighbour, Rose. She's as deaf as a post and a bit mental. You'll have to speak up.'

No Idea

I put my bag down and smiled at Rose.

'So what have you got in your bag, then?' Rose bellowed. 'I'm after a few dusters and some carpet shampoo.'

Mum put her arm around her and shouted in her ear, 'Rose, you dopy mare. This is my son, Rob. He's not a door-to-door salesman and he's not selling sponges!'

Rose replied, 'Oh, sorry about that, Sally. Good to meet you. So what are you selling then?'

I chuckled before Mum interrupted. 'No Rose. This is my son, Rob!'

'Of course you are.' Rose kissed me on the cheek. I felt like I'd just been licked by a large drooling mastiff. 'Your mum has told me all about you. I'll get the kettle on.'

A tall and grey skinny man walked down the stairs toward me.

Mum grabbed my hand and walked me to this ghostly figure with slick-backed hair. It must be Vince, I presumed, not least because he was similar in appearance to his namesake, Vincent Price, of Hammer House of Horror fame. The small moustache and hair product in particular, looked identical. Shave the fluff off, and he'd be a perfect match for Count Dracula, though that role was owned by Christopher Lee.

'Son, let me introduce you. This is Vince. He does all of the cooking!'

Having sampled my mother's cooking, albeit, fifteen years ago, I'd say the bloke had no other option.

'I hope he's giving you lessons,' I replied, remembering the burnt offerings of my childhood.

Mum winked at Vince and squeezed his bony cheek. 'Vince has taught me a thing or two, I can tell you.'

'Please don't,' I replied.

'What's all this commotion then?' asked Vince.

Mum put her arm around me. 'It's my Rob. He's come home!'

His eyebrows raise forty five degrees, startled.

Rose butted in. 'It's just like the bible, Vince... the probable son has returned!'

Vince replied, 'It's the prodigal son, not probable son, Rose. And anyway, that son set off for faraway lands, squandered his wealth and ended up living with pigs. Rob, on the other hand-'

I finished his sentence, '-Has run out of money and been living with pigs in Brixton, so that's two out of three.'

Mum smiled. 'You poor thing... I bet you're famished. Park your bum down here and I'll get Vince to cook you the lovely rib-eye steak I just bought him from the butchers.'

'That's my rib-eye!' said Vince, clearly sulking. I'd already decided to nickname him, 'The Count'. He looked like he belongs in some French chateau or castle.

No Idea

I joked to myself, 'You'd think the Count would avoid the stake every time?'

Note to self. NEVER attempt stand-up comedy.

Mum replied, 'Don't worry about your steak, Vince. This is just like the bible. Don't you remember the father celebrated the son's return by throwing a party and killing the fatted calf for him? So that's what we are going to do. Rob's getting the calf's rib-eye and that's the end of it!'

Vince's jaw dropped. He whispered in Mum's ear, 'While you're at it, why don't you give him my new cashmere robe and leather sandals for his feet?'

'Good idea! And another thing, we're gonna have a party as well!'

The Count asked Mum for a quiet word in the kitchen. She agreed, but I could still hear them talking.

'You've never once thrown a party for me, yet when Rob turns up after God knows how long, you want to throw a party for him... and give him my steak!'

I could see I'd put Vince's nose out of joint by simply turning up.

Mum laughed, 'He's getting your steak, robe and sandals as well. After all, isn't that what happened in the bible, Vince?'

Vince mumbled something before walking off in a huff. I decided to keep my mouth shut.

'Rose, while I get Vince cooking would you go run a hot bubble bath for my boy?'

'You want a bubble bath toy?'

After mum repeated herself, Rose heard correctly the second time and walked back down the hall and up the stairs croaking a tune like she was both stone and tone deaf.

'You don't have to do all this,' I replied, embarrassed at all the commotion and fuss.

'Son, this is the happiest day of my life and it's right we celebrate. Now, up you go. You'll find Vince's robe on the back of the door and I'll put his leather sandals and a clean pair of boxer shorts outside the door in a minute. Now, up you go and leave your clothes next to the basket. I'll get Vince to wash them for you after he's cooked your steak.'

I kicked my Crocs off in the hall and walked upstairs, enjoying the super lush, long piled carpet massaging my toes.

Rose was smiling, waiting for me in the bathroom.

'Let's be having you then,' she remarked. If I was guessing correctly, the wild look in her eye warned me to be careful with her.

'You're a handsome lad. A good warm bath will do you the world of good.'

'Erm, yeh, thanks.' I replied.

'Now, jump in and I'll give your back a scrub. There's plenty of bubbles in there, so I won't see anything I shouldn't see - not that I haven't seen it all before,' winked Rose.

I politely refused her offer and escorted her gently out of the bathroom.

No Idea

In no time at all, my head had sunk beneath the warm, fluffy bubbles. It definitely beat the cold showers I'd been having at the flat.

Everything was beautifully quiet, and the heated bath felt like a blanket for my tired muscles. My head rose from the water and I rested my arms either side of the bath, totally relaxed. A shower might get the job done, but a bath got you there in style.

I decided I wouldn't allow my feelings to get the better of me when I was getting the first bit of TLC in ages. If Mum wanted to make stuff up to me, I wasn't going to stop her. We needed to talk, but first, relax and then... the Count's rib-eye did sound good!

Chapter 11

Milking It

After the best night's sleep in living memory, I lay cushioned among soft, silky sheets on top of a king size Posturepedic mattress that worked wonders for my spine. When the only thing your posterior has known is the prod of metal coils that have separated from the collective and gone rogue, the experience of a quality bed was not only new, but quite overwhelming.

Instead of being woken to the smells of a damp and dingy flat, I was greeted by a row of warmly lit ceiling lights and a smell so fresh, I was lured by the scent. Taking deep breaths, I sniffed the sheets, something you couldn't pay me to do back at the flat.

The central heating kept the bedroom at a delightful, almost tropical temperature. Sleeping in the home of an astrophysicist, he would probably say the rays of our yellow dwarf that produced the energy of one trillion megaton bombs each second, were sending a gentle wave to me from 90 million miles away. I was only a few miles from my flat in Brixton, but a million miles away from the world I had known.

The alarm clock on the pine bedside cabinet told me it was a quarter to two in the afternoon. I didn't remember much after my long bubble bath followed by the culinary delights of the Count's rib-eye steak the day before. I went straight to bed after dinner, so my latest deep sleep marathon lasted almost 19 hours, my SAD symptoms conspicuous by their absence.

I was also aware of a warm presence in my room. It felt personal, inviting, even exciting. It was an old friend of mine who I hadn't seen in years. Hope.

I wasn't naive enough to think my SAD had just upped and gone, but I felt fresh and hopeful. Getting the best sleep of my life and waking up to a warm and brightly lit room certainly had something to do with it.

I reached for my laptop and booted it up. After discovering my story, The Collar, on an old floppy disk in Rupert's drawer, I emailed myself a backup and saved it to my laptop before leaving the flat. Curious to read the second chapter, I clicked on the saved file.

Before I proceeded to read chapter two, I was reminded of the time I came up with the idea. Along with lengthy discussions about religion with my granddad and after watching the Billy Elliot movie on TV, the story began with something that happened to me as a child.

I was seventeen years old when I awoke in the middle of the night with an entire draft of a story. It was partly biographical and fictional adventure. I ran down the stairs at 4.30am and grabbed my notebook and pen. Twenty minutes later, I had written six pages of notes. The outline for my story had begun. Here's the second chapter:

THE COLLAR – Chapter Two

'After bolting down what tasted like mouldy bread with cold spaghetti hoops, I hurried to the bathroom to wash the orange stains from my chin. Why the rush? Let me tell you. It was date night (well, afternoon) and I wanted to impress. What ten year old boy wouldn't want to 'strut his stuff' when he had a date with the best looking girl in the school?

I had a special relationship with Nicola Raishby. She knew nothing about it, mind you, but in my imagination we did the most incredible stuff together, Y'know, the kind of stuff ten year olds think up. Whether it was going to London on the train (and not getting lost), having enough cash in your pocket to buy two large McDonalds meals or walking hand in hand before stopping for an ice cream and then kissing like movie stars behind the outdoor toilets, it was all awesome.

The great thing about your imagination is you don't have to smell the pee when you're standing outside the public toilets. You can strip your mind of all the things you hate, and replace them with all the stuff you love. And I loved Nicola Raishby.

Now back to reality, this was my first 'real' date and I was scared. I didn't want to spoil the dream world I had created with anything like 'hard facts,' but what if she didn't want to kiss me? What if I just clammed up and didn't know what to say to her? What if she didn't like my clothes? She'd only seen me in my school uniform, which, I admit, levelled the playing field with the other boys.

Back to the kissing thing: 'That's what girls want from a boyfriend', said my brother, Mike. 'Kissing isn't kissing until you put your tongue inside her mouth and thrash it about.' He made it sound really gross, like an eel wriggling in a bucket or a fish flapping about while gasping for air.

I liked Nicola so much I was prepared to do anything -anything she wanted, and if that meant polishing her perfect white teeth I'd do it, though I wasn't sure if she would have to take out her dental braces first?

My mum had some lovey-dovey, black and white films where the only people kissing were gangsters with their dames, but I couldn't recall seeing one of them shove their tongue down a woman's throat. I doubted what Mike told me, until I came down the stairs one night while my dad was watching porn. 'Watch this stuff and you'll learn something,' he yelled, drunk as usual. At ten years old, I didn't want to learn any of it and I couldn't understand what they were trying to do anyway. Some of their moves reminded me of the Twister game that I played at my friend, Roland's house - but thankfully, everyone kept their clothes on.

Now ready for my date, I had slicked back my dark brown hair with huge dollops of my dad's Grecian 2000 gel product. I couldn't quite decide whether I looked like a cool mobster or count Dracula, but what mattered to me was that the most popular boy in the school (Martin Fisher) looked cool with his hair gelled back. He was the kid that all the nerds loved to hate and the cool kids loved to love.

News of my impending date with Nicola travelled around the school quicker than my classmate Nitty Nancy's nits, who scratched as often as she took breaths. I smile as I write these words again, but THE Nicola Raishby, the prettiest girl in the school, said yes to my date. It was without question, the greatest achievement any ten year old boy could wish for.

Woolworths didn't close till 5.30pm on Saturdays, so I had an hour before the shop closed. Eager to get some passport sized photos of us together from the photo booth, I parked my bicycle at the entrance of Nicola's drive and rang the doorbell. She answered the door immediately and I gasped. She looked more beautiful in her out of school clothes than I had imagined.

We made way to the shops on our bikes and within five minutes, and I had already arrived at Woolworths, a good few hundred yards ahead of Nicola. Like a typical half-wit ten year old boy, I hadn't thought of cycling alongside my date, but ahead of her. I was far too eager to impress with my speed and bunny hops as I negotiated several high curbs, raising the handlebars and kicking the bike sideways in the process. She didn't look best pleased. I realised immediately I had already cocked up the first part of my dream date.

Rule No. 1. Don't show off. FAILED.

I chained our bikes to the railings and took Nicola's hand and walked her into the store. She pulled a face. My hands were not only sweaty, but the rubber grips on my bike had left an unpleasant colour and smell on them.

Rule No. 2. Don't be sweaty or smelly. FAILED.

I apologised for the sweaty palms and she replied by raising her eyebrows. I think she was telling me not to ruin the date even further. There's no such thing as a cat with nine lives when you're dating.

We stood outside the photo booth. It was going to be so exciting. Nicola would sit on my lap while we both smiled at the camera. Five photos would be taken in quick succession, and I had decided to give her two of them - one to stick on her bedroom wall and one for the front of her school diary. I could tell, even at ten years of age, she wasn't too keen about taking photos on her first date with me. But then she didn't have the good fortune to have shared the fifty dates we'd already been on together – inside my head. Those magical moments only belonged to me, and here I was about to desecrate the memory of them all.

After some less than gentle nudging on my part, Nicola sat down in the booth while I put my hand in my pocket to retrieve the two 50ps needed for the coin operated machine. My pockets were empty! Amidst my dreaded nerves of getting ready for my first date, I had forgotten to take any money with me.

Rule No. 3. Never go on a date without money. FAILED.

I apologised and asked if Nicola would put her money in the machine. She replied, 'My mum said I wouldn't need any money, so I didn't bring any!' She looked embarrassed and I felt like a giant turd, so we both left the shop. She wanted me to take her home.

Rule No. 4. Don't ask the girl to pay for the first date. FAILED.

I cycled alongside Nicola on the way home, devastated. 'So, erm, I'm sorry about the money thing. Shall we go again after school on Monday?' I enquired, with some desperation.

'I'm busy this week,' she replied.

Not willing to give up so easily, I added, 'Oh, that's okay. I'll buy a disposable camera and bring it to school. Maybe we can get one of your friends to take photos of us at lunch time?' My request was met with silence. I realised I had unwittingly humiliated this delicate and sensitive girl.

Rule No. 5. Don't sound desperate on your first date. FAILED. LARGE.

I pulled up outside Nicola's house and walked her to the front door. My desperation to salvage something of our first date turned into lunacy. Before she had time to ring the door bell,

No Idea

I leaned over to kiss her goodbye. Startled and before she had time to move, I pushed my mouth onto hers and thrashed my tongue inside her mouth, just like my brother said. The poor lass choked and then pushed me away, crying. I was devastated. I didn't want to put my tongue in her mouth in the first place, but I naively listened to Mike's advice. I should have known better. I apologised and said goodbye.

Rule No. 6. Don't shove your tongue inside the mouth of someone who doesn't want it. FAILED.

After I returned home Mike wiggled his eyebrows and said, 'So... how far did you get with her then?'

'Woolworths,' I replied.

Getting to the kind of places that Mike was suggesting was the last thing on my ten year old mind.

I learned later from my friend Ginger Jim, that what I did to Nicola was called a French kiss. 'No wonder it didn't work,' I said to Jim. 'I'm flippin' English, ain't I?'

The experience was so traumatic for me, that to this day, I still call it, 'Tongue-gate.' That was my first date with Nicola Raishby.

Did I dare try and date anyone else during my entire time at school after that misadventure? Well, read on. You'll have to wait and see. But sadly, it wasn't the last time I listened to the advice of my brothers.'

I had a huge grin on my face after reading the second chapter of The Collar. And let me tell you – most of the story was true.

***

My bubble soon burst after I heard mum's voice raised downstairs.

'Look, I know he is your son, but this is my home as well.'

'How could you say that to me? You know how much I've longed to see Rob again. We've spoken about this before. And this is also my home, Vincent!'

I closed the lid of my laptop and crept outside the bedroom to listen more closely.

'I'm sorry. Of course this is your home and he is welcome to stay, but for how long?'

'He'll stay as long as I want him to stay. Rob has fallen on hard times. He's done little else but sleep since he arrived.'

The Count replied, 'Like I said, he is welcome and I want you to be happy. I just want to know what his plans are. That's all.'

As Mum cried, I recalled from my childhood how she would lock herself in her bedroom and try to muffle the sobbing with her pillow after an argument with my dad. As the years passed, it was impossible for her to disguise her pain. Before I reached my teens she tried to put a brave face on everything, but I knew she was desperately unhappy. I didn't want her to be. As a child, I wanted to see her smile and wished I could help her. For many years I even blamed myself and thought I was a part of the problem.

I loved my mum, but she broke my heart when she moved out. I don't know if it can ever truly be mended as far as we are both concerned, but she seems closer now to the happy mum I longed for as a kid.

When she left me with nothing other than a note on the table I said that I never wanted to see her again, but she seems different now. I love seeing her happy, but I'm not ready to tell her yet. We still have the past to deal with.

I am puzzled how the heck she has got to be so different, though? I couldn't imagine going to church making that kind of transformation in someone? And the Count didn't seem the type who inspired happiness.

I looked over the banister at the top of the stairs, careful to stay out of eyeshot. He placed her head on his chest and stroked it with one hand and embraced her with the other. My eyes welled up. I'd never seen a man show any kind of affection to Mum. Maybe I was wrong about this new bloke and there was more to him than meets the eye?

The Count deserves the benefit of the doubt. From now on, I will call him by his name, Vince.

***

'Is that you, Rob? Are you up now?'

Mum must have heard the creak on the landing floorboards. 'Erm, yeh.' I took a few steps back to the bedroom and after noticing my clothes were missing, I grabbed Vince's white dressing gown before putting it on and walking downstairs.

Mum put on a brave smile and wiped her eyes before hugging me.

'Ah, there you are, Rob. You must have needed that sleep! I didn't want to interrupt you, but I checked on you a few times and you still make that funny purring sound when you snore.'

Vince reached out for a handshake. I offered my limp-wristed hand, a little embarrassed at his formality.

'Morning, Rob. I hope you found the bed comfortable?'

'I did thanks. I think that's one of the reasons I overslept.'

Mum put her arm around my shoulders. 'That's alright, son. Anyway, I've washed the clothes you were wearing yesterday, but where are the rest of them? I went through your bag but I couldn't find any more?'

'Ah, yeh. Pit Bull's got my sweatshirt and I've got her Crocs.'

'Yes, I wondered about those shoes with flowers on! And who is this girl, Pit Bull?'

'She's my flatmate, Martin's girlfriend.'

Vince interrupted. 'So how long do you intend visiting us for?'

No Idea

'Just 'till I can get back on my feet,' I replied. 'You know, find a job... get writing again.'

'Ah, you're a writer,' said Vince. 'What have you written?'

'Erm... lots of unfinished stuff, to be honest.'

Mum smiled. 'I always knew you had it in you, Rob. You were always telling tales when you were a lad and you loved writing with Tom.'

Vince looked worried. 'So you want to finish your book here? How long do you think it'll take?'

'I'm not sure.'

Mum patted me on the back. 'How exciting, my boy is writing a book! What's it called?'

'No Idea.'

Mum clapped her hands together several times. 'What a lovely name for a book! No Idea! I like it.'

'No Mum, I mean I've no idea what my book will be called yet.'

Vince looked puzzled again. 'So what's your book about, Rob?'

I felt a sense of dread coming over me and refrained from saying 'No idea' once more.

'It's a bit complicated.' I replied.

'Ooh, like one of those mystery, thriller-type, novels?' said Mum.

'Something like that.' I smiled, remembering what my granddad used to say: 'Yer mother's as batty as a fruitcake.'

Mum continued, 'I can't stand the suspense so I always read the last chapter first, but then I can't be bothered to read the rest.'

'I didn't know you liked reading?' I replied.

'I'm not fussed love, but I like books with a nice cover and a pretty spine. They have to look nice on the shelf.'

Vince raised his eyes to the ceiling. 'Sally has put my science books in the attic.'

'That's because they look drab!' she retorted.

Mum grabbed my arm. 'I've got a surprise for you. Hilary and Grace will be here any minute now to give me a haircut and pedicure, but I've asked them to give you the full works first. Oh and Grace is single and she's really smart. She goes to my church as well. You'll love her.'

Before I could say, 'No thanks, I'm not into religious fanatics,' I took a good look in the hallway mirror. I looked like the bloke in the Turin Shroud, so I decided to take Mum up on her offer of a haircut. Hopefully, the girl could use her clippers on my beard, but I wasn't convinced about the pedicure. I hardly touched them myself.

'Okay, I could do with a haircut. Thanks.'

Mum picked up the telephone and dialled. 'Oh, and I'm sorting you some new clothes. Rose will pop to town for me. And don't worry. I've got your sizes and I'll send her somewhere decent – Maybe Marks and Sparks or Top Bloke?'

'I think you mean, Top Man? And thanks, but you don't have to do all this.'

Vince butted in. 'He's right, love. Let the lad chose his own clothes.'

'Don't you tell me what's best for my boy, Vincent! A mother knows her own son. Now put the kettle on and fetch Rob that ham sandwich I just made for you, will you, love.'

Vince retreated back into the kitchen. Smart bloke. He knew when it was best to keep quiet. That's another improvement on my absentee father.

Mum spoke into the handset. 'Ah, Giuseppe, be a love and fetch Rose for me, please.'

She held her hand over the phone receiver and whispered to me, 'He's only 42. We call him Rose's little play thing.'

The thought of Rose with someone nearly half her age was enough to turn the stomach.

Mum was still on the phone. 'Yes, Rose, listen love. Have you got your hearing aid turned up? Right, pop over for a minute will you. I've got a little job for you.'

I dreaded the thought of Rose choosing my clothes. After the bathroom episode, I couldn't escape the mental image of her buying me a few pairs of thongs, skinny trousers and fish net vests. I hoped I was wrong.

'Erm, Mum, keep the receipts won't you?'

'Don't worry, love. I'll give her a list.'

Before I made my way to the kitchen for Vince's ham sandwich, the door bell rang. Mum ran to the door, giggling on her way.

'Oh, Hilary, come in. Let me introduce you to my son.'

Hilary had to be the strangest looking beautician I'd ever seen. At least 6ft 4 with arms hairier than a gorilla and hands twice my size; Hilary, and by Hilary I mean a bloke with a girly name, looked more like a plumber or site contractor with a utility belt around his waist and trousers with multiple pockets for his tools.

I couldn't imagine relaxing if my feet were being caressed by a bloke who looked like he'd chin you with one misplaced look. I honestly didn't know where to look at 'Ruggers'. Yes, I called him Ruggers, because he had cauliflower ears, no neck and a wonky nose set at 45 degrees.

I was anxious. How could this bloke cup my feet without me cringing first? I didn't want to say the wrong thing to Ruggers, but I couldn't help but feel I was gonna put my foot in it, pardon the pun. Faux Pas were something I inherited from my mother.

Growing up, I lived next door to a guy called Jack who was a tank commander during the Second World War. Mum told me our neighbour lost his leg in a tank. As a young child, I was puzzled how he'd lost it in such a small space, but Mum always found a way of saying the wrong thing to Jack every time he visited. I can recall several incidents that made me laugh out loud, followed up by a clip round the ear from Mum.

Dad was digging out some foundations for a new garage and Mum managed to fall in one of the four-feet deep trenches. Looking startled, she said to our

No Idea

neighbour, 'Oh, Jack, can you give me a leg up. Oh! I mean, sorry, could you pull me up!' He just laughed.

On another occasion, she was looking out into the garden with Jack. She turned to him and said, 'I suppose we'll all be out in our shorts this summer, eh! Oh sorry, I mean, erm...'

Jack was a good sport and laughed it off. He even showed me his wooden leg, which I thought was cool. My funniest memory was when Jack said he had family visiting for the holidays, to which Mum replied, 'I suppose we'll all be getting legless at Christmas, then!' The more nervous she was about mentioning Jack's wooden leg, the more she put her foot in her mouth.

Mum's comical mishaps reminded me of the Fawlty Towers TV episode, The Germans, where the hotel owner, Basil Fawlty escaped from hospital and still suffering with concussion, returned to his hotel. Confused, he couldn't stop himself mentioning the Second World War to his German guests.

Mum walked me through to the conservatory and sat me down in front of a foot spa.

'Put your feet in there, love. Fifteen minutes in the warm water with Tea Tree and Peppermint oil, and your feet will be ready for Hilary to work on.'

'Mum, we need to talk later,' I replied, dinking my feet into the warm vibrating spa. The aroma almost instantly relaxed me.

'What about, Rob?'

'Us'.

Why was I saying this? Mum's kindness was making me nervous... like she was brushing over the past, as if I should just forget it all. I felt like I was letting my guard down, and that made me uncomfortable.

'We can chat later if you want. Vince is going out soon after he's finished watching the bowling on TV.'

'Where's erm, Hilary?'

'He's watching the bowling with Vince while your feet get a good soak.'

'What's the deal with him? He looks like he's come to mend your boiler. He's hardly the beautician type.'

Mum laughed, glad for the change of subject. 'Hilary is Vince's brother. They hardly spoke because Hilary lived up North, Lancaster, I think, for the last thirty years. He's moved back to London now, and yes, they are like chalk and cheese, but bizarrely they both like watching and playing bowls.'

I shook my head incredulously. 'I wouldn't have put him down as a bowling man?'

'I can't stand it. I said to Vince the other day, 'It's no wonder young people don't play this game. It's far too slow for them. If they shrink the green in half, the ball will get there twice as quick.' A bit like football.'

'Why is it like football?'

'Well, if they all had their own ball they'd be better off, don't you think? There's no need to make the game so hard. Anyway, let me go and pop the kettle on.'

No Idea

In no time at all, I closed my eyes and drifted off to some place new; somewhere safe...

* * *

'Right then, where are these feet your mother said I'll need bolt cutters for?'

'On the end of my legs,' I joked, as I opened my eyes to the explosion of personality that was Hilary.

'Next question and don't lie to me. Do you have any fungal infections – athlete's foot, warts like verrucas, corns or anything else I should know about?'

'Erm, I don't think so.'

Hilary scraped the inside of his nose with his finger. 'Do you have diabetes or any blood disorder? Are you on Warfarin or any other blood thinners?'

'Nope... this pedicure sounds more like a hospital procedure?'

'Less of the cheek, son. You wouldn't want a blood-bath on your hands if I nicked your feet with my blade or damaged the nerve endings because you can't feel my nippers.'

'I was banking on 'not feeling anything', kind of thing.'

Hilary bent over my feet and dried them with a towel, before opening a large leather pouch resembling a torturer's tool kit bursting at the seams with a large set of instruments.

'Erm, can you tell me what you're gonna be doing with my feet?' I asked.

'Okay, you've had the Tea Tree and Peppermint soak, so I'm going to remove all of your dead skin and then use my scalpel to get your feet smoother than a baby's arse. Then I'll give you a deep tissue massage, wax and remove all of the hair on your toes and then use my sharp cuticle nippers and scissors to tidy up these little Piggies! We'll be done within the hour.'

I was still puzzled why a bloke who looked better suited to door security had chosen to be a beautician.

'Hilary, if you don't mind me asking, but you don't seem the beautician type? How did you get into this work?'

'I used to work in a care home, and the ol' buggers had nails that needed a chainsaw to cut them. Instead of wiping their arse for £7 per hour, I learnt I could earn four times that cutting their nails.'

'That makes sense,' I grinned, before thinking, 'I hope he sterilizes his toolkit!'

'I like to think of myself as a chiropodist. I ask them all the right questions and line them up in the dining room. It's like cutting a hedge row. I can get through a few dozen of them and earn a day's wage in a few hours.'

'Did you have to go to University to get your qualifications?'

'Na, I did a seven day Foot Practitioner's course, online.'

'I'd give the job a go myself,' I replied, 'If I didn't hate feet.'

No Idea

Hilary frowned. 'My mate unblocks drains for Dyno-Rod, but it doesn't mean he loves shite! You can always find a job no-one likes doing. I do feet, and cheaper than everyone else.'

***

Hilary was half way through my pedicure before my mobile phone beeped. It was a text from Pit Bull: 'Hi Rob, the boys and I are just round the corner. See you in a minute. X'

'What the...!' I shouted, staring at my phone. 'Mum, how did Pit Bull get this address? She just texted to say she's coming over with the lads!'

'Ah, she sounds a lovely girl. We had quite a chat while you were asleep.'

'You answered my phone? When was this?'

'She called a few hours ago and said she needed to see you urgently. I remember you mentioning her yesterday, so I invited her over. You're welcome to have friends over, Rob.'

'Mum, I'm not a kid. I need some space, and inviting the dossers over isn't going to do me any favours!'

The door bell rang several times.

'Ah, that must be Grace. Are you ready for your haircut?'

Grace walked in and I blushed. She looked just like the girl I wrote about in the Bistro, without the Adam's apple, meat and two veg, of course. She was gorgeous, and here I was, sitting between mum's potted plants and palm branches and wearing nothing but a white dressing gown while a 6ft 4 inch hairy gorilla sat on a stool and gave me a foot job.

She said hi to Hilary before walking over to me.

'Nice to meet you, Rob, your mum's told me all about you.'

I couldn't imagine what Mum told her? Was it the, 'Ah Rob, he's unemployed, been living with a bunch of dossers for years, and he's always unlucky in love,' kinda thing?

Grace stepped closer toward me. I could smell her perfume and was feeling intoxicated, but in a good way. My forehead was getting moist and I hoped that was my only physical reaction. Wearing nothing but a bathrobe, I dared not employ my imagination on anything else other than football or an episode of Top Gear.

I stammered like an imbecile. 'Erm, yeh... hi, Grace.'

Grace chuckled. She could see I was nervous.

'Well Rob, what would you like me to do for you?'

I screamed aloud in my head, 'Top Gear, Jeremy Clarkson, Wayne Rooney.'

'Erm, could you cut it, like, er, how you would like it to, erm, cut it?'

Grace laughed again. 'Sure. How about I take a good few inches off, clipper the sides, say, number three, and take the weight out of your hair?'

No Idea

I nodded. I had no idea what she was on about, but Grace could do whatever she wanted with me, of that, I was sure.

'Don't mind me, Hilary. I won't get in your way,' she said.

'I've nearly finished with his plates of meat,' he replied.

I tried not to wince as he push my cuticles back on my toes with his shiny tool and let out a high-pitched squeal that made me look an even bigger tit.

Grace snorted with laughter. Even that sounded cute.

'Rob, would you like some Indian Head Massage before I start cutting?'

'Would I like a head massage? Is the Pope Catholic?'

'That's okay, Rob. I don't have to. It just helps you to relax and stimulate the blood vessels.'

It wasn't the blood vessels in my head I was concerned about.

'No, please, that would be amazing.' I was definitely not thinking with my head now.

'I'm just massaging your head, Rob.'

'Of course,' I stuttered, blushing again, somewhat relieved the blood was now rushing to my cheeks this time.

Grace's hands felt so good on my head, I immediately conjured up memories of Top Gear episodes.

My voice was hurried as I shouted to mum for a glass of water. If I didn't cool down soon, I might have exploded. I wasn't sure if she could hear me, because she'd put on one of her religious CDs. It sounded like Jewish music.

'Do you like this kind of music?' asked Grace.

'Erm, I'm not sure what it is, but it's very relaxing, especially with your massage. You'll have to pull me down from the ceiling in a minute.'

I was surprised at my boldness. This girl had me so relaxed I couldn't be held responsible for anything that popped out.

'It's Messianic Praise,' she said. 'This is one of our CDs from church.'

Mum walked in with a glass of water for me.

'See, I told you, Grace, he's gorgeous, isn't he!'

'He's a bit rough round the edges, but he'll brush up,' Grace joked.

The door bell rang before Mum greeted Pit Bull and the lads at the door.

'Welcome to my home. Rob's just getting a few beauty treatments in the conservatory, so go on through and I'll put the kettle on!'

'It's nice to meet you,' said Pit Bull. I could hear Martin grunt. Social skills were never quite his forte, unlike, grunting.

Pit Bull walked between the palm branches into the conservatory and held her hands over her mouth.

'Rob, I never thought I'd see you like this,' she chuckled.

'Bloody 'eck, Rob,' said Martin, trying to hide his smirk. 'Ye loch like Jesus oan th' throne!'

No Idea

Rupert was holding a can of beer in his left hand and trying hard not to spit the contents onto the conservatory floor.

I could see it from their point of view. I was reclining on a high backed, golden armchair with the light shining down on me from the skylight above. I was also wearing a white robe, while a beautiful woman massaged my head and a large creature filed my toe nails... and all to the sound of orchestral, praise music.

After introducing Grace and Hilary, I asked, 'What are you doing here?'

Martin nodded at Rupert before he spoke up. 'Erm, Rob, we wanted tae say somethin'... we're, y'knaw, sorry abit th' rent hin'... Ah spoke tae mah ol' man, an' he's gonna gezz thes month's rent money.'

'That's great, Martin, but what's that got to do with me?'

He continued. 'An' Rupert took his drum kit tae pawn shop. He got sixty quid fur it, sae th' fridge is foo ay food, an' th' elecy is workin'.'

Pit Bull looked tearful. I knew the lads were trying to make the effort, but it was too little, too late. I was worried that if I went soft on them again, I'd end up in the same hole I'd been in for so long.

'And what happens after this month?' I replied. 'Who's going to pay the rent then?'

Mum waltzed into the room, oblivious to the change of atmosphere while Hilary announced he was off out for a fag break.

'There you are my dears. There's a pot of tea, coffee, sugar, milk and chocolate biscuits. Help yourselves.'

Rupert spoke up. 'If you're cross with me about those naughty Viagra pills, I'm sorry.'

'I thought you were giving me Aspirin, not Viagra!' I replied.

Rupert looked up from the floor. 'Yes, I know we've been taking the Michael. I do understand. But Pit Bull said she'll pop along with me to an AA meeting next week. I can't promise anything, but I'll try.'

'But you have to do this for yourself, Rupert. Don't you want to make something of your life?'

Rupert lowered his head. 'I thought we could all do that together.'

'It's too little, too late, don't you think? I need to move on, and the flat depresses me... frankly, you lot depress me. Not you, Pit Bull, love.'

Pit Bull wiped the tears away from her eyes. 'Rob, Mrs Popov has already visited twice, and after I told her you left, she looked devastated. You need to visit her.'

'Blimey, I only have a cup of tea with her a few times a week!'

'Exactly, Rob. And since her boy went missing, who else does she chat to? I don't think I've ever seen her leave her house. Does she have to lose you as well?'

Grace jolted my neck back to make a point, before she began clippering my hair. 'Rob, I know

No Idea

it's none of my business, but if you mean so much to her, you should visit her. I wish I could still visit my grandmother, but she died when I was twelve.'

'You're right, Grace, it isn't any of your business, and she's not family,' I replied, shocked at my own heartless response.

Pit Bull looked angry. 'So who are your family these days, Rob?'

Apart from the whir of the hair clippers, the room was quiet, and to be honest, I didn't know how to answer her question.

Grace spoke into the awkward silence. 'Is it really so hard to love your neighbour, Rob?'

'It's alright for you religious lot,' I snapped. 'You've got it all worked out. Everything is rosy and you can just forgive everyone! Well life ain't like that.'

Mum had been silently listening, but she was animated now.

'Rob, don't talk to Grace like that! You've no idea what she's been through.'

'And you've no idea what I've been through either.'

'That's right, Rob. I've been a terrible mother,' she wailed, leaving the conservatory.

Pit Bull stood up and motioned to the lads to do the same. 'We came here to see you, Rob, because we miss you and we wanted to try and work things out together. We've been like family for a long time. Call us if you ever remember that.'

Martin avoided eye contact with me and took hold of Pit Bull's hand before walking out, while Rupert grabbed half a dozen chocolate biscuits from the tray and left the room.

It was just Grace and I in the room now.

'Rob, I know you're hurt but you were a bit harsh with your friends.'

I got up from the chair in a strop. 'I'm sorry, but you know nothing about my life, so I'd appreciate it if you didn't judge me!'

'Rob, I'm not judging you. And I've only clippered one side of your hair. Don't you want me to finish?'

I slammed the conservatory door on my way out like a petulant brat and sprinted up to my bedroom. You know what they say:

Pride comes before a fall... and a fool.

No Idea

Chapter 12

Wake Up and Smell the Coffee

A few loud thuds reverberated through my door.

'Come in,' I replied.

It was Vince and he didn't look too happy.

'Rob, you and I need to have a talk.'

He was right, of course. I was a guest in his house and I acted like a selfish idiot earlier.

'Rob, I know there is history between you and your mum, but you have to give it time. You both need a lot of healing.'

'I'm sorry. I just wasn't ready to see the dossers, and then Grace interfered and, well, it went downhill from there.'

'I think Sally was trying so hard to please you, she didn't think before inviting them over. But please tread carefully. She already feels bad about the past and she wants to make it up to you.'

I nodded my head and rolled out of bed in Vince's white bathrobe. To be fair to him, apart from a frosty introduction (and I could understand why), he was being gracious with me. It couldn't be an easy thing welcoming a total stranger into his home for an unspecified length of time. After all, he married my mother, without the baggage of her family.

No Idea

'I presume Grace has already gone?' I asked. 'I need to apologise to her. Oh, and get the other half of my hair cut.'

'Your mother left Grace's number for you by the phone. She thought you might ask for it.' Vince's demeanour was beginning to thaw again.

I thanked Vince and took my mobile from the bedside cabinet before running down the stairs and bumping into Mum.

'Rob, I'm sorry about earlier. I thought you might have wanted to see your friends.'

'Not so soon, Mum. I need space to think.'

I grabbed the number next to the house phone and dialled it on my mobile. Grace's number was busy, so I walked inside the lounge and took a nose at the DVDs on the shelf.

They must belong to Vince because I couldn't see a single film I fancied watching. Most of them were black and white movies, and the only colour ones I could see were of the John Wayne, Cowboys and Indians, variety.

His mostly 'U' and 'PG' certificate collection made sense when I noticed the framed bible verse hanging above the TV set:

"The eye is the lamp of the body; so then if your eye is clear, your whole body will be full of light. "But if your eye is bad, your whole body will be full of darkness. If then the light that is in you is darkness, how great is the darkness!' Matthew 6:22-23.

'Crikey. That sounds like SAD,' I muttered.

Vince appeared beside me. 'I don't think Jesus was talking about SAD, but I understand your metaphor, Rob. We need both natural and spiritual light in our lives.'

'I suppose you're right,' I replied. 'Sorry. I didn't see you there. I was just looking at your DVD collection.'

'That's okay,' said Vince. 'Feel free to watch whatever you want.'

I thanked him before trying Grace's number again. This time, she answered.

'Hi, Grace, it's Rob. Listen, I'm really sorry about earlier. I acted like a total jerk.'

She was silent and I felt awkward. 'I was wondering if it was possible to come over to yours now and get the other half of my haircut?'

Grace snorted. 'Sure. Your mum has my address, but you'll need to come right now as I'm going out soon.'

I thanked her and headed for the door.

Mum stopped me. 'Rob, before you go... don't you think you should change out of your bathrobe? You don't want to give Grace the wrong impression?'

I could see the devilish glint in her eye. She hadn't lost her cheek, and that made me smile.

She thrust a twenty pound note into my hand. 'Pop in the lounge. I've ironed your new clothes. Oh, and there's a new pair of shoes and trainers as well.'

'Thanks Mum. That's really kind of you.'

I was curious what clothes Mum's neighbour, Rose, picked up for me in town, hoping she'd avoided the string vests and thongs and chose clothing from the men's section. After arriving in Pit Bull's lime green Crocs with flowers on, the new clothes should be an improvement on my Fred Perry grey tracksuit that was so worn you'd think it had a dozen owners before me.

The provenance of the tracksuit suited the 'dozen owners' theory. Rupert needed beer money, so he sold it to me with the words, 'Listen old boy, she's been round the clock but she's in fair condition, and looking for one careful owner to restore her to showroom condition.' By that he meant, washing and ironing the tracksuit, I imagined.

I looked over at the ironing board in the lounge and was pleasantly surprised... no, shocked. There were half a dozen sweatshirts, long-sleeved shirts, t-shirts, a few pair of stonewashed light and dark blue Jeans, a large pile of decent boxer shorts and socks and a pair of black and white Adidas Samba trainers and brogue leather boots.

'Mum, did you choose this stuff?' I asked, stunned at her impeccable taste.

'While you were asleep, Grace told me she was free for the afternoon, so we popped into town to buy your clothes. Rose had forgotten to go for me, so we went instead of her. Aren't you glad?' she chuckled.

The cute, snorting hairdresser had become all the more attractive, if that were indeed, possible.

Chapter 13

Doing God

The butterflies fluttered inside my stomach as I made my way to Grace's house. I felt embarrassed – not merely because of the way I had acted, but sporting half of a haircut and fancying the pants off the girl (quite literally), was like having a tattoo that said, 'Unstable, Proceed with Care,' written on my forehead.

I took a deep breath and knocked on her door, before checking my reflection in the glass pane. Yep, a half-clippered head looked ridiculous.

Grace answered the door. 'You're looking sharp, Rob.'

'You mean the clothes?'

She pulled a face. 'Well, I wasn't talking about your IQ.'

'I deserve that,' I laughed. 'But I do have to thank you for the clothes. If Mum's batty neighbour, Rose has bought them, I could have turned up in a stringed vest, leather trousers and cowboy boots.'

'Ha! Or worse, Vince's dressing gown?'

'Erm, yeh that was a bit embarrassing, I admit.'

'But not as funny as those Crocs with flowers on,' she mocked, snorting loudly.

No Idea

'Yeh, I borrowed them off Pit Bull after she lost my trainers.'

Grace pointed to a leather stool in the kitchen. 'Take a seat, Rob.'

'Grace, I owe you a sincere apology. I'm really sorry about earlier.'

'It's okay. Your mum explained stuff to me while we were in town. I get why you're angry.'

'I'm more confused at the moment, rather than angry,' I replied.

'Yep, I get that too, but maybe your mum isn't the same person?'

I took a deep breath before pondering her thought.

'I'm glad she's happy. I just want to make sense of my life now, coz I've made a balls-up of it so far.'

Note to self: Suggesting you're a total failure may not be the best way to impress a woman.

I closed my eyes and rested my head back as she clippered my hair. There was silence, but it didn't feel awkward, and the aroma of Grace's perfume helped me to relax again.

'Thanks Grace. The truth is I've never spoken to anyone about my past.'

'Your mum's told me a lot about you. I've been cutting her hair for a few years now. That's a lot of girl chat.'

'That'll be the son she remembers from fifteen years ago. People change,' I replied.

'Just like your mum, then?'

'Fair comment,' I replied.

I wasn't sure if I could voice what I wanted to say to Grace, but I decided what the heck.

'Maybe it's a bloke thing, but talking about my family feels like I'll end up doing cold turkey with no promise of a cure at the end of it. And the last time I tried to speak about stuff, my ex told me to just get over it. She wasn't the listening type.'

'I don't think we just 'get over' stuff. We're not robots. We have feelings. Sometimes we just have to let them out.'

'I wouldn't want to open Pandora's Box on you.'

Grace smiled. 'According to Pandora's Box, when she opened her jar all the evil flew away and only hope was left inside. Isn't confession supposed to be good for the soul?'

'Is that why Catholics do it?' I said. 'They get sloshed on Saturday night, see the priest on Sunday, say three Hail Marys and a dozen how's your fathers, and their conscience is clean.'

'I can't speak for Catholics, I'm not one, but I know the bible teaches us to be sincere and not to take God's forgiveness like it's a free pass to carry on screwing up.'

'It all sounds too simple for me. I thought you lot believe the Big Man forgives everything you do, no questions asked?'

'Rob, if you love someone, would you betray them if you thought you'd get away with it?'

'I get that, but how can you believe in someone you can't see?'

No Idea

'Do you have to see everything you believe in? What about love? What does that look like to you?' replied Grace, with a gentle tone.

'Love hasn't looked like anything for a long time. As for the Big Man upstairs pulling all the strings, I'm just not sure.'

She nodded. 'I understand. I just find it much harder to believe the idea that there was nothing, and this nothing happened to magically explode for no reason into something, creating everything and coincidentally and conveniently rearranging itself into self-replicating bits that turned into the hugely complex and amazing world we see today.'

'That's an impressive summary for a hairdresser,' I replied. 'Sorry, that came out totally wrong! I mean, you sound like a counsellor with a degree in Physics, and not your average hairdresser.'

'Oh, I'm just warming up. I was just going to ask if you were going anywhere nice on holiday, what you thought of the last episode of Towie, or the front cover of Hello magazine?'

'Point taken,' I laughed.

'Rob, we all make wrong assumptions when we don't know the person or the thing we are talking about. I didn't leave my brain at the door when I became a Christian.'

'So how did you get to learn all this stuff anyway?'

'I did an Honours Degree in Theology,' she replied.

'Well, you might be the only person I'd enjoy talking about religion with.'

'We aren't all morons. There are loads of intelligent people who believe in God. That's how I became a believer, after having some seriously long chats with Vince.'

'Vince! You mean my mum's new husband?'

'Yes, Uncle Vince is my mother's brother.'

'Flipping heck, I thought you just knew my mum through church. So an astrophysicist convinced you to believe in the man upstairs?'

'Vince just helped me join the dots. I think science shows why a belief in an intelligent designer makes sense.'

'I'm not sure how a belief in God will help me make sense of my life, just yet. I find it hard enough making sense of my own head.'

Grace smiled. 'I understand. And your mum hasn't put me up to anything. I guess everyone's healing has to begin somewhere, and bottling stuff up just makes it toxic.'

I took a deep breath and decided to remain quiet for a moment. I felt like I could talk to this girl for hours, but I didn't want to rush anything.

'Grace, for years I wanted to understand why stuff happened in my family. I believed if I asked any questions it would only make things worse.'

'Forgiveness isn't easy, Rob, but bitterness is far harder to live with.'

Grace stood in front of me trimming my fringe with her scissors. 'I used to talk to my mum about everything,' she said. 'She always gave me good advice, even if I didn't want to hear it.'

'My parents weren't the best for advice,' I replied. 'I remember Mum being so spaced out on valium, she told my first girlfriend that birth control meant reducing the number of boys she slept with. Then Dad did the drugs talk with me... and told me where to get them. My upbringing was hardly balanced.'

Grace snorted again. 'Sorry, I shouldn't laugh. That's pretty grim. So who did you hang out with when you were growing up?'

'There was an old school mate, Tom - until he got his first publishing contract and stopped returning my calls. And there was my Granddad, but he died a month after Mum moved out. He was more of a father to me than my own Dad. He buggered off a year before Mum did.'

'I'm sorry to hear that. When my Grandma died, I was devastated, and then, only last year... my mother passed away.'

'Oh crap, I didn't know. Sorry.'

'It happened quickly. I was planning to travel and work abroad, but the cancer came last summer, and within a few months, she died.'

I felt awful and a bit self-absorbed, so I remained silent, encouraging Grace to continue.

'Count your blessings, Rob. If you are always looking back, you'll never move forward. At least you have a chance to turn your life around now. At least your mum is still alive.'

Grace finished cutting my hair, removed the kitchen towel from around my neck and held a mirror up to my face. 'There you are. What do you think?'

'I think you've removed enough hair to fill a sofa. It hasn't been this short in years, but it looks good. Cheers.'

Grace's eyes sparkled in my direction. She looked gorgeous. No more than thirty years old, she reminded me of the London singer and songwriter, Jess Glynne. Her auburn-red, curly hair waved at me every time she moved, while her deep blue eyes drew me in every time I captured her gaze.

I laughed inwardly at the thought of squeezing her perfectly formed, button nose, but I really wanted to kiss her soft, pink lips. I figured if this girl was hot even though she was a 'God botherer', I couldn't imagine how hooked I'd be if she was sitting on my lap and watching a chic-flick with me.

I diverted my thoughts back to Jeremy Clarkson and Wayne Rooney, for safe measure.

'I think your attitude to life is infectious. I like it,' I added. 'So where are you off out tonight?'

'There's a comedy night in Brixton. I'm going with my friend, Sarah.'

'Nice one. Can I ask you a small favour, if you don't mind?'

'Sure.'

'Would you drop me off in Brixton? I think this would be a good time to visit my neighbour, Mrs Popov.'

No Idea

'From what your friends said, I'm sure she'd appreciate it. Be back at mine for seven o'clock.'

I was emboldened now.

'Can I make another wish?'

'I'm not your fairy godmother... but, as it's you, go on then.'

'Would you like to visit her with me... before your show starts?'

Grace flicked the kettle on and grabbed a packet of chocolate Hobnob biscuits. This girl had impeccable taste.

'Hmm. Do you normally invite girls to old ladies' homes for tea and biscuits? I'll hand it to you, Rob. You're different!' Grace snorted several times at her own joke. I loved this girl's confidence.

'No, I was just thinking, erm, y'know, you might-'

'Sure. But you'll have to tell me all about her before we leave... in ten minutes!'

Twenty four hours ago I thought my life was going down the toilet. Now I was daring to believe that it might be changing for the better. Maybe I did have some faith, after all?

Chapter 14

The Adventure Begins

After giving Grace the full run-down about Mrs Popov and her missing grandson, Alexei, she seemed all the more excited to visit her. We'd taken the bus to Brixton and I made sure we spent most of the time talking about Grace and her family.

Grace was 28 years old and an only child of Jewish parents, Jacob and Kitty Stein. That was another surprise. She was Jewish but she believed in Jesus? 'How does that work?' I asked. She reminded me that Jesus was a Jew. I couldn't argue with that.

Thankfully, she changed the subject and moved on to talk about her own family. The way she spoke about her relationship and how she loved her mum, Kitty, made my eyes filled up more than once.

I won't pretend I wasn't jealous of the relationship she had with her parents. I wished things were different in my own childhood, but Grace was also coping with a different kind of grief. Her father, Jacob Stein, was only sixty eight years old when he was diagnosed with Alzheimer's disease, and lived in a dementia care home a few miles away. I guessed this was what Mum meant when she said that I had no idea what Grace had been through.

I wondered if I ever wrote a book about my life, I should call it, 'No Idea'. No idea how to heal the past

- no idea what do with my life - and no idea what to write next, bar these words.

Grace seemed so confident and self assured that I expected she liked guys who knew where they were going in life; blokes different from me, the kind with decent jobs and their own apartments, minus any dossers.

It was our stop and time to get off the 133 bus near Sudbourne Road to make our way to Mrs Popov's house. I felt I needed to explain a few things to my elderly neighbour about why I left. She was already missing Alexei, and I didn't want to make things harder for her. And I was happy to meet up with her once a week for a cuppa.

After the rebuke from Pit Bull and Grace earlier, I regretted saying that Mrs Popov wasn't family to me. Apart from her younger brother, I didn't think she had any living relatives in the UK, so I became a bit of a lifeline for her, ordering her groceries online and having the supermarket deliver them to her door. On further reflection, she was more than just a neighbour, and I decided I would look out for her.

I tapped my knuckles gently on Mrs Popov's window. We had a special knock. I would knock twice, then three times quickly followed by two more gentle knocks. That way she felt safe coming to the door.

She opened her letterbox. 'Rob, secret knocking are ve?'

'Yes. I've popped by to say hi with a friend. Is it a good time to come in?'

'Your timing, good always,' she said, opening her door with a beaming smile.

I winked at Grace to remind her of Mrs Popov's nickname, Yoda, and how she said most things backwards. Grace smiled at me, and I wondered how the heck I'd persuaded this girl to go anywhere with me.

Mrs Popov walked us through to her lounge and we warmed up quickly in front of her gas fire, before she tottered into the kitchen to make some tea.

'Aw, Rob, look at her photos. Is that her grandson, Alexei?' she asked, pointing at the photo above the fireplace.

'Yes, though I haven't seen the one in the middle before. It looks like a more recent photo.'

I leaned back on the sofa and rested my head on the large fluffy cushion. The TV volume was quite loud, so I took a few deep breaths and cupped my right hand around my cheek with my little finger underneath my chin and closed my eyes.

'You okay?' asked Grace.

'Yeh, I was just thinking before Mrs Popov comes back in.'

'What were you thinking about?'

'I was thinking... maybe I could do some research on Alexei's disappearance? I know it would encourage her, and it's not like I don't have any time now.'

I found myself staring at the photo on the mantelpiece. There was something different about it that I couldn't quite put my finger on.

No Idea

Mrs Popov returned with her rose-patterned tray and china cups.

'Lump for you, one or two?'

Grace politely declined the sugar and took her cup holding the small handle with her index finger. I hadn't noticed her nails before, but they were perfectly manicured and painted the cutest pink.

'Sugars are three for you, Rob?' She smiled, handing me the cup before sitting down in front of me and leaning forward in her Parker Knoll rocking chair. 'Beautiful is your girlfriend, Rob.'

I looked at Grace and raised my eyebrows, more in hope than expectation, and offered a cheeky wink in her direction before giving Mrs Popov my attention. 'Grace is a friend. She is the niece of my mum's new husband, and the one responsible for my new haircut.'

My neighbour chuckled. 'For life, a special friend is.'

Mrs Popov got up from her chair and walked over to Grace, taking her by the hand. 'Come, beautiful girl. Show you something, I must.'

I figured she was taking Grace to see her huge collection of framed photos in the dining room, so I stayed seated and allowed my thoughts to wander for a moment.

My attention was drawn to the photo of Alexei again, but this time I spotted something interesting. Alexei was sitting at a table and smoking a cigarette while staring down at something. I stood up from the sofa to look closer and underneath a newspaper I noticed what looked like the corner of a tablet or iPad. I didn't know why I was interested in this fact, until I remembered Mrs Popov telling me the only computer or device her grandson had was his mobile phone and laptop.

I could hear Grace chatting away in the next room, so I decided to join them.

'Mrs Popov, do you mind if I ask you a question?'

She turned to me and smiled. 'My Rob, always you must.'

'The photo in the lounge with Alexei smoking at the table... do you know when it was taken and who took it? Do you know if Alexei owned an iPad or something like it?'

'Eye pad? No eye problem he had, I think?' she replied.

I rephrased my question. 'No, I mean the electronic tablet that's called an iPad. I think it's an iPad I can see underneath the newspaper in this photo.'

'I didn't know if he had eye patch, and electric things missing with Alexei.'

I tried not to smirk while Grace looked at me inquisitively. 'What are you thinking, Rob?'

'Well, apparently Alexei was a tech genius. I'm just wondering if that was Alexei's iPad in this photo. What if we found his Apple ID and cracked his password, Apple could trace the last place he was online with it. All we need is to convince Apple we're him.'

No Idea

Mrs Popov shrugged her shoulders, apparently clueless to what I've just said.

Grace nodded. 'Even if we found Alexei's email address, how would we crack his password?'

I took a few moments to think carefully before I replied. 'Mrs Popov, would you happen to know what Alexei's email address was? If you're not sure, do you know who he spoke to on the internet?'

'Clues, I have none,' she replied. 'I never liking N'internet. But try look for me, there you must.'

Grace looked at me intently. 'Rob, I remember when I forgot my Apple password I just had to give my email address, date of birth and answer a few security questions to get back into my account.'

'Exactly,' I replied.

'Mrs Popov, do you still have any of Alexei's paperwork or notes?' I asked.

She bowed her head while rubbing her wet eyes.

I put my hand on her shoulder. 'I'm sorry I don't want to upset you...'

'Upset I am always, but worry, don't. Upstairs, go, first room.'

I took Grace by the hand before we took to the stairs. 'Oh, sorry, I don't know why I did that,' I said, embarrassed.

'Rob, if you want to be the perfect gentleman, be my guest!' Her eyes sparkled in my direction again.

We climbed the stairs and entered Alexei's bedroom... the one he had never slept in.

***

Mrs Popov told me that Alexei lived in Wolverhampton with her before he went missing after a trip to London. Feeling useless and estranged from her grandson, she moved to London to search for him, and in the hope they would be reunited again, she'd lovingly prepared Alexei's bedroom.

The room was meticulously arranged, more of a shrine to his memory than a room he might ever sleep in. To the left of the bed was a writing desk with table lamp, a pot of new pens/pencils, notebook and what looked like an unboxed 10.1" HP laptop.

Apart from a few cupboards for his clothes, some distasteful Nazi memorabilia and posters on the wall, a shelf of books above the bed grabbed my attention.

There were various books on psychology, advanced mathematics, computing and philosophy. I looked carefully at each item to see if there were any loose notes among them, but found nothing.

'Grace, do you want to check the drawers in the dressing table?'

'Sure,' she replied, while I looked inside Alexei's coat pockets inside the wardrobe. Nothing turned up.

We walked back down the stairs and after obtaining Alexei's date of birth, I made a record of Mrs Popov's telephone number. If we could find his Apple ID, we'd only need the answers to two out of three security questions that Alexei chose in order to reset the Apple ID password. Then we would have access to his iCloud account with no need to access his email.

No Idea

My neighbour handed me a photo of Alexei and her together. The photo looked like it was taken somewhere in London. 'Have this for me, when you are looking, Rob. See him, call me you must.'

'Thank you. I'll look after it,' I replied. 'This photo appears to be a quite recent one. Is this in London?' I asked, pointing to the photo. 'Were you on holiday together?'

'Yes, only photo taken before missing. Imperial War Museum he was seeing. He liked war.'

Grace touched my arm. 'Rob, should we just go to the police about your iPad theory?'

'Not yet. Let's see if we can find it first. You never know where it might lead.'

Chapter 15

Chat Show

After I said goodnight to Grace, her friend picked her up from Mrs Popov's address for their night out to the Comedy Club, while I took the bus back to Mum's house. I stood at the entrance of the lounge and stared at Mum and Vince as they held hands and laughed at the TV.

'Honey, how did you get on with Grace?' she asked, sporting a cheeky grin.

'Fine, we just talked about the usual stuff - planning our wedding and discussing how many children we'd like to have together.'

'You haven't lost your sense of humour,' she giggled. 'Come in and join us. Vince has recorded The Jonathan Woss show for me. It's got my favourite hottie on next... the Butler bloke.'

'Do you mean Princess Di's butler, Paul Burrell?' I joked.

Mum nearly spat out her tea. 'No you silly sod. I mean him who plays James Bond!'

'Daniel Craig?'

'No, I don't mean him. The Scottish one-'

'Sean Connery?' I replied.

'No, what's his name – plays for that Liverpool football team.'

No Idea

I laughed. 'So let me get this straight... he's a Scottish bloke who, when he's not playing a butler, he's playing Bond in the movies, and only when he isn't playing for Liverpool?'

'Steven Gerrard. That's it!' she shouted.

'Mum, Steven Gerrard has never played James Bond!'

'No, I mean Gerard Butler.'

Vince's eyeballs hit the ceiling before chuckling. 'Your mother's away with the fairies, as usual!'

'No mum, Gerard Butler has never been Bond or played for Liverpool Football Club. Do you mean someone else?'

'You're right, love. It's not Gerard Butler. I meant Mel Gibson.'

I couldn't hide the grin on my face. 'Nope, Mel hasn't played Bond either.' I recalled my own gaffe with the hot-blooded Scandinavian Astrid and my drunken comment about Mel playing a Viking. Maybe I was more like my mother than I realised?

Mum scrunched up her forehead in determined fashion. 'Yes he has! It was when he had permed hair and his partner was a black bloke with a moustache. I remember the ending... he shot some South African bloke on a boat.'

I couldn't stop myself laughing. 'Mum, you're thinking of the film, Lethal Weapon. Mel Gibson was Sergeant Riggs and his partner, Danny Glover, was called Sergeant Murtaugh.'

'That's the one,' she replied. 'Oh and Vince, I want to see that film where Mel plays the Lord... I think it's called The Passion. I bet he makes a lovely Jesus.'

'I'll go get the kettle on, love,' smirked Vince, leaving the room.

Mum tapped the cushion next to her. 'Come and sit down here, love.'

I sat down at the end of the sofa, an extra bottom length away.

'So Rob, I know it must seem like you've only been here five minutes, but how are you? We can chat about stuff as soon as you're ready.'

I paused for a moment before standing up and replying, 'Sure, maybe later, but I'm gonna go up and do some work on my laptop if you don't mind.'

'Okay, love. I've made you some Chilli Con Carne with rice. I'll just go and heat it up in the microwave.'

As Mum popped into the kitchen, an unmistakable voice grabbed my attention. I looked up at the TV screen, blinked twice and did a double take as the guest was about to be interviewed by Jonathan Woss:

'Ladies and Gentlemen, let's give a huge welcome to Tom Davey (audience wolf-whistles and claps furiously). So Tom, what's it like being the No.1 chick-flick writer who isn't a chick? How does that work, and how do you cope with all of the female attention?'

I'm as disgusted as I am intrigued, and sit down on the sofa again.

Tom replied, 'I like to think of myself as the modern metrosexual man, y'know, groomed, rather than brutish, a tad narcissistic but not Neanderthal, and girlfriends, I can shop like the best of you.'

Jonathan laughed. 'I'm loving the man bag! It's definitely you, Tom! So... it must be very satisfying to be the pin-up boy of the literary world?'

'What can I say? I love my fans from all over the world, I really do.' The audience screamed in delight, and it wasn't just the women. If I could've reached into the studio and slapped the adoring blokes, I would.

Jonathan leant forward. 'Well, after selling nearly five million copies of your last book, 'Once Bitten, Twice Ravenous,' you must know more about women than the legend (Mel Gibson) sitting next to you?'

Mel chuckled and put his arm around Tom. 'Everything I know, I learned from this dude.'

Tom raised his hand in an act of false modesty.

'So, is it true your 'Love Coaching' is a great hit with the stars?' asked Jonathan. 'Care to share some of the names of your famous clients with us?' He raised his eyebrows several times for effect.

I grabbed the cushion next to me and squeezed it tightly before cussing at the screen as Tom crossed his grey mottled drainpipe trouser leg over his knee.

'Well, Jonathan, you know I don't like to brag, and of course, some of my A-listers prefer to remain anonymous, but let's just say it would probably be harder for me to name five celebs I haven't seen.'

Jonathan threw his head back in laughter. 'For the record, ladies and gentlemen, my wife has been a client of Tom's for some time, and I can tell you, I'm very happy to pay for her visits. The benefits are out of this world!' The audience laughed hysterically as Jonathan licked his lips.

'Oh, you are too kind,' replied Tom. 'Let's just say my work is largely theoretical and my readers are the practitioners. I like to think my words are like nectar – my fans suck them up and make their own honey lovin' with it! In fact, this may be the perfect time to announce my new book coming out for Christmas. It's called... yes you guessed it... 'Honey Lovin'- How To Be a Sweet Success!'

Mum returned with a tray of Chilli Con Carne, while Vince handed me a mug of coffee. I smiled politely and thanked them both before moving to the end of the sofa where I could balance the tray of food on the large square arm.

'Oh, Rob. Look who it is on the TV! It's your old mate, Tom,' yelped Mum. 'And you'll never guess what? I called his mum today and told her you were back in town. I still keep in touch with her. Apparently, Tom spends most of his time now in LA. You know - the one in America.'

I muttered a few choice words and turned up the volume on the remote control. In all fairness, I always found Ruth to be a kind person and I know she felt awkward when her son stopped all contact with me. But I didn't want Mum meddling in the past. It was bad enough knowing we'd have to talk about it soon enough.

No Idea

The audience calmed down, primed for Jonathan's next question:

'I'm sure Honey Lovin' will be a 'sweet success,' but tell us... when did you decide to become a writer and who were the biggest influences in your life?'

Tom fiddled with his thin black tie and leaned back into the sofa before considering his reply. I held my breath anticipating his answer.

'Jonathan, I'd have to say I've wanted to be a writer ever since I was a child. I devoured the classic children's stories and grew to love and admire the giants of literature as a teen, but I wanted to write something fresh, different, even irreverent, y'know, push the boundaries-'

'You, irreverent? Pushing boundaries? Surely never,' replied Jonathan, to a cacophony of laughter.

Tom replied, 'But my biggest and only influence in my young life as a writer? That's not hard...'

Time stood still before Tom would surely mention my name. Would this be the first occasion in fifteen years he'd finally acknowledge our friendship and talk about the hundreds of hours we spent writing together? Would I find anything in his words that might soothe the ruined memories of our friendship?

'The single most and only personal influence in my young life as a writer has to be... my mother.'

I glared at the television in shock and disbelief. Mum saw the effect Tom's words had on me and turned the TV off.

I sucked hard on my bottom lip and tried to stop the rush of unwelcome memories flooding back. I clenched my teeth in defiance, but nothing stopped a solitary tear from running down my left cheek and on to my shirt.

I tried to avoid looking at Mum and shoved a fork into my dinner before slowly sucking the contents off the stainless steel ridges. Nothing I did masked the hurt.

Mum put her arm around my shoulder while I coughed a little to clear the back of my throat.

'It's okay, Mum. It's like you've said in your letters, 'the past doesn't have to determine the present,' eh?'

I thought about my words. I was sitting next to the Mum that walked out on me fifteen years ago, and it felt okay. It didn't excuse the past, but neither did it have to dictate the present.

I had lived with the idea that it didn't seem right or fair to forgive my mum, but since seeing her again, I began to think differently. What about my crap? Who forgives that? What about my wasted life since Granddad died? Maybe that was it. The person who has been forgiven much, loves much? Maybe this is who Mum wanted to be, but what of myself? Could I expect to move on with my life without giving her another chance?

Mum held a tissue to her nose and blew it several times. 'Son, I'm sorry. You didn't deserve what Tom did to you... and you didn't deserve what I did, either.' She kissed my cheek, now wet again with her own tears. We both had more in common than I realised. We both hurt. We both needed to forgive. We both needed a second chance.

No Idea

'Hurt people, hurt people,' I'd heard it said, but what about those who forgive each other?

I managed to snort and cough within milliseconds of each other, and nearly choked on my food. I leaned over to the small coffee table and grabbed a large tissue to deposit the contents of my mouth.

Vince stood up from his armchair. 'I'll give you both some space. If you need me, I'll be in the conservatory.'

Though there was silence, I couldn't stop my tears. My chest tightened as I sensed this might be the right time to talk openly. I took a few deep breaths and tried to calm myself before speaking.

'Mum, I'm glad you are happy with Vince.' I swallowed hard again to stop the stinging sensation in my throat, before continuing, 'You never deserved to be treated so badly by Dad. And I know now, after thinking about stuff, that you were unhappy. I used to think it was something I'd done, but-'

'Rob,' she interrupted. 'It was never your fault, none of it, but I'm ashamed to say, you were let down by bad parents. Me, your dad, we were both hurting each other, and you were caught in the middle of it. And I'm not sure if you know, but I had a terrible addiction to Valium pills.'

'I know. Wasn't it called, 'The pill for every ill?'

'Yep, it was also called Mummy's little helper. They dished it out to anyone who was struggling. My doctor said I needed it. At first it did what it was supposed to do... make you calm, but then I felt more spaced-out than ever, having to up the tablets to try and escape the depression. Ten years later and a few years before I met Vince, I was way past the maximum dose and a total wreck.'

I listened empathetically. 'I heard it can be more addictive than heroin. How did you get off it?'

'It took a good few months. I cut the tablets into quarters and gradually reduced the dose, but the withdrawal symptoms were terrible. I could hardly climb the stairs and the panic attacks and agoraphobia kept me pretty much housebound, apart from going out for the essentials.

'Before I met the Lord, the only inner strength I found was in a medicine cabinet or drinking alcohol. I felt powerless.'

I listened carefully. 'So this Jesus talk – are you sure you haven't just swapped one opium high for another,' I replied. 'No offense intended.'

'None taken, love. I understand how it must all seem, but I'm not the person I used to be. I'm not perfect, but I know what I want in my life – who I want in my life, and I want you, son. I want us.'

'Why didn't you think about the consequences of leaving me? First Dad, then you. I returned to an empty house and thought we'd been burgled. You cleared the house and all you left me was a note. What was I supposed to think?'

'I wasn't in a fit state to understand the consequences of anything. And moving in with Trevor was the only option I could think of – the only one that might keep me alive. I couldn't cope, Rob. I wanted to do myself in. I tried it a few times with pills and the second time with booze, but I ended up in hospital. And I wasn't in for some blood disorder like I told your father to tell you. I had a seizure. I nearly killed myself.'

Mum put her head on my shoulder and sobbed quietly. I tried to stop my own tears, but it proved futile. I turned to face her and looked at her complexion. I couldn't bear her tears. Now I knew I loved my mum. Despite the pain and disappointment, my love was stronger than any hate or unforgiveness I had felt when she left me.

'Son, when I went through your bag yesterday to sort your washing, I saw all the letters I'd sent you. I cried when I saw you'd kept them. I'd hoped you were receiving them from your previous landlord. But I found a letter you had addressed to me – one obviously, you never sent. Please don't be angry with me, but I read it. And I understand your feelings, Rob. It broke my heart to read how you felt about me, but I needed to hear it.'

'You had no right to go through my letters,' I snapped, before pausing a few seconds and regaining some composure. 'I wrote that letter with my angry head on. And I didn't know I had the letter in my bag... but I don't feel like that now. I know it'll take us time to talk through stuff. Just be patient with me, Mum. I've screwed up my life since Granddad died. I really miss him.'

'Take as much time as you want, son. I miss him too.'

I excused myself and took the tray and hot drink with me to my bedroom. I had a lot to process and needed some space. Keen to change the subject, I focused my thoughts on Mrs Popov's boy, Alexei. I was determined to try and find his email address and crack his Apple password. If he or someone else was using the iPad, I figured it might lead to clues of his disappearance.

No Idea

Chapter 16

Wi-Fi Boost

Several loud beeps from my phone notified me of a text message. I leaned over to the side table and clicked on the screen. It was from Grace:

'Hi Rob. Hope you're okay? Comedy show was wicked. I'll bring you next time if you're up for it? Any news yet re Alexei's email address? Heading home soon. x'

I replied to Grace's text: 'I'm fine. Had awkward chat with Mum but went better than expected. I might be up for going out. No news yet on email address. I'm going through the notes in Alexei's book to see if any more clues. Rob.'

After obtaining Vince's Wi-Fi password, I surfed the internet and visited a number of forums and chat groups focused on Alexei's interests, but found nothing. There were no Google records for his full name, and no links on Friends Reunited or Facebook that traced him back to his school or college in Wolverhampton. I couldn't tie anything in with Alexei, apart from a few amateur sleuth pages that cast wild guesses from kidnapping to paedophilia.

The only thing that caught my attention was a Missing Persons website offering a £50,000 cash reward for information leading to his whereabouts. Such was the devotion of Mrs Popov, I wouldn't be

No Idea

surprised if she'd stumped up the money herself. She didn't have much of a clue how she might find her grandson.

The only information I had to go on was a sheet of paper found inside one of Alexei's books. I held it up and the bright ceiling light illuminated the paper. Apart from some sketchy notes about bitcoins and the Dark Web, a rough cartoon sketch of a Badger wearing a t-shirt that read, 'dark web riot', stood out to me on the page. I wondered if Alexei might have used those three words as a username on the web or as an email address?

I grabbed my laptop and typed the words 'dark web riot' into Google. Nothing, so I tried a variation of @darkwebriot, darkwebriot@yahoo.com darkwebriot@gmail.com, wondering if these addresses ever posted anything on the net? Nothing, so one last shot... I logged onto the icloud.com website to see if Alexei might have used this as part of an email address:

A message appeared: 'darkwebriot is not an Apple ID.' So I tried again, this time adding the gmail.com address to the end, and received the following message:

Select how you want to reset your password: Choose from the options below to reset the password for darkwebriot@gmail.com

I stared at the screen for a few seconds. Someone had registered this email address with Apple! I was now offered two options to recover the password: 1. Receive an email or 2. Answer security questions. I knew I couldn't ask Apple to send an email as that would notify Alexei or the person controlling his account.

If this was Alexei's email address, I was about to see the security questions he chose when he set up this account. The screen asked me to verify Alexei's birthday to continue, so having already written this down at Mrs Popov's earlier, I entered his month, day and year. This would definitely show if Alexei and darkwebriot was the same person.

I shook my head in disbelief. This had to be Alexei's account, because I was presented with two security questions. 1. What was his favourite childhood friend? 2. In what city did his mother and father meet?' If I could find these answers, I'd be able reset the password and see if Apple could track his iPad, so I dialled Mrs Popov's telephone number.

'Hi, Mrs Popov, It's Rob. I've been thinking about Alexei and wanted ask you a few questions. Is that okay?'

'My dear, you must,' she replied, rather insistent.

'First question, I mean, I was wondering... who was Alexei's best childhood friend?'

'Rob, not sure, I am. Sorry. Why asking? Finding something you have?'

I needed to think on my feet. I didn't want to get Mrs Popov's hopes up just yet, so I replied, 'No, I was just wondering if I could find any of his friends on the internet. That's all. How many friends did Alexei have growing up? Do you know the names of any of them?'

'Alexei had difficult child time. I can think not of any. Lonely boy, he was.'

No Idea

'So he had no friends at all that you can think of?' I asked. I found it strange why Alexei would chose this particular security question, if he had no friends.

Mrs Popov continued. 'Sad his time in Russia. Mother died in birth and father away he went. This why moving to England with him, I did.'

I moved on to the second security question: 'So where did Alexei's mother and father first meet?'

'Ah, yes. They meeting Sochi, Russia,' she answered.

I knew the name, Sochi. The Winter Olympics was held there a few years ago and I remember watching some of it on the television.

'Thank you Mrs Popov. I will speak to you again soon,' I replied, before ending the call.

Though I was unable to access Alexei's account with just one of the answers to the security questions, my appetite for amateur sleuthing hadn't abated. I'd cracked his email address and one of the two required security questions and I was determined to find out who Alexei's childhood friend might be.

I dialled Grace to update her with the news. 'Hi. Guess what... I've found Alexei's email address and one of his security questions. I'm just stuck on who his childhood friend might be. Mrs Popov said she didn't think he had any.'

'You're kidding me?' she replied.

'Nope, he went by the Gmail address, darkwebriot. But this thing about his childhood friend – why would Alexei choose that security question if he didn't have any friends?'

'Maybe he meant an imaginary friend?'

'Hang on a minute,' I replied. Turning back to the laptop, I typed in the Russian City, Sochi, for the first security question, before typing the word, imaginary, for the answer to his childhood friend.

'Grace, you aren't going to believe this,' I shrieked with excitement. 'You're amazing!'

'Why, thank you, Rob.'

'It worked!' I replied.

'You're kidding me?'

'No, I'm deadly serious. You better come over now.'

'I'm on my way, but don't do anything till I get there. I remember when I logged in a few weeks ago Apple sent me an email message saying that someone just accessed my account. If Alexei is still alive or his email account is being watched, we'll need to act quickly.'

'Should we just call the police and let them check this out?' I asked, nervous I could be out of my depth.

'And tell them what? That you just hacked a missing person's account?'

I could see Grace's point. And what if the missing iPad couldn't be located anyway?

I replied, 'Okay. Once we log in, we won't have long to see where it's located on the map, and that's only if he is connected to the Internet with it. His emails, contacts, photos and stuff might also be backed up in the cloud.'

No Idea

'Rob, if we find anything interesting, we will have to pass it on to the police. Anyway, I'm starting the car now. See you in a minute.'

My heart thumped loudly as I contemplated my next step. Things were about to get very, very interesting.

***

Grace walked into my room and sat on the bed. 'I can't believe we've come so far already.'

'Me neither,' I replied, my heart banging, but for a different reason, daring to believe that I might have the slightest chance of making a romantic connection with Grace. I didn't want my hopes dashed, but it was hard to stop thinking about her. If all she wanted was a friendship, I didn't want to scupper that by making any sort of play or display of interest.

'We might have a problem,' I said. 'Are you saying the moment we reset the password, a message will be sent to Alexei's email account?'

'Correct,' replied Grace.

'So if Alexei's emails are being monitored, they will change the password again and we will be won't be able to get back in?'

'Exactly.'

'We will need to move quickly before we're locked out of the account or whoever has the iPad does a runner,' I replied.

'Well, I've got the car outside, so I'm ready to go.'

'Sounds like a plan,' I replied. 'I'll choose a new password, and if we get the location of his iPad, we can log in from your iPhone and follow the signal in your car.'

I reset the password and gained immediate access to Alexei's iCloud account. My finger hovered over the mouse pad button before I clicked on the Find iPhone app. 'Here we go,' I muttered before clicking.

'Flippin' eck! His iPad is connected to Wi-Fi now!' The map on the screen showed a green circle hovering over an address in High Street, Croydon. I clicked on 'Satellite' mode on the screen and the map changed to a photographic display of the street, shops and an accurate location.

'Rob, that looks like it's either the Italian restaurant or the night club under the flyover. I think it's called the Ponte Nuovo.'

We rushed out to Grace's Mini Cooper and jumped in. 'It might take us half an hour to get there, so we need to be quick. Pass me your phone and I'll login to the iCloud.'

Grace replied, 'We won't be able to park in the High Street, but there's a multi-storey a few minutes away. We'll go there.'

'That's fine,' I replied. 'When we arrive, you go order a table for two in the restaurant and I'll check out the night club next door. I'll come and find you when I've checked the club. If you see anyone who looks like Alexei or someone holding an iPad, take some discreet photos and come and get me.'

No Idea

'No problem,' she replied. 'But will you just try to scan everyone inside? What if they aren't using the iPad or you can't see it?'

'I won't hear the iPad in a nightclub, so I'll just have to take a chance and see if I spot Alexei or anyone with an iPad in there. If I find nothing, I'll join you in the restaurant and we can send an alert to his device. It will go off like an alarm and the noise won't stop until someone clicks on the screen. That should be long enough to see where the noise is coming from.'

Grace nodded as she drove at speed down Leigham Court Road. 'Another thing, Rob. What if we find Alexei? That might suggest he doesn't want to be found, and we could be in a world of trouble if we confront him?'

'Whether it's Alexei or someone else with his iPad, we get some photos and call the police.'

***

We arrived at the multi storey car park and crossed the road toward the Ponte Nuovo. Grace took my hand as we approached the entrance. 'Rob, I'm nervous.'

'Don't worry, we won't do anything stupid, and remember - if we have to set off the iPad alarm, there's no way anyone will know we sent it. I'll see you in the restaurant in the next five or ten minutes. Just get a table for two.'

Grace entered the Ponte Nuovo and was greeted by a waiter who took her to a table located roughly in the middle of the restaurant, while I headed next door to Club 88.

***

After scouring the club, I hadn't seen Alexei or anyone with an iPad or a 'man bag' to carry one in, so I made my way back to the Ponte Nuovo.

I approached Grace's table and kissed her on the cheek before sitting down. 'Sorry to keep you waiting,' I said. My language may have been for show, but the kiss wasn't. Grace seemed perfectly happy with my performance as she smiled and handed me a J_2O Orange juice.

'I saw nothing next door. Have you seen anything interesting here?'

'Nothing,' she replied.

I scanned the restaurant in front of me. There were plenty of couples and a few families with children eating together, but no one resembling Alexei or anyone holding an iPad. I leaned over toward Grace. 'I can't see anything, either.'

Grace took a small mirror out of her handbag and pouted into the reflection to apply her soft red lipstick. She scanned her half of the restaurant again and lowered her voice. 'I can't see the package.'

'You sound like you're working for MI5,' I whispered, before continuing, 'I want you to leave the restaurant now and bring the car outside. Stop a few shops away. If the iPad's in here, whoever has it may want to leave quickly when I set the alarm off. Then we'll try to follow them when they leave.'

No Idea

Grace finished her drink and left for the front door, while the waiter approached me.

'Is everything okay, sir? Would you like to order anything else?'

'Erm, my girlfriend isn't feeling well, so I'll settle the bill now, please.'

I paid for the drinks with the cash and waited a few extra minutes in my seat to give Grace enough time to park outside. I pressed the icon on my phone screen that said, 'Play Sound,' and quickly switched on the camera app, ready to take photos.

A sonar sound from an iPad rang from a table in front of me, barely a few meters away. A lady reached for her handbag. She was sitting next to a young child who tried to grab the iPad, and was refused. An older man (who I presume to be her partner) sitting opposite the woman saw the flashing alert on the iPad. Clearly startled, he snatched it from her hand and touched the screen. The alarm stopped.

I heard him say, 'Why did you bring this to the restaurant?' The woman replied, 'I'm sorry, but I brought it for Bertina just in case she was bored and needed something to play with.'

I had already taken a dozen or so photos of the three of them, so I held the glass to my face and watched him as he looked around the restaurant. Seconds later I left my chair and walked calmly out of the front door and toward Grace's car.

She flashed her car lights at me before I walked over to her and climbed in the front seat. 'I found the bloody iPad!' I exclaimed, a little out of breath from excitement than any fatigue. 'Some fat guy with, I presume his wife and daughter, had the iPad. The guy looked startled when the alarm went off.'

'So what do we do now?' asked Grace.

'Just move the car forward enough so I can see inside the restaurant. I want to see what he's doing.'

The Mini Cooper moved along the pavement. 'Stop here. I can see him. He's on the phone to someone. Okay, here's the idea. Pull over on the other side of the road, just out of sight for now. Let's follow them at a safe distance when they leave the restaurant.'

Five minutes passed before a black cab stopped outside the Ponte Nuovo and the three of them stepped into the cab. 'Follow them Grace, but remember: don't get too close to the cab. I don't want them to think they're being tailed.'

We'd been following the cab for about ten minutes when we pulled up about fifty yards away from a large, gated property in the wealthy area of Sandilands, East Croydon. The two adults and child hurried out of the taxi and entered a property I presume was their home. 'Whoever these people are, they're not short of a few quid,' I said.

'So what are they doing with Alexei's iPad then?' Grace asked.

'Okay, here are a few theories. When the woman was questioned by her partner why she brought the iPad to the restaurant, she said it was for her daughter to play with. So, first - maybe Alexei knows them and for whatever strange reason, he gave it or sold it to them? Second, Alexei pawned it and the bloke or his missus bought it from a shop or stall somewhere.

No Idea

Third, they are in some way responsible for his disappearance, and foolishly gave his iPad to their daughter.'

'You told me Alexei lived in Wolverhampton when he went missing,' she replied. 'So if Alexei knows them, how? And why would he give his iPad to someone who looks like they could afford to buy thousands of them? Also, do rich people buy second hand iPads? Maybe they had something to do with his disappearance? We need to call the police now, Rob.'

'There is another option, Grace. When I was searching online for information on Alexei Popov, I came across a website asking for any information that might lead to his discovery. They are also offering a reward of fifty grand if he's found.'

'Rob, if you think this family might have something to do with his disappearance, don't you think it's a police matter?'

'Of course I do, but surely the information would be passed on to the police when we submit it on the website?'

'What does the website say? How do we know the information will be fed through to the police?'

I searched Google for the web page again. 'Here it is. I'll read it out...'

'Let me read it,' she replied. 'Okay... it says they work with the families of missing children and respective agencies, including police forces throughout the UK, Scotland Yard, the National Crime Agency, Child Exploitation Online Protection Centre, among others. And there's a 24 hour helpline for us to call.'

'I've got an idea,' I replied. 'Why don't we ask Mrs Popov if she knows anything about this Missing Persons charity website? I remember that the Alexei posters I put up for her mentioned a reward on them. If she gives it the all clear, then we contact them.'

'Good idea, but it's nearly eleven o'clock, Rob. She'll be asleep.'

'Maybe, but it's worth waking her up. We need to act now.'

Grace agreed, so I dialled Mrs Popov's number from my phone. The number rang half a dozen times before it was answered.

'Rob, you, this is?' asked Mrs Popov.

'Yes, I am sorry to call you so late, but I found a website called, Missing Person Overseas and it's offering a reward for any information leading to Alexei's discovery. Did you know about this?'

'Rob, these people my only help. Police not help.'

'So if we find anything, should we contact this Missing Persons charity or the police?'

'My Alexei is found?' she asked.

'No Mrs Popov, but we are trying to use the Internet to help find him. That is all.'

'Any ideas, please tell them to me or Charity. They quickly act.'

I agreed with Mrs Popov and ended the call. 'Grace, she said we should contact the website. Can you dial the 24 hour emergency number on your iPhone. Mine is running out of battery.'

The line rang loudly as the call was amplified through her car speakers.

No Idea

'Good evening. This is the Missing Persons Overseas helpline. Can we help you?'

'I hope so. I have information on the Missing Person, Alexei Popov...'

Chapter 17

Old Wounds

After giving the Missing Persons Overseas charity the full story of our escapades, Grace dropped me home just before midnight. They said a police officer would probably contact us today to collect the photos we took in the restaurant, so I was up early and joined Mum and Vince for breakfast. Thankfully it was uneventful, with just the predictable teasing from her about the amount of time I was spending with Grace. Of course I told her nothing about last night and even less about what Grace and I were doing together.

Mrs Popov was the first to call me on my mobile and asked if Grace and I would visit her as soon as possible. The wobble in her voice suggested she had been crying again and I was keen to visit her and find out more of Alexei's back story. I presumed the people at the Missing Persons charity had called her.

Grace cancelled her mobile hair appointments for the day and seemed wholly committed to finding Alexei, clearly fond of Mrs Popov as well. After the Ponte Nuovo adventure and trip to Sandilands, all I could think and hope for was that Alexei would be reconciled with his grandma again, even though we had no idea whether he was alive or dead.

***

No Idea

Mrs Popov passed us a cup and saucer from her trolley and poured the tea before offering an assortment of biscuits on a china plate.

'I have some important questions I'd like to ask you, Mrs Popov, if you don't mind.'

'Questions I have also,' she replied. 'But first, yours.'

'Okay, I've written them down here. My first question is, 'Why did Alexei leave Russia and when?'

'Fifteen old years. He had cracking habit,' she replied.

'Oh, drugs?'

'No... maybe? I meant computers cracking.'

'Ah you mean hacking? Was he involved in computer hacking before he came to the UK? Did he get into trouble? Is that why he had a copy of the book, Cybersecurity and Cyberwar?'

'Yes. In Russia, it like small crime and young people doing it, but Mafia worse. Money, girls, drugs - it killing him nearly.'

'I'm sorry,' I replied.

'And credit cards, bags of them I find. We escape to England then. Afraid for him, I was.' Grace stood up from the sofa and walked over to Mrs Popov to hug her as she sobbed quietly, rocking to and fro in her chair.

'Do you know why there is so little information on the Internet about his disappearance?' I asked.

'I know not, but I also tell newspaper lady and crazy she thinks I am.'

Si Page

'Grace, I think we should show her the photos on my phone?' She nodded in approval.

'Mrs Popov, last night we tracked the signal of Alexei's iPad to a restaurant in Croydon. We went there and took photos of the man who had Alexei's iPad. If we show them to you, will you tell me if you recognise anyone in the photos?'

'Yes, see them I must.'

I walked over to her chair and scrolled through the images on my phone with Mrs Popov.

'Holy Mary!' she screamed.

'Who is it?' I asked.

'My brother, Peter... Peter Popov. Crook, he is!' She imitated a spitting action, clearly disgusted.

My eyes widened before I took a deep breath. 'That explains why I've never seen a photo of your brother. What is his line of work? Did you know he lived here? And has he had any involvement in Alexei's life before?'

'My brother in computers and banks. Russia he only live, St. Petersburg. Here I did not know. I take Alexei from him, away.'

Grace asked, 'So you haven't had contact with your brother, Peter, for a long time?'

'Not after Russia. For Alexei, he was bad person.'

I leaned forward to make a point. 'Do you think Alexei might have taken a train to London to meet up with your brother?'

'If Peter here, living. Then yes.'

I continued. 'You told me before that Alexei was a mathematics genius and a computer hacker. I think he might be a huge business asset for someone, so I'm sure he is safe.'

'He knows thing about Mafia. Not safe, it make him. Afraid, I am. Help him, we must.'

'The Missing Persons Overseas charity said they will pass on our information to the police and we may be contacted soon. I will let you know everything I can after they have seen us.'

'Thank you, Rob. Know the truth of my precious Alexei, I must.'

***

Mum gave Grace and me some space in the lounge. 'I'll be in the kitchen if you need me,' she said. I thanked her and sat next to Grace on the sofa.

'We need to keep our voices down. I don't want Mum or Vince hearing our conversation.' Grace nodded, before I continued. 'I feel bad that I've dragged you into this and I don't want you to put your life on hold because of me.'

Grace lifted her head, slightly confused. 'Rob, you haven't dragged me into anything. Neither of us could have predicted what happened yesterday. And as for visiting your neighbour - I wanted to help you get your feet off the ground and give you some hope.'

Grace's words wounded me, like our friendship was no more than a coincidence and mattered little to her. 'I didn't know I was a charity case,' I replied.

Her face softened as the brightness of her ocean blue eyes captured mine. 'Rob, I didn't mean it like that. Of course you aren't a charity case. What I meant was neither of us had any idea we'd be spending so much time together, and I'm cool with that. The Lord moves in mysterious ways,' she smiled, before sending me a gentle wink.

I felt powerless to resist a tsunami of emotions and decided to do nothing, say nothing, but remain locked into her eyes. I wanted to feel her breath on my face and I was intoxicated with the thought of her lips touching mine. My eyes became wet as I was overcome with affection for my new friend. I sighed before looking down and composing myself.

'Are you okay?' she asked.

'I'm afraid to say what I feel. I know we've only known each other for what seems like 'five minutes,' and I don't want to spoil our friendship.'

'Sometimes you have to trust your gut instinct, Rob, and say what's in your heart.'

I took her words as an invitation to open up. 'I love being around you, Grace. You inspire me and I feel a different person when I'm with you.' I watched her reaction to my words and it was positive.

'Thank you, Rob.' Grace leaned over and kissed my cheek.

I closed my eyes, overwhelmed with emotions I had never felt so deeply before. She hadn't pulled her face away from mine. A tear rolled down from my left eye onto her cheek and I moved my head back a few inches and looked up at her face. She was smiling and my eyes gave the game away. I wiped the tear from my cheek, and she kissed it again. I cupped her face in my hands and kissed her right cheek.

No Idea

She moved her face toward me and gently placed her lips upon mine. The faint scent of perfume on her skin was like a magical elixir stirring inside of me each time her moist lips brushed against mine. I ran my hands through her long curly hair and moved my cheek against hers.

'Thank you,' I whispered in her ear. 'I didn't want you to feel awkward with me, but I really wanted to kiss you.'

Grace leaned back and offered me a cheeky smile as two cute dimples waved back at me from the corner of her mouth. 'Does it look like I feel awkward?' she asked.

'No, but I thought maybe you just wanted to be friends.'

'Of course I want us to be friends, and I'm not the kind of girl who would normally kiss a guy after knowing him for just a few days, either. But I'm not afraid to show my feelings or who I really am.'

I hoped we shared the same experience when we kissed. It was like a lifetime of disappointing relationships had been washed away and replaced with the real thing and love kissed my lips for the first time. Only now I realised that everything that came before was a poor imitation.

I squeezed my lips together and grinned. 'So I take it you don't have a boyfriend, then?'

Grace laughed. 'Of course not, dummy. I wouldn't have kissed you if I did.'

'Why don't you have a boyfriend? You look gorgeous to me.'

'Maybe I was waiting for someone who thinks I'm gorgeous,' she giggled, throwing her legs across my lap and reclining on the sofa.

I tickled her feet and grabbed the calf of her leg while she tried to kick away. 'Ah so you're ticklish then,' I laughed.

Her face scrunched up with a look of determination. 'Nope, I'm not ticklish at all. I was just having you on.'

'We'll see about that,' I replied, leaning over to tickle her tummy. The girl was in hysterics as my fingers worked their magic just above her waist.

'Stop Rob, or I'll-'

'You'll what,' I replied, before grabbing her feet and pulling her pink socks off and throwing them into the fire place. We were both laughing hysterically when Mum walked in with two mugs of tea.

'I wondered what you were getting up to.'

'Sorry Mum, but the girl can't keep her hands off me.'

'Hmm I very much doubt that, Rob. She's far too good for you,' she smiled.

'Exactly,' replied Grace as she sat up to take her mug of tea.

'I'm so glad you two are getting on well together. Hey, Vince, it's like we've got two kids here,' she shouted.

Vince walked into the room. 'So my niece is knocking you into shape is she?'

'Er, yeh, she's a knockout alright.'

No Idea

Grace took a cushion and threw it at me. 'Enough of the flattery, Mr Wise.'

I stared at Grace and asked Father Time to stand still for just a moment. I didn't want to stop looking at her. She was the sole reason for the joy I was feeling inside.

I excused us both and walked upstairs with Grace to my room. I didn't want my experience with her to end so quickly, so I took her by the hand as we sat together on the bed. 'I hope you don't think I'm being too forward, but I haven't finished kissing you.'

She rested her head on my pillow and flicked her wavy hair away from her cheeks. 'My, my, Rob Wise, where's all this confidence coming from?' she teased.

I caressed the nape of her neck and kissed her soft pink lips. She responded in kind and I felt aroused, but I wasn't about to overstep the mark. Just being with Grace was more than enough.

Thanks to Grace, I had discovered something new and precious.

Life can be beautiful.

Chapter 18

The Daily Telegraph

It may have been first thing in the morning, but Grace looked stunning. Clearly a morning person, her skin was bright and full of vitality with no evidence of a late night and her eyes sparkled a magnificent blue as they refracted the natural light in the conservatory. Despite trying to brush myself up for Grace's early morning visit, the black sacks under my eyes hung like a pair of saggy underpants and my 'break of dawn' face was only fit for a pillow and a dark room.

Grace and I mulled over last night's adventure while Mum and Vince popped out to do some shopping, so we had the privacy we needed.

'What I don't understand is why there's basically nothing online about Alexei's disappearance. Something doesn't add up. What do you think?' I asked, biting into a slice of toast.

'I know what you mean. I spent last night on the Internet looking at websites for missing people. I can't believe how many people are missing in the UK. There seem to be thousands, but only a couple I saw mentioned Alexei.'

'Like I said, something smells a bit fishy to me.'

'Rob, one of my friends, Kaisha Holloway, is a journalist at The Daily Telegraph. I think we should ask her if she can find anything on Alexei. What do you think?'

'It can't do any harm, can it? Maybe she will find something before we speak to the police?'

Grace nodded and picked up her mobile. 'I'll ring her now.'

While she scrolled through the address book in her phone, I smiled at her cute feet as they wriggled on my lap. Last night they were sporting the perfect pedicure with pink nail varnished toes, but this morning they were wrapped inside woollen rainbow-coloured socks, and her legs were clothed inside a pair of blue frayed denim jeans. Not one for guessing a woman's dress size, I'd say Grace has a curvy 32 inch waist, and her green knitted jumper complete with a giant embroidered daisy, was a size 12. I'd always believed beauty was skin deep, but to me, her physical appearance was only a reflection of what was shining on the inside of her.

'Hi Kaisha, it's Grace, long time no speak,' she said on the speakerphone so we could both hear.

After they shared a few pleasantries, Grace continued, 'Kaisha, something freakish happened to us last night and I need your help. My friend, Rob, and I may have found a missing person who is either being held against their will or working for a criminal organisation. His name is Alexei Popov. Can you see what you can find on that name?'

'Sure, Grace. What can you tell me about Alexei?'

'He was born in a place called Sochi in Russia, he's twenty one years old and he came to live in the

UK with his grandmother. Apparently he was involved with some dangerous people in Russia, something to do with computer hacking, and he disappeared after taking a train from Wolverhampton to Kings Cross station, London, about three years ago.'

Kaisha replied, 'Got it. So what happened last night? What made you think you found him?'

'Mrs Popov is Rob's next door neighbour and Alexei's grandmother, and Rob has been helping her look for him. When he discovered that Alexei owned an iPad, he found the guy's email address and managed to get into his Apple iCloud account. We then traced the iPad to a restaurant in Croydon and triggered an alarm remotely that rang on the iPad. A man with Alexei's iPad then panicked and ran out of the restaurant with his wife and kid. We followed their taxi to a gated house in Sandilands, Croydon.'

'Grace, you have to call the police with this,' replied Kaisha. 'They might want to act fast on this information, but don't get me wrong, I'm interested in this story and I'll look into this name.'

Grace replied, 'We gave all the info to a Missing Person's website last night, and they said it would be passed onto the police. I think we will be hearing from them today, so will you give us a ring if you find anything on Alexei?'

The line went quiet for a moment, before Kaisha replied, 'Did you say the property you ended up at last night was in Sandilands, Croydon?'

'Yes, why?' replied Grace.

No Idea

'There was a huge fire reported there early this morning.'

A chill ran down my back as I retrieved the phone from Grace. 'Hi Kaisha, this is Rob. Can you tell me what information you have on the house fire?'

'I'll read you the article we've written online,' she replied.

'Emergency Services were called to a property in Sandilands, East Croydon, at 4am this morning, after local residents raised the alarm, with one describing the fire as 'a towering inferno.' Initial reports suggest that two bodies have been recovered from the fire, though no formal identification has taken place as of yet. With temperatures well in excess of 1100 degrees Fahrenheit, it could be some time before the remains of the victims are formally identified. Police are looking for four people who were said by neighbours to reside at the property.

Neighbour, Philippa Mckenna, 45, who has lived adjacent to the burned out property for the past five years, was the first to call the emergency services. She said, 'By the time the fire engines arrived, the whole house was ablaze. It took them some time to enter the grounds of the property and break through the large security gates, because the man who lived there had it secured like Fort Knox. We used to joke that he must have been hiding Gold bullion there, it was so secure. It's awful. There's nothing left of the house now. I just hope the family managed to escape.'

A spokesperson from the London Fire Brigade said, 'Our firefighters tried to enter the building, but were beaten back by the intense heat and flames. The crew worked tirelessly to extinguish the fire and make the site safe, but little has survived the blaze. Inquiries into the cause of the fire continue, and investigators have not ruled out foul play at this time.

The local community are said to be in shock, and dozens of flowers and bouquets have been laid outside the property in respect of those who died in the fire.'

'Thank you Kaisha,' I replied. 'Do you have a photo of the property before the fire? I'm sure it's the house we saw last night.'

'I'm pulling up Google Street View as we speak,' replied Kaisha. 'I'll take a screenshot of the property and text it to the mobile you're calling me from. Call me back when you've seen it.'

I thanked Kaisha before handing the phone back to Grace. We waited less than a minute for the photo before the phone beeped with an attached photo. It was a perfect match and the same property we saw the man, woman and child enter last night.

'Rob, this is terrible, and it's more than a coincidence we called the website last night? What if they didn't pass on our information to the police, but to someone else who did this? How are we supposed to know who we can trust?'

'I agree, though as fanciful as it sounds, what if Alexei's uncle did this before they left the property? What if they were covering their tracks and destroying evidence? If he is as wealthy as Mrs Popov has suggested, this will only be a nose bleed for him.'

No Idea

'Maybe, but who are the two bodies inside, then? I'll text Kaisha first, and then we call the police.'

Chapter 19

Official Business

Several hours passed since we'd called the police and left a message on a detective's answer phone, but we were still waiting for their reply. It was now late afternoon and Mrs Popov had called my mobile and asked us both to visit her as a police officer had arrived at her home.

We made our way to Brixton and parked outside Mrs Popov's home. Pit Bull ran out of the house to greet me. 'Rob, how are you doing, mate?' she asked, embracing me. 'What are you doing here? I just saw a copper go next door. Are you visiting Yoda or coming to see us?'

'Erm, it's a bit awkward to explain,' I replied. 'The police have asked me to sit with Mrs Popov while they talk to her. You know her problem with the English language.'

'Fair enough mate,' she replied. 'Will you pop in and see us when you're done?'

'Of course we will,' replied Grace.

I nodded in agreement before knocking on Mrs Popov's window. She answered quickly and invited us in to the lounge before introducing us to the officer.

No Idea

'Good afternoon. You are Rob Wise and Grace Stein, I presume?'

'Yes, and you are...'

'I'm an officer working with Specialist Operations for the Metropolitan Police Service. I've been assigned to you for your protection.'

'Why would we need protecting?' I asked. 'I thought Alexei's situation was just that of a missing person, is it not?'

'Please take a seat. We have much to discuss.'

The officer looked a bit too 'thug' for the MET police, sporting a large scar on his left cheek and a muscular build maintained by a firm dedication to the gym each day. But then, what I knew about the roles of the police and British Intelligence was limited to watching Spooks on the BBC.

Grace sat next to me on the settee looking somewhat unsettled. I held her hand and whispered, 'It's okay.'

Mrs Popov listened intently to our conversation while we went over recent events with the officer.

'Have you told anyone else about last night?' He asked. 'Have you discussed Alexei or anything related to him with anyone?'

I hesitated before deciding in the circumstances, it might be best to lie. 'No, neither of us has discussed Alexei outside of this room.'

'Good. We don't want to endanger anyone else in this investigation. Now, I will require you both to sign the Official Secrets Act before we discuss anything else. Do you have any objections?'

'I thought the Official Secrets Act was only for people who work for the government and in some sensitive position where Intelligence is discussed?' I asked.

'Mr Wise, what I must ask of you will require you both to be servants of the Crown, and as such, I am required to ask this of you before discussing any sensitive information.'

Grace and I made it clear we had no objections signing an official document, if it meant protecting Alexei and of course, ourselves. The officer then walked over to us and confiscated both of our phones before returning to his seat.

He continued, 'Mrs Popov has told me that outside of Alexei, you are her next of kin. This is why she has asked me to make you privy to our conversation, along with your partner, Miss Stein.'

I'm not surprised, but saddened that my neighbour had no one else to support her. I hoped our conversation wouldn't hurt her. The officer said nothing about the fire yet. Maybe they wanted to do DNA tests on the bodies before they spoke her?

The officer continued, 'Alexei's uncle is well known to us and his criminal network spans across Western Europe. We have information linking him to the hiring of over fifty university students from Russia for the purpose of hacking and organised crime. Popov has been on our radar for some time.'

'So do you think Alexei might be working for him?' I asked.

'It is possible, though we have reason to believe Alexei obtained sensitive information that threatened

No Idea

to expose his uncle. Alexei may be in grave danger. However, with your help last night we have locked down the property in Sandilands and are going through the site for evidence now.'

'So what kind of danger is Alexei in?' I asked.

'His uncle is under investigation for the extortion and theft of financial information pertaining to some of the largest Fortune 500 companies in the world. We believe he hired teams of young hackers who created worms and Trojans to steal highly sensitive information that would send the markets into chaos. It was a brave thing you both did, but I'm afraid, an extremely dangerous one. We have already wiped the security feed of a number of premises to protect your identities.'

'So if his uncle knows that someone's on to him, Alexei might be in even more danger?' I asked.

'I'm afraid so. This is why we must get to him as fast as we can.'

'So what is it you want Grace and me to do?'

'We can't be sure your vehicle number plate or photographs weren't taken when you followed the taxi to the address in Sandilands. I'm afraid both of you are in danger.'

I looked at Grace who appeared understandably concerned.

'So should I change my car, or something?' she asked.

'I'm afraid it's not as simple as that,' he replied. 'If they have photos of either of you or the registration number of the car, they will find you.'

'Grace, you can stay with me at my mum's house,' I suggested. 'They have more than enough room.'

'For your own safety, you won't be able to stay with family,' said the officer. 'We can put you in a safe house, but you will not be able to leave it until we find Alexei.'

Mrs Popov had been listening carefully, but now she stood up to speak. 'Rob, pay for you I will, to go away with lovely Grace, anywhere for long break. No problem money. Safe, you must be,' she said, beginning to cry. 'Please go, long time away to be safe. Sorry, your life ruined, I have.'

'You haven't ruined my life, Mrs Popov, and that's a lovely gesture, but I certainly don't want to take your money.'

The officer spoke up. 'I'm sorry, Mrs Popov, but I'm afraid they won't be safe wherever they travel. The only option we have is the safe house and they will be well taken care of there.'

'Rob, my dad has dementia and is in a care home. I can't just up and leave him,' said Grace with a croaky voice. This formidable girl has a weak spot – her dad.

'I'm sorry,' said the officer. 'If they know who you are, they will be watching your Father's care home.'

Now it was Grace's turn to cry, and her sobbing broke my heart. Every tear she shed was like a stab in my own heart. 'Grace, maybe we can set up a Skype link and you can talk to him by video link or something?'

'But he doesn't recognise me in the home, and the video would just confuse him.'

'We must relocate you now, but you will not be permitted to talk with anyone outside for some time. That includes the use of the telephone and internet, I'm afraid.'

'How long will this be for?' She asked.

'Until we find Alexei. There are no other options. Now, I will follow you back to your house to get some clothes, but you must take nothing that gives the appearance you have left the property; and the same for you, Mr Wise. Then we will take you both to your safe house.'

I turned to Grace and kissed her while she hugged me and I could feel her clinging to me. This was scary for us both, but this time, Grace was looking to me for comfort and I knew it was time for Rob Wise to step up to the plate.

Mrs Popov hugged us both before walking to the front door with Grace. 'Don't be afraid. I'm sure they will find Alexei,' I said.

'Rob, for you and Grace, sorry it has ended this way, I am.'

Grace and I were followed by the agent in his blacked-out 4x4, en-route to her home to gather a few things.

'Rob, what will you tell your mum and Vince?'

'We can't tell them the truth. We'll have to use the only excuse we both have.'

'What's that?' she asked.

'Each other.'

Chapter 20

Cover Story

After Grace quickly filled two suitcases from her home, we arrived at my mum's and waited to talk to her and Vince in the lounge. Somehow we both had to pull off the biggest act of our lives, and all in the next fifteen minutes or so.

'So you want to talk to us both?' asked Vince, intrigued.

'You're not tying the knot already?' laughed Mum.

'Erm, not quite,' I replied. 'Last night we both had dinner with a friend of mine who was visiting London. He's about to leave for work in Los Angeles for the next year or so, and he's offered me the chance to take a writing break and look after his house and dogs in Scotland, while he's away.'

'That sounds marvellous,' said Vince.

Mum shot Vince a scornful glare. 'No it doesn't! Son, you've only been home a few days, and you want to be off already?'

'Mum, I understand, but you see, Grace and I-'

'What's Grace to do with this?' interrupted Vince.

Grace took my hand and spoke up. 'Well, we've both decided to take this break together. I need a change of scenery, what with Mum passing away and

No Idea

Dad who hasn't recognised me for a very long time now. And I can do some hairdressing there while Rob finishes his book.'

'Have you prayed about this, Grace?' asked Vince. 'And you hardly know Rob.'

'You know I'll be praying, Vince. I just know I have to get away for a bit. And the house has three bedrooms. You don't have to worry about my integrity, but I appreciate your concern.'

Now was the time to play my ace card. 'I want to be honest with you both. Grace and I have become close over the last few days and she's told me a lot about her faith. I know I have issues that need dealing with, and I believe Grace can help me move forward with my life. Maybe it's all part of a divine plan?' I suggested.

Mum's expression changed, though I wasn't sure Vince was convinced.

'Son, if this is the path the Lord has chosen for you then you must follow his lead. But you must look after Grace and respect her. She is a godly woman, and I'm sure you know what I mean by that. If He wants to bless you both it will be in His timing, so don't rush things?'

'I understand, Mum. This is an opportunity for the both of us to take stock of our lives.'

'So when do you plan on leaving?' asked Vince.

'That's, erm, a little more difficult. You see, my friend is waiting outside in his car to drive us back with him. He's catching a flight tomorrow, so he wanted to fill us in with the house before he left for the airport. I was just going to grab my things and head off. I'm sorry if it seems so sudden, but we have to leave in the next five minutes or so.'

Mum walked over and threw her arms around my shoulders. 'Rob, I will miss you. Please stay in touch with me, love. Oh, hang on, before you go, let me give you some money.'

'It's okay, Mum. I'll be fine.'

'Nonsense, you came here with nothing and you're not leaving the same way you came. Vince, go open the wall safe and bring me my Christmas envelope, will you?'

'Mum, I'm not leaving the way I came. Since I arrived things have been happening for me. And to see you so happy has helped me to see, believe, that there is a light at the end of the tunnel.'

Vince handed Mum an envelope which she passed to me. 'Rob, it's not a lot, but there's five hundred quid in there. It should help you get started.'

'Mum, really, you don't have to do-'

'What? I can't bless my own boy?'

Grace smiled and walked over to kiss my mum before turning to me. 'Rob, I'll go pack your bag upstairs while you say goodbye to your mum.' She'd already seen my scant belongings, so I nodded in appreciation while she ran upstairs.

'Make sure you call me, Rob. Oh, and leave your mobile number with me before you go.'

'Sure, mum,' I replied, knowing full well I'd be unable to contact her until Alexei was found. 'The signal might be a bit iffy there, but I'll be in touch as soon as I can.'

'I'll be praying for you both.'

'Mum, we need your prayers. This will be a life-changing experience for us both.'

The reality of my predicament hadn't escaped me for a second. I'd been trying to keep it together for my mum and especially, Grace, but I was scared. Scared more than I'd ever been before, and my mother's last words carried more weight than she realised. This was the first time in my life that I wanted her to pray for my future.

Grace walked back down the stairs with my black bag stuffed with the new clothes Mum bought for me. 'I've put your laptop, books and clothes in here, Rob. We have to go now.'

Before I opened the front door, I offered up a silent prayer to a God I had never known: 'Erm, Lord, if you can hear my thoughts... please be with us both cos I'm crapping myself. Sorry, Lord. I meant no offence and I'm new to this prayer-thing. Yours sincerely, Rob Wise. Amen.'

Chapter 21

Game Changer

Grace and I sat belted into the rear seats of the 4x4 en-route to the safe house. I looked into her eyes, but all I saw was pain. Whether it was the pain of not knowing when or if she would see her father again I wasn't sure, but I knew I wanted to comfort Grace, be a man and step up to the plate. This was time for Rob Wise to put some backbone where his wishbone had been.

I cleared my throat before speaking up. 'I was reading the news online this morning about the fire at Sandilands. I didn't want to mention it in front of Mrs Popov and upset her, but is it true – did they find two bodies inside the house?'

The officer remained quiet for a few seconds before replying. 'Yes, two bodies. Only if and when we learn one of the bodies is Alexei, will we break the news to Mrs Popov.'

'Makes sense,' I replied. 'But back at the house you said you'd locked down the property and were going through the site for evidence. If no-one was present at the address when you arrived, how did two bodies end up there? How did the fire happen if you had men at the house?'

'Mr Wise, you called us just after 11pm, and we arrived at the premises within fifteen minutes of your call. After we gained access to the property, we were on site for about three hours, before making it secure. We left the premises before 3am and received a report of a fire an hour or so later.'

'It doesn't sound like you made it very secure?' I replied, overstepping the mark.

He replied, 'We are dealing with highly skilled operatives.'

'Did you retrieve computers and stuff before the fire started?' asked Grace.

'I'm not at liberty to discuss the contents of any seized property with you.'

'Then whoever started the fire must have been watching the house and waiting for your officers to leave?' she replied. 'Maybe a neighbour spotted something suspicious after you left?'

I interrupted. 'Grace, I doubt anyone was sitting up at their bedroom window between three and four in the morning watching the house.'

'If the police were outside my neighbour's house at 3am, I'd want to know what was going on,' she replied. 'What do you think, erm, sorry, I don't know your name?'

'The name is Mortimer and that's enough with the questions please. I've told you all you need to know.'

We'd been travelling for about an hour when our vehicle pulled off the A3 motorway and into a petrol station forecourt. 'Wait here,' he said. 'I need to fuel up. Oh, and don't worry. The glass is bullet-proof,' he mocked, trying to defuse the tension.

He stepped out of the vehicle and locked the doors before reaching for the fuel pump.

I whispered, 'Grace, I need to call Pit Bull and tell her our cover story. We don't know how long we'll be away and I don't want them thinking I don't care about them... cos I do.'

She smiled, 'Aw, you're going soft, Mr Wise. Anyway, we can't because Mortimer has our phones.'

'I know, but he's left his on the passenger seat. I'll use that one and then delete the record of my call after.'

Mortimer holstered the pump and walked toward the kiosk to pay for the fuel, so I grabbed the phone and dialled Pit Bull's number. I received the message, 'This number is unobtainable. Please try later.' I needed to act quickly before he returned to the car. 'Grace, I'll call Mrs Popov and ask her to tell them our cover story.'

Fortunately I could still make out the faint outline of her telephone number inked on my hand so I punched the number in the phone and pressed the loud speaker button so Grace could hear the conversation.

A woman with a strong London accent answered the phone and spoke immediately. 'That was quick. Now bag up the bodies and I'll send Alistair over to dispose of them. He'll be with you in an hour or so. I have to tidy up a few loose ends here and then we're done.'

'Who is this?' I asked.

Grace snatched the phone and ended the call abruptly before throwing it back on the passenger seat. 'Rob, that woman must have seen the number ringing and presumed you were Mortimer. Now she'll know something's up. Oh my God, Rob. Why did she answer Mrs Popov's phone? The bodies she was talking about must be ours? And what if she's killed Mrs Popov?' She began to cry. 'We need to grab the phone and get out of the car. We'll call the police when we get out of here.'

The passenger doors were locked. 'The child safety locks must be engaged,' I said. 'We need to climb out through the front, quickly.'

We clambered over the seats but the front doors were also locked. I spotted Mortimer walking away from the cashier and toward the double doors. 'Grace, he's coming! We need to get back in our seats and play the game until we can figure a way out of here.'

'What are you doing?' screamed the officer as he ran back to our vehicle. He snatched the phone from my grip and slammed the passenger door shut.

Grace winced and squeezed her long fingers into my clammy palm. After learning we'd been betrayed, fear seized my muscles like deadly venom.

He scrolled through the caller list on his mobile and turned his thick-set neck from the driver's seat. 'Why did you call Mrs Popov?'

I screamed inside, 'Oh no, I forgot to delete the calls.' My chest tightened as my breathing became shallow. I replied, 'If my friends thought I was missing, they'd start looking for me, and that could cause problems, so I wanted Mrs Popov to tell them our cover story. She's the only person I can trust who knows our plan.'

The officer turned away and started the engine before engaging the central locking and flooring the accelerator. He glared back in his rear view mirror. 'Don't compromise this situation again. You have no idea who you're dealing with.'

On the contrary, I knew exactly who we were dealing with, thanks to the call with my neighbour.

An incoming call rang through the car speakers and was answered quickly by our driver. A wave of nausea surged through me as I recognised the chilling voice: 'Go to plan B. We've been compromised...'

Grace whispered in my ear, 'Rob, if we don't get out now, we're dead.'

Like a snitch clad with cement shoes, I was sinking beneath the waves without a plan of escape.

***

After taking a slip road in the direction of Chessington, our vehicle turned into a country lane and pulled over to a secluded area of greenery and heavy bushes. The officer brandished a weapon from his jacket and leaned back. 'Both of you - step out of the vehicle, now.'

First Grace stepped on to the curb, and I followed before slamming the door loudly in a desperate attempt to draw some attention. He struck the back of my head with his weapon and led us down a path, a hundred yards or so away from the main road.

I turned my head around at the man who was pointing a gun at my face. 'Where are you taking us,' I asked.

No Idea

He said nothing and waved his weapon at me in the direction of a large shed. I'd already decided that at the first opportune moment I would launch myself at him and try and grab the gun, while screaming at Grace to make a run for it. I didn't fancy my chances, but I was praying I'd find enough strength to hold the man down for just long enough to give Grace a running start. I loved this girl more than my own life, that much I was sure.

Mortimer led us inside the shed so I scanned the room quickly for anything I could use against him. The wooden building was large, with numerous tools fixed to the wall, while another door to the left of me led to another room.

'Both of you, quiet,' he said. 'You, boy, kneel down on the plastic sheets and put your hands behind your back. And sweetheart, go and get the pieces of rope over there and tie lover boy's hands and feet. Do it properly and remember... I'm watching you.'

Grace snivelled as she tied my hands and then my feet. 'Please... Mortimer. Show compassion to us. We don't even know the missing boy. We were only trying to help Rob's elderly neighbour find him. If you let us go, we won't say a word. We just want our lives back. Please.'

Mortimer remained silent for a while, before replying, 'And what will you give me if I let you go?' he asked, in a suggestive and despicable manner.

'What do you want?' she replied, knowing full well what he wanted.

'You know what I want. It's what every man wants, isn't that right, lover boy,' he laughed. 'I felt him pull the rope tight around my wrists before stepping back. 'Over here girl,' he snapped. 'Take it all off, and I mean, everything, and go lay down in that room.'

I could see in the reflection of a small mirror on the wall that Grace lifted her knitted jumper off, followed by her bra. I couldn't remain silent. 'Please, Mortimer, don't do this. If you have to finish me then do it, but let Grace go. She means the world to me. Let her live, I beg you. She doesn't deserve this.'

'Shut your mouth or I'll make you watch the fun.'

I screamed out to an unknown God to intervene. I pledged my life to serving Him and to regular church attendance, charity work and the pursuit of world peace – basically I conjured up every word I thought might please Him.

I could see from the corner of the mirror that Mortimer had removed his trousers and was about to lie down on top of Grace. Since he had a gun pointed at my head, I hadn't seen an opportunity to grab his weapon and make a fight of it. Now, more than ever, I wish I'd tried. Now, I begged Grace's God to help us. I didn't care for my own life, only hers, and her dignity.

My desperation grew into rage. I tried to stand up on my legs, while wriggling my wrists violently, but I fell sideways into a pile of scrap wood. I spotted an upturned axe firmly wedged in some firewood and tried to stand up again, while leaning against the wall. I rubbed the rope on my wrists furiously against the edge of the axe blade. I felt a surge of adrenaline running through me. If I could free my hands, I wanted to crush Mortimer's windpipe.

Grace cried out my name before I heard a thud. Her voice fell silent, like he'd banged her head on the floor. I rubbed the rope violently against the sharp edge of the axe blade, but my time was running out. The agent saw me standing up and ran toward me. The rope still hadn't frayed enough to release my hands. He removed his gun and pointed it at me while I propelled my head like a torpedo at his face. He pulled the trigger while I dived toward him with such ferocity that the top of my head met with the bridge of his nose. A flash of pain followed with a loud crack as I fell on top of his body. He'd shot me alright, but I'd still managed to knock him out with a flying head butt.

I shouted out to Grace and heard a murmur. 'Quick Grace, quick,' I yelled. 'Untie my hands.'

She slowly came to, and then ran toward me, leaning over the bloodied face of Mortimer to untie my hands.

'Grace, grab his gun and keep it pointed at him while I grab the rope. This time, we'll tie him up and find out who he's really working for.'

As the adrenaline wore off, I tried to ignore the throb in the side of my head while I tied his ankles, legs, wrists and arms together. I'd never had the good fortune of reading the 'How to Immobilise a Trained Killer,' manual, so I thought it best to tie some rope around his neck as well. I dragged his body toward a metal Snap On tool chest and wrapped the rope around the legs. He wasn't going anywhere fast.

Grace wiped the tears off her face. Traumatised and shaking, she was oblivious to the fact she was wearing nothing but her rainbow socks. I picked up her clothes and pulled the jumper over her head before placing each arm inside. I kissed her lips tightly and wiped the tears from her cheeks. 'Are you okay, Grace?'

I was crying now as I squeezed my cheeks against hers. I don't know how, but by some miracle, Mortimer's bullet hadn't killed me, and I'd planted my concrete forehead on the top of his nose. His face was a bloody mess and I wasn't sure if he was dead - I'd hit him so hard - but I had two people to thank for that. The first person was obvious, because miraculously, there wasn't a gaping hole between my eyes. The second person to thank was my flat mate, Martin. He'd told me so many stories about 'The Glasgow Kiss' and the kind of damage the head butt did, that subconsciously I'd used it as the only weapon at my disposal.

Grace was now dressed as I passed her shoes to her. 'Is your head okay?'

'I think I'm fine, Rob, but your earlobe's a mess.'

I felt the sticky, congealed blood. 'I think it's just the bottom part missing.' Grace wiped my ear with a tissue from her pocket. 'Yes, you look like an Amazon warrior now,' she smiled. I put my hands around her waist and kissed her forehead.

I grabbed Mortimer's phone from a small table by the door. 'Grace, I think we need to call the police now.'

No Idea

'I wouldn't do that if I were you,' replied Mortimer, as he regained consciousness. He wasn't going anywhere with the rope around his neck and his limbs tied, but Grace still kept the gun firmly pointed at him.

He continued, 'If you call the police, you can kiss your family goodbye. We know where they live, Rob. Telford Avenue, isn't it?'

I swung my left foot into his crotch. 'Don't threaten me, you sick pervert!'

Mortimer screamed in pain as his rigid frame shuddered. 'I told you before... you don't know who you are dealing with. It's not just me... there's a network of people looking for Alexei,' he gasped repeatedly, trying to catch his breath.

Mortimer's phone rang. I showed Grace the caller ID. It was Mrs Popov's phone. Grace put the gun into the eye socket of her attacker. 'You tell the woman we are both dead. If you don't, I'll shoot you, limb by limb myself, and claim it was all in self-defence. Do you hear me?' she yelled. Mortimer nodded.

I pressed loudspeaker and accepted the call, holding the phone to his mouth. 'It's done,' he answered.

'Good,' replied the woman. 'Alistair should be with you in the next half hour and he'll dump the bodies. You make your way back here.'

Grace pushed the gun further into his eye socket.

'Fine,' he replied, before I ended the call.

'Where is she expecting you back?' I asked.

'Brixton,' he replied. 'Your neighbour's home.'

'Mrs Popov?' I asked.

Grace grabbed my arm. 'Rob, I say we just call the police now and send them to Mrs Popov's. They're bound to find her body in the house.'

I agreed and dialled 999. 'What emergency service do you require?' asked the operator.

'Police,' I yelled down the phone.

The telephone operator patched my call through to another operator. 'What is the location of the emergency please?'

I proceeded to give Mrs Popov's address.

'And what is the emergency?' he asked.

'There's been a murder. You'll find the body of Mrs Popov at the house, and the woman who murdered her is inside. Please hurry. They are responsible for the death of Alexei Popov and the fire at the Sandilands property in East Croydon. I can't tell you any more as I have to get out of here, but I'm going straight to a police station now. Bye.'

While Grace pointed the gun at Mortimer, I released the rope from the metal tool chest and yanked him up, tugging the rope around his neck. He made a choking noise. 'Any grief from you, and I'll pull this rope so tight it'll be lights out for you. Understand?' Mortimer nodded as he made small steps with the rope around his ankles.

I walked him out of the shed and toward the boot of the 4x4 while Grace kept the gun on him. I raised the boot lid and standing behind him, struck him across the back of his head with a thick plank of

No Idea

wood from the shed. He was out cold, so I rolled his limp body over the lip of the boot and tucked his legs inside. There I found some extra rope, Gaffer tape and ties in an open bag, so I made two more rope ties around his legs and arms and wrapped the tape around his mouth and the back of his head, several times. There was no way he was doing a Houdini before we handed him over to the police. His large frame filled the rear boot floor and there was little room for any movement.

I hadn't driven for nearly ten years, but I wanted to take control of the situation, so I jumped in the driver's seat and started the engine. The manual gearbox suited me as I pulled away at some speed toward the nearest police station.

Grace reached over and placed her hand on my shoulder. 'I can't believe what you did back there. You were incredibly brave,' she said.

'If it wasn't for Martin always going on about the Glasgow kiss, I might not have thought about it, but I wasn't going to let him hurt you, Grace. I love you,' I uttered, before shuddering at the words that left my mouth. I was a little startled and felt I should offer an apology for overstepping the mark. 'Sorry Grace, I can't believe I... oh that wasn't cool... erm, I wasn't expecting that-'

Her face was flushed a deep pink and I could see her eyes were wet. She smiled and touched my cheek with the palm of her hand.

'Thank you for taking care of me, Rob.'

Her words struck a deep chord within me. I'd lived for too long with the notion I could barely take care of myself, but now I'd not only saved my own life, but the life of someone I had hopelessly fallen in love with.

Grace tactfully changed the subject, sparing me from sharing any more of the feelings growing inside of me.

'And thank God for the Glasgow kiss,' she grinned.

'I never thought I'd be thanking anyone for my flat mates, but you're right - thank God, indeed.'

No Idea

Chapter 22

Saving Grace

I held Grace's hand as we arrived at the Police Station and approached the front desk. Not wanting to join the small queue of people ahead of me, I tapped several times on the glass.

'Oi, get behind and join the queue, Muppet,' yelled an angry teen, eyeballing me.

'I can't do that,' I replied. 'I need to talk to someone now. I've got a hit man tied up inside my car boot.'

The teenager laughed. 'Yeh, right, and I'm wearing a suicide vest, mate. Now get lost.' The officers ignored the commotion while I returned to Grace at the back of the line.

'Rob, we can't just stand here. Go knock on the glass again,' she said.

I pushed in front of the line again, this time banging loudly on the glass.

'What do you think you're doing?' barked the duty sergeant. 'Carry on like that and the only thing you'll be knocking on is the inside of a police cell. Now join the line. You'll be seen after these people.'

'I can't do that,' I replied. 'I've got a hit man tied up in my car boot. Oh, and I've got his gun. Here you are.' I removed the weapon from my coat and placed it on the counter.

The female officer reached over and snatched the weapon before the two remaining officers leapt from their seats in the office and burst through the side door. They seized my arms and threw me to the floor before pinning me down and searching me for any more weapons.

'Please listen,' I cried. 'If you don't believe me, take the keys out of my pocket. You'll find a 4x4 with black windows parked outside, and the man's tied up in the boot. Be careful, though. He's already tried to kill us once. Just look at my earlobe. He shot that earlier.'

***

'My name is Detective Inspector Ankers and in accordance with the Police and Criminal Evidence Act, this interview will be recorded. Please state your full name...'

I sat upright on the wooden chair hoping we could make some progress and the police would link Mortimer and his gang to the murder of Mrs Popov and Alexei.

Ankers continued, 'Tell me, do you normally tie people up and carry them round in your car boot? We have the gentleman being interviewed at the moment and we'll get his side of the story, but do you have any idea just how much trouble you could be in for possessing a loaded firearm and bringing it into a police station?'

'The car doesn't belong to me, I have no idea how to unload a gun, or for that matter, how much trouble I could be in. But I doubt it's worse than being shot at.'

'Tell me, Mr Wise... why did you make an emergency call directing police to an address in Brixton? Why didn't you ask the police to attend the scene you claim you were taken to in Chessington?'

'We needed to get out of there quickly and decided to drive straight to a police station.'

Over the next fifteen minutes I relayed the full story of Alexei, the tracked iPad and the so-called safe house to Detective Ankers, before adding, 'When we called Mrs Popov's mobile, a different woman answered. Before I had time to speak, she must have noticed I was using Mortimer's phone, because she told me to bag up the bodies and that someone called Alistair was coming to dispose of them. The bodies she was talking about were mine and Grace's. You see, she thought I was Mortimer, your man in custody.'

The detective stared intensely at me while tapping his pen on the side of the table. 'The problem I have with your account, Mr Wise, is we sent officers to Mrs Popov's home. She is alive and well and denies knowing anything about this 'Mortimer' character of yours. She said that no officer had visited her home and she knew nothing about a safe house.'

'Why would she do that?' I replied. 'She must be scared. Maybe someone's threatened her to keep quiet? I don't understand.'

No Idea

'However,' Ankers replied, 'You have made an allegation of abduction which is a serious offence and we will investigate this fully. We are also talking to your partner, Miss Stein to see whether she backs up your story.'

'And what is Mortimer saying about everything?'

'I'm not at liberty to discuss that, but I can tell you the man we have in custody is not speaking to us at the moment.'

'I'm telling you, either the man you have or the people he works for are responsible for the fire in Sandilands,' I replied.

'We will be making thorough enquiries, Mr Wise.'

After writing a four page statement and asking me to sign it, Ankers informed me I was free to go. 'We will need to speak to you again, Mr Wise, so don't go too far away, and Miss Stein is waiting in the reception area for you.'

'Oh, before I go,' I asked. 'Did Mrs Popov mention anything to you about her missing grandson, Alexei?'

'I'm not sure what's going on here, but we'll get to the bottom of it. For now, I suggest you both keep your heads down and stay out of trouble.'

'But what did she tell you about Alexei?' I asked.

'Mr Wise, that's one of the problems I'm looking into - she denied ever having a grandson.'

***

Grace and I were puzzled why Mrs Popov denied all knowledge of our conversation with Mortimer, not to mention, denying the existence of her grandson, Alexei, so we decided to take a train back to Brixton to see her and find out what happened after we left.

'Here are the facts as I see them,' I said to Grace. 'First, Mrs Popov was introduced to Mortimer who we now know was posing as an officer, so he tricked us all. Two, she was only introduced to him after we gave the Missing Persons Overseas website information about Alexei. Three, the property in Sandilands was reduced to ashes as a result of our call, and four, she must have been threatened and told to lie by someone who has information on Alexei, probably the woman who answered her phone. The bad link in all of this is the Missing Persons Overseas Charity.'

'Rob, I'll give Kaisha a call at the Daily Telegraph. She might have found something on Alexei and she could look into this website for us.'

'Sure,' I agreed, passing her the phone. We were only a few train stops away from Brixton Station. 'If you say we can trust Kaisha, we need to tell her what's happened, because if we go missing again, she might be our only lifeline.'

'Crikey, you're a morbid one aren't you?' she snapped.

'Sorry. I'm thinking that after we've seen Mrs Popov we need to get away somewhere safe for a while – at least until the police can give us more information. What do you think?'

No Idea

She nodded. 'As far as your mum and Vince are concerned, we've gone away. We've still got our luggage, so after we see Mrs Popov and your flat mates, then we see my dad. We can take a hire car and get out of London, maybe somewhere an hour or two away.'

Grace turned on her mobile phone and pressed the speaker phone button as she dialled Kaisha's number.

'Grace, is that you?' answered Kaisha. 'I've been trying your number for the last few hours. Are you guys okay?'

'It's a long story, Kaisha. Where do I start? Since we tracked Alexei's iPad, we've been double-crossed, Rob was shot but thankfully, only grazed, a so-called police officer tried to rape me and we've just left the police station and are on our way to Brixton to see Rob's neighbour, Mrs Popov.'

'Oh... my... are you alright? I wish I got hold of you earlier. After what I've discovered, I think you guys need to lie low for a while.'

'What have you learnt about Alexei?' I asked.

'I couldn't find anything new from the web or archived articles on missing people, but I've spoken to Dimitri, a friend of mine who works for a hedge fund in the city. He's told me before that some of his clients are Russians, so I ran your story by him. Ten minutes ago, I had a disturbing reply from him. Apparently, your boy has a serious bounty on his head. Dimitri wouldn't go into details, but he said I should think twice before running a story on him.'

'I understand if you can't help us,' I replied.

'Nonsense, of course I'll help. And Grace is my friend. As for not running a story, you should never say that to a journalist and expect them to walk away. It's the very thing that fires up their interest.'

Grace spoke up. 'Kaisha, did you find anything on The Missing Persons Overseas charity? The moment we gave information to them, the whole thing kicked off.'

'That's why I said I tried to get hold of you earlier. The website has domain privacy on it, but a colleague here looked into it. It's owned and hosted by someone in Russia, but the only contact details we could find was the telephone number on the website. I called it earlier but the number is now unavailable and the website is offline. I can only guess that the people who put a price on Alexei's head have something to do with it.'

Grace replied, 'Rob and I are going away somewhere safe. I'll call you when we get there, but don't run a story yet until we meet up. Don't mention our names or anything to anyone who might tag us in the investigation. The police are doing their investigations as well, so we need to be careful.'

'Of course I won't compromise you. You give me the green light when you're ready.'

'Okay, thanks. Now we are going to see Rob's elderly neighbour, Mrs Popov. We think she's already been threatened, so if we learn anything else, we'll call you.'

No Idea

Chapter 23

The Disguise

We arrived in a taxi at Mrs Popov's home and pulled up five or six houses away from her door. Everything looked normal. There were no suspicious vehicles parked up, and as far as we could tell, no one was sitting in them or keeping watch on her property.

'Rob, I'm having second thoughts. Are you sure it's safe for us to go in now? What if the woman who answered Mrs Popov's phone is still inside the house?'

'How could she be? The police have already been inside and interviewed her.'

I walked down the path and used my secret knock on her window before waiting a minute or so and then trying again. Mrs Popov eventually opened the door and invited us in.

'Mrs Popov, are you alone in the house?' I asked.

She nodded and walked us into the lounge. She was clearly shaken up, because there was no greeting at the door and she said nothing to us while we took a seat on the sofa. Grace reached out for my hand while Mrs Popov sat silently, staring at us, as if waiting for something to happen.

Grace leaned over and whispered, 'Rob, something isn't right.'

No Idea

'You are correct,' said a male voice from behind me, as he thrust a hood over my face. Grace screamed. Whoever was behind us must have done the same to her. The room became pitch black.

'Who are you? What do you want from us,' I yelled in panic.

'Shut up,' said the male voice. 'I'll be asking questions. First, who are you and why are you looking for me?'

'Who are you? Wait, are you Alexei Popov? How did you find us?' I asked.

'I'll be asking questions. Who are you both?'

'My name is Rob and this is my girlfriend, Grace. I'm Mrs Popov's neighbour. I live next door with Rupert, Martin and his girlfriend, Pit Bull.

The man whispered to another male voice. I couldn't make out what they were saying as the language sounded like Eastern European, maybe Russian.

'You were spotted with woman following taxi to house in Croydon. Why did you do this, and where did you get information to hack Apple account and track iPad?' he asked.

'I was just helping my neighbour to find you. I saw a photo of you with an iPad and figured we might still be able to track it. Mrs Popov handed me a book of yours called, Cybersecurity and Cyberwar. Inside were some notes you'd made and I took a wild guess the cartoon sketch you drew of a Badger wearing a t-shirt that read, 'dark web riot,' might have been your email or username ID. I just got lucky, but I honestly thought your life was in danger. I was trying to help you.'

Alexei removed both of our hoods. He was definitely Alexei, the guy in Mrs Popov's photos.

'Yes, this woman who calls herself, Mrs Popov, took my things after I left Russia. She is no relative of mine. She has many names and disguises and hired many times by people trying to kill me. Isn't that right, Laura Pontin, Sarah Hardy, Karan Peta, Deborah Dobrin, and whatever name you use! Mrs Popov is new one to me, but my uncle say she has many false identities. He expected she try to kill us.'

'Boss, I remember other names – Suzanne Appleton, Hayley Slaughter, Donna Jago-'

'Yes, who cares, whatever!' Alexei interrupted.

'And her husband goes by nice English boy name, Craig Gillan, Ben Groves and Peter Best when in UK.'

'Dmitry, shut up!'

'Yes boss. Sorry, boss.'

Now I was totally confused. I could hardly imagine my elderly neighbour as anyone other than Mrs Popov, but now I learn she has dozens of names and is a killer for hire.

'But Alexei, I've seen photos of you both together?' I replied. 'Mrs Popov even showed me your bedroom with your posters and Nazi memorabilia?'

Alexei laughed. 'Really? You mean she Photoshop me? Yes, I heard rumours about her passion for Nazis. Those aren't my things.' He turned

No Idea

and glared at Mrs Popov. 'Tell them who you really are!'

'You shouldn't have come back here you gullible fools,' she screamed.

I was startled. Her voice was different and her English was perfect. I felt the acid rise from my gut and burn my throat as I recognised her London accent. It was the same voice who answered the call I made from Mortimer's phone. I coughed to clear my airways while Grace squeezed my hand.

'Alexei, I had absolutely no idea Mrs Popov had been lying to us the whole time. Now I know she was the one who told Mortimer to kill us. I thought you were her grandson and I just offered to help her find you. I swear.'

'I believe you, Mr Rob Wise. You have been with a Detective Inspector Ankers, have you not?

'How do you know that?' I replied.

'We were notified of interview at police station. I like you disabled attacker with flying head butt and tie him up in car boot. I must say I'm impressed. And then you ask police to check Mrs Popov. We followed up lead. And I will tell you... this Mortimer who try to kill you both is Mrs Popov's husband,' he said.

'Husband? You gotta be kidding me?' I replied.

Grace spoke up. 'So what is your connection with the police?'

'My uncle has friend in high places.'

'So why didn't the police arrest Mrs Popov if they knew Mortimer was her husband?' I asked.

'They haven't joined dots, but we heard transcript of interview at station and we knew 'Mrs Popov' was fake. We wanted talk to her first.'

'How did you know she was a fake?' I asked.

'Because I don't have grandmother still breathing,' he laughed.

Alexei was interrupted by another man who entered the room. 'Boss, I have Tall Decaf Soya Vanilla Ice Latte at 120 degrees with extra shot, cream and sprinkle of chocolate with caramel twist.'

'Did you get Lemon Whisper cupcake with butter cream icing on side?'

'Sorry, they were out, so I got plain Flapjack.'

'What, no chocolate? Am I Neanderthal?'

'Sorry, boss.'

Alexei made a loud sipping noise, before addressing Mrs Popov. 'Tell them truth, or I ask Franco to make you,' he shouted.

Mrs Popov removed the wig from her head and pulled out a few pins from her hair, before shaking her long brown and curly locks out. She then removed some fake dentures from her mouth, followed by a layer of skin from her face that made her look thirty years older. Now I figured my evil neighbour had only put on her disguise when she called at our flat or was expecting my visit.

Mrs Popov spoke up. 'It's true, boy. I was playing you. You told me what a whiz you were with the internet and computers, so I wondered if you'd find anything on Alexei that I'd missed. When you knew too much, I had no choice but to ask my husband to take care of you both. It was nothing personal. Purely business, you understand. Alexei and his uncle aren't the first people I've been hired to find, and they won't be the last.'

So much was being revealed now I felt I was starring in a TV episode of Columbo.

Grace walked over to Mrs Popov and slapped her face. 'You evil cow, how dare you. Do you know your husband tried to rape me?'

'He always likes to have some fun before he finishes the job,' she replied.

Alexei's two henchmen focused their weapons on my neighbour.

'Say goodbye to Mrs Popov,' said Alexei. He nodded his head at two of his men who taped her mouth, wrists and ankles. 'She will go to sleep for few hours,' he smiled, as a needle was pushed into her left arm. Within seconds, she was unconscious.

'What are you going to do with her?' I asked.

'The police know nothing of her connection with Mortimer. We keep it that way and take her to my uncle. He will decide what next for her.'

I'd never had such mixed emotions. I couldn't stomach the thought of someone hurting the elderly neighbour I'd enjoyed cups of tea with, but this wasn't the Mrs Popov I was led to believe. Before me was a cold, heartless killer and I couldn't reconcile that in my head. How someone could put on such a compassionate front one minute, only to act despicably the next, was beyond my comprehension.

'Rob, before you and girlfriend leave, I must insist several things for safety. First, take money from her suitcase. There is about twenty thousand there. I don't need her money. She won't need it where her or husband will go. Second, you must both leave UK for month or two. Then, news of my death and uncle from house fire is enough to discourage those looking to silence us. Then it is safe for you to return.'

'So you staged the fire at the house in Croydon?' asked Grace.

'Yes. When iPad alert went off and my uncle knew he was followed, we weren't sure who you worked for, so the fire was our way out. It was only matter of time before we fake our deaths, so we set fire to house. Whether our enemies would believe reports of our death, we could not be sure, but now, everything perfect.'

'I don't understand. What's perfect?' I asked.

'You and Grace will confirm story. You to tell papers that neighbour you helped was girlfriend looking for me. You helped find me with iPad and Mafia think she was killer who saw bounty on our heads and trying to track us. But you must not call her Mrs Popov. You must give her a nice and simple English name. Now take this phone. I will call you and give you story you must tell newspapers. Maybe we write good fiction together,' he chuckled.

'Won't the Mafia hear that Mortimer has been arrested?' asked Grace.

'No one will see or hear from them again,' replied Alexei. 'But there will be newspaper story that both

No Idea

of them with two unidentified men, died in tragic road crash. My uncle's people work on story now.'

'How on earth will you fake that?' I asked.

'Rob, some news stories are made up. We have her belongings to place at crash scene. Imagine - Impact of crash so severe that suitcase exploded and showered belongings across road. It will be shocking photograph for newspaper,' he grinned, before continuing, 'Mortimer's DNA found at Sandilands property, and reports in media that dental records match my uncle and I. Our enemies will believe we are dead.'

'I wondered why you were telling us so much,' I replied. 'So who were the two bodies inside the house?' I asked. 'What happened to the woman and the girl?'

'They left rear of house after your car moved away. And the two bodies – they worked for your neighbour. My uncle's men took care of them when they broke into house and tried to kill us. That's when we agreed to use cover story of us dying in fire.'

'But how would the police buy the story?' I asked. 'They won't have your DNA or dental records.'

Alexei sipped from his Costa cup. 'It's taken care of. I told you my uncle has friend in high places. He made deal with your government when he was chief accountant for Mafia. He raised me after my parents died and he couldn't leave me in Russia. So he 'blew whistle' as you English say, and stop sale of highly dangerous information to some bad people. Your government gave us safe refuge and let us keep money that uncle took from them 'for expenses' before we left Russia.'

I turned to Grace and hugged her, before replying to Alexei. 'So, we are free to go?'

'First, your flat mates and nosey neighbours see Mrs Popov carried out on a stretcher to ambulance. I will ask my men to put her wig back on before ambulance arrives. Then you must text your friends next door that she had heart attack while you were visiting. They will see and hear the ambulance and look out of window and see her carried off in stretcher. You will visit flatmates after ambulance leaves and tell them she died. Then you will be free to go.'

'You should definitely write fiction,' I smirked. 'So when will you contact us and tell us to run your story?'

'Soon,' he replied. 'But when I tell you to speak to newspapers, you must not reveal your identities. The journalist will agree to keep your identity safe after they receive a phone call from my uncle's contact.'

Alexei opened Mrs Popov's suitcase. 'After ambulance leaves, you take this cash,' he said, pointing to a dozen or so rolls of wrapped twenty pound notes. He added, 'Now text your friends. They must see her carried out to ambulance when it arrives.'

To be sure I'd reach someone in the flat, I sent the following text message to Martin, Rupert and Pit Bull: 'It's Rob. I'm with Mrs Popov and she's had a heart attack! An ambulance is on its way but I don't think it's any use. She's dead.'

My phone rang. It was Pit Bull. 'Rob, what the heck - what happened?'

'The short and the long of it is we came by to see Mrs Popov before visiting you. She just hit the floor and that was it. Game over.'

'Shall I bring the boys over now?' she asked.

'No, an ambulance will be here any minute. I'll come over with Grace once the ambulance has left. Bye for now.'

The ambulance siren became louder as it approached the house before parking outside.

I took Grace's hand, and opened the front door to the paramedics. One of the men walked straight past me and into the lounge. He shook Alexei's hand and spoke quietly to him. I couldn't fathom how, but they both seemed to know each other. 'Maybe Alexei asked a few of his contacts to steal the ambulance?' I wondered. Anyway, it didn't matter. The ambulance was all for show, and she'd soon be taken to Alexei's uncle.

It was a well-staged affair. These Russians didn't like loose ends.

Chapter 24

Farewell

Pit Bull threw her arms around me as we stood at the door. 'Rob, I'm so sorry about Mrs Popov, mate... oh, hi Grace, lovely to see you again.'

Grace kissed Pit Bull on the cheek.

'Did you see Mrs Popov being stretchered into the back of the vehicle?' I replied.

'That's a weird thing to say, Rob,' replied Pit Bull.

'Sorry, I meant it like you said your goodbyes.'

'Yeh, I saw her. I didn't really know her that well, but I know she meant a lot to you.'

'She certainly played a role in my life,' I replied, trying to look somewhat sorrowful.

'I saw a few blokes go into her house earlier,' she said. 'Was everything alright?'

I had to think quickly on my feet. 'Yep, she let a few blokes in who were selling kitchen stuff.'

'That's not like her to open the door to strangers?' she replied.

'Maybe it was because we were with her and she needed some, erm, house cleaning stuff?'

'Ah, that's what the huge black sports bag was? I saw some lump of a bloke in a suit carry it in.'

No Idea

'That'll be it,' I replied. 'He was just selling cloths, sponges, detergents, mops and stuff. I asked them to leave when Mrs Popov decided she didn't want any of it. Anyway, let's go in. I want to see the boys.'

The hall was almost unrecognisable. Someone had bought a few tins of paint and had decorated two thirds of the hallway, and there was a new, small chandelier with a working light bulb inside.

'Has the landlord been in?' I asked. 'Is he decorating for new tenants?'

'Erm, something like it,' she replied. 'I told him I'd probably be taking over the lease of the flat, so the boys and I have spent hours tidying and giving it a lick of paint. I didn't think the landlord would take me seriously if he saw the flat in a mess, and I didn't think you'd mind, what with your new life and everything.'

'I'll have a word with him,' I replied. 'How are you going to be able to afford the rent?'

'It's two hundred quid a week more than what I'm paying now, but I'm doing extra hours at Wong's Chinese and I just got Martin a job there as the delivery driver. Working nights will suit him, and even Rupert's looking for work. I guess miracles do happen, Rob.'

'But Martin hasn't got a motor though?' I said.

'He has now! My dad gave his car to his friend, Roger. The old boy has had a few strokes and has stopped using it now, so Martin's insured to drive it and he's even got the use of his council garage. You ought to see it, Rob. It's hilarious - it's only got three wheels and it's got go-fast white racing stripes on it.'

Martin strolled in. 'Rob, it diz nooght tae sixty in abit ten minutes! Th' grub will be cold by th' time Ah deliver it, but I'll gie it a try!'

'It sounds amazing,' I laughed. 'You'll have to send me a photo of it.'

'Ye dornt want tae see it. It's a Robin Reliant!'

'Sounds more like a death trap,' I laughed. I had never felt so proud of my friends. I whispered discreetly to Grace, 'Would you mind if I give them a month's rent with Mrs Popov's money? I want to help them get off the ground and we've got more than enough to last us.'

'Aw, I knew you were a big softie. Of course, Rob. These are your friends. We should do all the good we can with her money,' she winked.

The lounge was the cleanest I'd seen it, and someone had bought a huge rug to decorate the centre of the wooden floor. Less than a week ago, I wouldn't have dared to bring a girlfriend back to the flat. How things had changed so quickly.

Rupert walked in, his hair erect and recently styled by his pillow. 'How are you, old chap?'

'Good to see you,' I smiled. At this moment, I knew I'd missed them and they had been family to me, even if our friendship had been tepid most of the time.

'I'm doing fine and I'm chuffed for you all. The flat looks good, and Pit Bull told me about the job,

No Idea

Martin, and that you're looking for work again, Rupert.' They both nodded.

'Aam sorry tae hear abit Mrs Popov,' said Martin.

I sighed somewhat theatrically. 'What with her missing grandson and stuff, she didn't have much else to live for. It is sad, but she's where she deserves to be now.'

Pit Bull walked into the lounge with five glasses and a bottle of Pepsi. 'Blimey, Rob. You're almost sounding religious,' she jibed.

'I'm sure she'll get her reward,' I replied.

Pit Bull looked at me puzzled. 'That's a strange way of putting it? Anyway, what's new in your world?'

'Well, what with the depression and stuff I get in the winter, Grace and I've decided to spend a few months away in the sunshine. We're both going to Tenerife in Spain.'

'Aw, that sounds amazing, Rob,' smiled Pit Bull. 'But I thought you'd run out of money n' stuff?'

'I had. But I went back to see my mum and she's given me some of Granddad's money to get away. It'll do me the world of good, and Grace will look after me, won't you, love?'

'Rob, I'm not your mother,' she laughed. 'Would you like her to come as well?'

The lads high-fived each other. 'That's you told, ol' chap.' said Rupert.

'I suppose I asked for that. Anyway, we can't stop because we have to visit Grace's dad before we hit the airport. Oh, and before I go... if you see or hear from my mother, I told her we are going to Scotland. She doesn't like me flying n' stuff and she doesn't like the Spanish.'

'You better not come back with a suntan then, Rob. You can't get one of them in Scotland,' said Pit Bull.

'Never mind, I'll tell her I've been using a tanning salon.'

'Wa diz she hate th' Spanish,' asked Martin.

'No idea. Maybe she tried to do a Shirley Valentine and it went tits up?'

'Don't be horrible,' teased Grace.

'Anyway, we'll be in touch. Pit Bull, will you see us out? I need to give you something before we leave.'

I gave the lads a hug before walking to the front door with Grace. 'I want you to have this,' I said, handing Pit Bull a bundle of twenty pound notes tied with an elastic band. 'There's about two grand there. But don't argue with me. I want you to have this for the rent. It should be the head start you need to get going.'

'Rob, you can't do this,' she said hugging me tightly.

'I can,' I replied. 'And one thing you've taught me... If family don't look after each other, who else will?'

***

No Idea

After leaving the flat, Grace and I felt safe enough to make a visit to her father, Mr Stein, before we left the UK. Grace's car was parked up outside her home in Streatham, so we used a taxi to stop off for dinner at a pub restaurant just a few miles away from Mr Stein before we would make our way to Heathrow airport for a 10.30pm departure.

Both of our passports were up-to-date (I still had a year left on mine) and Grace had booked First Class flights for us to Tel Aviv, Israel. I remarked that First Class seemed a bit extravagant, but Grace said we had Mrs Popov to thank for that.

Grace told me her father had a close friend, Mr Goldwyn, who owned a café in Tel Aviv along with a several rental properties in Netanya, a short taxi ride away. She had visited there many times and was familiar with the place. I was excited at the thought of going anywhere with Grace and would have gladly settled for a caravan in soggy Skegness, but with upwards of twenty grand of Mrs Popov's money, sunny Israel sounded a far more benevolent choice.

'Rob, Tel Aviv is great because I'll feel like I'm near family, and the only other person who knows about our friend, Jacob Goldwyn, is my dad. We'll be safe there, and we can stay for up to three months with a tourist Visa.'

'Cool, so he can help us find somewhere to stay?' I asked.

'It's already sorted. He has a holiday apartment available and we can stay in it for as long as we want.'

I knew little about Israel apart from what I'd seen on the news, and even less about Tel Aviv, other than it was a Mediterranean coastal resort with plenty of beaches and nightlife. 'Sounds like it might be the perfect cure for my winter blues,' I said.

'Exactly, it gets over 300 days of sunshine a year and even in October it can reach 30 degrees. You'll love the architecture and museums, and when you take me out for dinner, you'll be spoilt for choice,' she smiled, holding up a wine glass. 'Here's to sunshine and happiness, some great writing, good health and erm... the death of our enemies!' Grace let out a loud laugh. Seeing her smile again made me feel like I was the luckiest man alive.

The chink of our glasses raised a fond memory of summertime at Granddad's house. He often left the back door open, and as you walked through the rustle of the long multi-coloured beaded curtain that hung over the door, you could hear the wind chimes just outside. I was grateful for those magical memories and was excited about creating new ones with Grace. The thought of spending my winter in a warm and sunny climate washed over me like a spoken blessing.

I winked at her. 'Sounds like you'll have to do some serious shopping for me at the airport. Shorts, t-shirts, flip flops, sun lotion - I'm up for the lot.'

'With your pasty skin, we'd better start with factor 50,' she laughed. 'And aren't you glad Hilary gave you a pedicure as well?'

'Ah, yes, who can forget the butcher from oop North? I certainly won't.'

No Idea

***

It was 6.30pm and we had just finished our meal at the restaurant and were en-route to visit Mr Stein. We didn't talk much in the taxi. I think we both needed some quiet space to comprehend what had happened to us in the past few days and also what we were about to embark upon.

I held Grace's hand in the back seat and leaned over to kiss her. I loved the smell of her skin and hair, and closed my eyes and inhaled, trying to capture every sweet scent that was so uniquely hers. With a gun pointing to my head, I had been willing to die for this girl. Now I was given the chance to live for her, and I was overwhelmed with gratitude.

Barely a week ago I might have given a quick wink or thumbs up to the cold and impersonal universe, but now, on the contrary, my feelings were all the more personal, like I wanted to thank someone, rather than something. I've never been the religious type, but my thoughts were beginning to crystallise, no doubt encouraged by the sense of joy and adventure I was experiencing. I previously had no idea where I was going, but now I felt a sense of purpose and destiny, like some higher power was actually looking over, even rooting for us.

Maybe Grace's faith and Mum's prayers were playing a part in my life? I wasn't entirely comfortable with the thought of religion, yet I'd began to perceive that my life was like a tapestry woven with trials and failures; only now, a few new threads had been added - threads of hope and opportunity.

Religion always felt so impersonal. Whether it was the pompous ritual of clergy in fancy dress or the stale smell of my classroom RE lessons and the accompanied boredom, these feelings were now being replaced with something far more tangible. Fuelled with hope, or dare I say it, faith, I wanted to thank this unknown God - maybe Grace's God - for helping me to experience something rather than just hear about it. Despite the turmoil of the last few days, I felt like something fresh and new was about to happen in my life.

My thoughts were interrupted by Grace as she withdrew a tissue from her pocket and wiped her eyes.

'Grace, what's up?'

She remained quiet for a few moments before replying. 'I was just wondering whether my dad would recognise me today.'

I had never known anyone with dementia and could only hazard a guess at just how lonely Grace must have felt. My voice was quiet and gentle. 'I do hope so, Grace, but if he doesn't, you must cherish the precious memories you have of your dad. The times when he told you how proud he was of you, how he loved you. I'm sure you were always his princess.'

'You make it sound like he's already dead,' she replied.

'Sorry, I didn't mean to. I'm just saying you have to remember who your dad really is, and not just someone with dementia. Oh crap... here I am talking to you about an illness I know nothing about.'

'I know you mean well, Rob. It's okay. Now it's sinking in that we're going to be away for a month or two, I don't want this to be the last time I see him. Won't he wonder where his daughter is?'

'I say we get a Pay as You Go phone at the airport and you can call him regularly at the home. I'm sure it'll be safe enough for us to do that.'

Grace nodded and wiped her eyes. 'Thanks, Rob.'

'We'll create some special memories that we can share with him when we return.'

***

We pulled up outside Mr Stein's care home and pressed the buzzer.

A lady who suited the description of an old hospital matron, opened the door. 'Hi Grace. Your dad's in the Rose lounge... would you and your friend like a cup of tea?'

We both politely declined before making our way to one of the communal lounges to be met by the tune of an old wartime chorus:

'Roll out the barrel – we'll have a barrel of fun.

Roll out the barrel – we've got the blues on the run.

Zing! Boom! Tarrarel! – ring out a song of good cheer.

Now's the time to roll the barrel – for the gang's all here.'

We stood at the entrance watching the residents while Grace pointed out her dad sitting on the left hand side of the room by the window. She smiled as he joined in the song. It mattered little whether the music reflected his generation. This was a happy communal experience.

It was the first time I had visited any type of nursing/care or retirement home. I was struck by the shared activities listed by day and time on the wall, and from bingo and card games through to visits from local musicians and trips out, there was something for everyone. The word dignity sprang to mind. Whether they dozed in the lounge, watched the television or engaged themselves in the activities, every person appeared to be treated with dignity and respect.

Grace took my hand and walked over to greet her father.

'Hi Daddy, how are you?'

Mr Stein looked up and smiled, but I wasn't altogether sure if he knew who Grace was.

'I've brought a friend with me today. His name is Rob, and he's a writer. You like books, don't you?'

I remembered Grace's words. 'You have to treat them as a person and look past the illness. He may not know who I am now, but I know who he is. That is enough.'

Grace spoke to her father with gentleness, demonstrating great patience in her tone of voice. 'What did you have for your dinner this evening?'

No Idea

Mr Stein cupped his daughter's face in his hand. 'How was school today, my dear? Did you hand in your homework?'

'Papa, of course I did. I handed in my painting of our garden with the flower beds and your favourite Ranunculus flowers. You remember them, don't you?'

Though their conversation was rooted in the past, I loved the willing role Grace played in her father's memories. For the next ten minutes their conversation was lucid, even if it belonged to another time.

'Papa, I'm going on holiday and I'm going to see your friend, Mr Goldwyn. Won't that be lovely, and I will call you from his home. Is that okay? Can we chat on the telephone?' she asked.

'Who is Mr Goldwyn?' he replied. 'You be careful, my dear. You know what your mother and I have taught you about strangers.'

Grace smiled. 'Don't worry, Papa. I will be careful. And Rob will look after me, won't you?'

I nodded. 'Mr Stein, I promise to take good care of your daughter.'

'Good care? She's not a china plate, my lad, though fragile she may well be. And rinse the plates after dinner, won't you. I don't like soapy suds on the dishes. Wash it all off. Anyway, what's for dessert?'

'Erm, would you like some dessert?' I replied. What a stupid response. Grace had mastered the art of making conversation with her father make any sense, but I'd just offered him dessert and only after I'd rinsed the dinner plates in the kitchen.

'Who are you?' he replied.

'Sorry, my name is Rob Wise. I am, erm...' I froze for a moment, not knowing whether to say that I was Grace's boyfriend or go fetch some pudding.

'Ah yes, of course you are,' he replied.

'Papa, Rob is my boyfriend. And he takes good care of me.'

'Well, I don't know who he is, but if he's honourable, we shall have to see. I should like to meet his parents, my dear. Then I will give you my blessing or not.'

I gently reminded Grace of the time and that we needed to check in three hours before our British Airways flight. She stood up from her chair and hugged her father and kissed him on the cheek. 'Papa, I'll call you soon. You will come to the telephone won't you? And don't forget – I love you.'

Her last three words of love and affection seemed to hover in time. I imagined hearing those same three words again, but this time, with my name added on the end. 'I love you, Rob.'

Mr Stein stood up from his chair and thrust his hand out in front of me. 'Thank you for coming to see me, doctor. I'll be as right as rain in the morning,' he chirped, before shaking my hand.

'I'm sure you will, Mr Stein, I'm sure you will.'

No Idea

Chapter 25

Tel Aviv, Israel

Less than a week ago we arrived at Ben Gurion, a large modern airport with a buzzing cosmopolitan feel and a swagger that made Heathrow look a little less ordinary. Spotlessly clean and bustling with life, we walked past people holding up greeting signs and were welcomed by a plethora of fashionable shops and restaurants. First impressions were dazzling, and the signs written in Hebrew, English and Arabic added to the delicious atmosphere.

Our accommodation was in the beautiful city of Netanya, only 30km from Tel Aviv, so travelling in by taxi had been easy. Our apartment was perfect, with spacious rooms and a balcony overlooking the Sironit Beach and its beautiful coastline. I had looked forward to meeting Mr Goldberg and thanking him for the kind use of his apartment, but ironically, the day we arrived in Tel Aviv, he was leaving for a family holiday in New York. He left a letter for Grace with directions to the nearest supermarket, along with a fully stocked fridge and half a dozen bottles of (according to Mr Goldberg) the finest wines grown in Israel.

People watching (a habit of mine) had been a fascinating experience while I sat in the diverse selection of international cafés. Having already visited the four areas of Tel Aviv (North, Centre, South and Beach), we had enjoyed conversations with Russians, French, Ethiopians, Brits, Canadians, Americans, Australians and South Africans, among many more.

Grace looked at home among the many beautiful girls that visited or lived in this small Mediterranean coast, but I only had eyes for Grace. I was hoping my recent grooming efforts made me fit in a little better with the summer bodies I'd seen on the beach, but I wasn't so sure.

'So how do I brush up against the Kens with their six packs and sports cars?' I asked Grace.

'Well, the Factor 50 Sun Lotion has kept you from cooking like a lobster and I'm hoping you'll turn from a soft pink to a healthy brown. Otherwise, I'm not sure you'd look right with this Barbie Doll,' she giggled from the bathroom.

'At least this Ken doesn't wear socks and sandals together like some Brits,' I chuckled.

'Do that and you'll be flying home on your own and sooner than you think.'

Thankfully, Grace wasn't the shallow type, and seemed happy with me. How could I tell? Every day she looked into my eyes for longer than I dared hope for.

I was looking forward to taking Grace to dinner at the Azrieli Towers and I read in a brochure that from the observatory on the round tower you could see the entire coastal plain for miles. I wanted tonight to be special, just as our days had been since we arrived.

Grace stepped out of the bathroom in a stunning halter neck white dress with open toed brown leather sandals. Her feet had tanned in the week since we arrived, and were decorated with silver diamante stones, not so dissimilar to the dreamy girl I wrote about in the first two thirds of my short story at the Noire Bistro in Chancery Lane. Thankfully, Grace didn't have a pickaxe in her throat and my fairy tale was becoming a reality.

Sitting on the corner of the bed I couldn't help but stare at Grace. 'You'll need to put some more lipstick on in a minute,' I smiled.

Her eyes sparkled. 'And why is that, Mr Wise?'

I took the palm of her hand and with my other arm, drew her waist against mine. I kissed her lips and wrapped my arms around her, my kiss lingering, her fresh minty breath enticing me to explore her soft lips. I moved her body against the wall.

'Rob, let's not rush,' she said. 'I'm an old fashioned girl, if you know what I mean.'

I had never pictured myself as a married man, and I was quite sure that I had plenty to learn, and not just about Grace. But one thing had become crystal clear to me in the past week - I wanted to be with this girl forever.

I ran my fingers through her long curly hair and looked deeply into her eyes. My body stirred again, aroused, as I pressed my body against hers.

Grace pulled away slowly. 'That's good timing,' she teased. 'I think that's our taxi outside.'

I promised Grace that I would master my natural urges if it meant doing things right by her. It was proving almost impossible, but I respected her wishes. The bottom line was I wanted to be with her, body and soul. To my surprise, I was also learning to love why she didn't want to rush into bed with me. In just a short time, Grace had taught me that building a deep friendship was the key to laying a strong foundation for our future.

***

Our taxi took us past side streets with the names of those who had inspired generations. Tel Aviv had clearly evolved way beyond the impression that an unfamiliar traveller like myself had of Israel. Even though the West Bank with all of its insurmountable difficulties was only an hour's travel away, it seemed almost forgotten by the people who shared the kilometres of beaches and shops throughout the city.

I'd previously imagined Israel as a land of artefacts and antagonised people, a contradiction of Arabs and Israelis and a tinder bomb waiting to happen. But here, a giddy optimism breezed through the streets. I learned from Grace that in Jaffa, Jews, Christians and Arab Muslims lived side by side, and the people of Tel Aviv made no distinction between orthodox Jews or secular ones. Tel Aviv was clearly the contradiction, an oasis in the eye of the storm, where the people lived like they hadn't time to stop and think about their problems.

Since our arrival we used the same taxi driver when traveling in from Netanya. I loved to ask him questions, and especially because his spoken English was good and he seemed to enjoy talking with me.

'How do you feel about the way Israel is portrayed in the media?' I asked.

'Contrary to your BBC, most Israelis do not wish the death of their enemies,' said our taxi driver. 'We wish only for another day. And in that moment we try to forget what divides us. And then we wish for another day.'

'But aren't you tired of people's perception of Israel?' I asked.

'If you don't ask, we don't care,' he replied.

I loved the directness of the Israelis I'd met. Not deliberately rude, but economical, even stoic with their views.

Our driver continued, 'What can we do? There will always be conflict. Why worry, when you can live? This is the way of Tel Aviv.'

Before we made our way on foot to Azrieli Towers, we stood at the corner of Dizengoff Street and Ben Gurion Boulevard enjoying a fresh fruit shake at a corner kiosk. I was in playful mood and stood in front of Grace and mimicked holding a microphone to my mouth:

'Madam, here in Tel Aviv the blue Mediterranean water and golden sand is home to the most beautiful sunsets... it's a place where the street musicians serenade you with singing and dancing and kittens playfully chase each other in the cobbled alleys. In this magical land, the sunshine lights up the many rows of cafes and bars ready to indulge your every desire,' I said.

She replied, 'So now you want to be my tour guide?' she giggled, slapping my rear.

No Idea

'Tel Aviv is a joyous place where the pitter-patter of tiny feet reverberates around the restaurants and the elderly are given first place, rather than ignored or forgotten. Welcome to the beautiful land of Israel!'

'Rob, have you been drinking too much of Mr Goldberg's wine?' she laughed.

'I just feel so happy here,' I replied. 'Like my senses are engulfed in a cacophony of sounds - water, sea, birds, cars, mopeds, bicycles, shoppers, street entertainers, and of course, let's not forget the food. If I eat another Falafel, I'll end up looking like one.'

'Fat chance of that, skinny ribs,' she replied.

We'd spent our week walking and cycling around Tel Aviv. We rented bikes every day and getting around the city was easy. There were automated pavement rental stations everywhere which made it convenient for us to pick up a bike and drop one off whenever we fancied.

The bike lanes stretched for miles, so this holiday was proving to be the fittest time of my life. Eating so well and exercising, I was toned and looking well for the first time in years, even if my pink skin threatened to turn dangerously red.

Ben Yehuda street was a favourite haunt with Grace. With all of its exuberance for life, fashion and art stalls I envisaged leaving Ben Gurion airport with a few suitcases more than we arrived with. She was clearly enjoying our holiday every bit as much as me.

If watching people was a sport, then Tel Aviv was the Grand Slam of the year. The people dressed carefree while others perfected decorum, and in this city, the two complemented each other. The incandescent love for life here was infectious, and I couldn't imagine myself leaving. I was enchanted and sharing the experience with someone I loved.

It has been said, 'an English man's home is his castle.' Here I imagined that most Tel Avivians only used their homes for BBQs and sleep, as the street cafes and bars were filled with people every evening. The thought of spending much of their time outside of the home was invigorating, and coming from someone who had suffered from agoraphobia, Tel Aviv's charms already had me spellbound.

We arrived at the Azrieli Tower and were led to our table. The view was stunning from the 49th floor in the 2C Mediterranean gourmet restaurant and dining just before sunset was perfect. Fortune definitely favoured the brave tonight, as I wasn't normally someone for heights, but Grace loved the window seat.

We decided to skip a starter and opted for a fish main course with roasted nuts and a Tataki roll of Beef tenderloin coated in fresh herbs, served on Pineapple Carpaccio and accompanied by a baby leaf salad. We often sampled each other's food in Tel Aviv, and tonight's dishes would be no different.

'Grace, I'm just a simple lad from South London whose aspirations never amounted to much before I met you, but you've opened my eyes to see just how beautiful life can be. Thank you,' I said, raising my glass to her.

She smiled before sipping from her white wine. 'Rob, you do sound so dramatic, sometimes. But thank you. You're not so bad yourself.'

No Idea

I tried to relax while I considered the words that threatened to spill out of my mouth.

'So, are you still okay chatting with my friend Kaisha, tomorrow?' she asked. 'Her flight comes in about 5pm and she's meeting us at one of my dad's favourite restaurants in Jaffa, if that's okay with you?'

Kaisha had agreed to stay with us for a few days in Netanya, before flying back to London and writing up the story responsible for sending us to Tel Aviv.

'Sounds good,' I replied. 'I can't quite believe we're going public with Alexei's story, but his email was clear enough about what we were to say and not to say.'

'To be honest, I'm still a bit nervous about the whole thing, but what with Mrs Popov and her husband out of the picture and then the newspaper article confirming Alexei and his uncle's death, I'm hoping we can start a new life when we get back home,' replied Grace.

'Together?' I asked.

She took several sips from her glass and stared at her crystal reflection before replying. 'What do you think, Rob?'

I felt my cheeks flush. I'd been planning this moment and didn't want to ruin it, yet my mouth opened as the words poured out of me.

'I want to be with you and I want to make you happy. You are my soul mate, Grace. I want to be with you when you wake up, and watch your eyes close when you go to sleep. I want to be the kind of man who makes you proud.'

I paused, as if needing to replay in my mind the words I had just said.

Grace lifted her serviette and wiped her eyes.

'I'm sorry. Have I said something wrong?' I asked.

'No, Rob. You've said everything right.'

I lifted her hand and kissed it. 'I always hoped someone would inspire me to find love. I just never believed it could happen.'

'Now do you believe?' she asked.

'Yes, I do. I believe that without love, I was stumbling around in the dark. You've helped me to see my life more clearly than I could have imagined, and in such a short time.'

I reached inside my jacket pocket for the Neta Wolpe Art Deco 14k Gold Diamond Ring I had secretly purchased in Tel Aviv while Grace was busy shopping in some chic fashion store. I hoped that one day I would know when to present this ring to her, but I hadn't figured it might be so soon. However, with newfound optimism, I'd decided to carry the ring in my pocket, ready for that special moment.

I continued, 'I want you to have this, Grace, with all of my love.'

I handed the petite jewellery box to Grace. She looked astonished, and at first glance, didn't appear ready for what was inside.

'Is this what I think it is?' She opened the box and gasped before looking up at me. A small tear trickled down the side of her left eye. I leaned over and wiped her tear with my finger.

No Idea

'Yes, it's an oval shaped diamond ring set upon an openwork floral design,' if that's what you mean?'

'But when did you get this, Rob?'

'I snuck out when you were shopping and collected it yesterday after I had our names engraved on the inside. I got your size right n' everything after I took a ring from your jewellery bag.'

I could tell she was confused whether this was an engagement ring or just a lovely gift.

'So why did you buy this for me?' she replied with an open-ended question.

'I want to be with you for the rest of my life. Will you marry me, Grace Stein? Will you make me the happiest man in the world?'

My attention was drawn to a young couple next to me who sighed loudly in adoration, waiting for Grace's reply. She snivelled and then cried a little louder. I didn't know whether to express shock or delight so I did both.

'Rob, my answer is...' Her pause was deliberate until the corners of her mouth widened into the most beautiful smile.

'Yes. I will marry you.'

In one chorus, the restaurant erupted in applause. It wasn't just the couple sitting next to me who were listening.

While Grace continued to sob and I wiped my own eyes, a waiter appeared with a bottle of champagne on ice. 'Compliments of the gentleman and the lady to the right of you, sir,' he said. I nodded in grateful appreciation in the direction of the generous diners and voiced my appreciation, before the music grew louder. I think someone notified the staff of my proposal, because a song befitting the moment with Hebrew vocals and accompanied by a classical guitar, filled the restaurant.

Grace leaned over and whispered in my ear, 'Rob, there's something important that I've wanted to tell you before this evening, but I've been waiting for the right time.'

'Can it wait until we get home?' I asked. 'Let's enjoy this evening. More wine?'

No Idea

Chapter 26

Bombshell

After celebrating our surprise engagement and drinking far too much wine, we returned to our apartment and slept soundly until 10am.

Netanya was the perfect place to relax. A beautiful city with 10km of beach and promenade strip with many superb ethnic restaurants, I was also looking forward to visiting the heritage sites and understanding more of Israel's history.

Grace joined me on the balcony wrapped in a large towel and lifted a jug of fruit juice from the table. The sound of the ice rolling inside the glass reminded me - as if I needed any reminding - this was also a time for rest, relaxation and hopefully, writing.

'Do you remember last night when I said I needed to talk to you about something important?'

'I remember it was the best night of my life,' I replied, pouting my lips and blowing a playful kiss in her direction.

'I'm serious, Rob. Do you remember?'

'I think so, but I was a bit bladdered so I only remember the good bits. What's up?'

'This isn't easy for me to talk about, so please be patient with me. You promise?'

No Idea

My cheeky grin was replaced by a sober gaze. 'Of course I promise. You can talk to me about anything. What's up?'

'It's about your mum. She called me yesterday on my mobile.'

'Grace, I thought we agreed we wouldn't give our number out? What did she want?'

She sighed deeply, before taking a sip of her drink. 'She wanted to know if I'd spoken to you about stuff.'

Grace looked worried, almost afraid to talk. Now I was concerned. 'What stuff? Is my mum sick or something?' I asked.

'No, she's fine... kind of. Oh Rob, this is hard. I don't know where to start.'

I stood up from my white plastic chair and hugged her. 'It's okay Grace. Just take your time.'

'After your mum married my uncle Vince, we became close friends. We used to chat all the time, and then she started to confide in me...'

'I figured that much,' I replied. 'So you know plenty about my childhood then?'

'That's it, Rob... your mum's asked me to talk to you about that. She wanted to do it herself, but since we left her so soon, she told me yesterday time was running out and I had no choice but to try and talk to you about...' she paused.

'Talk about what?'

'It's about your dad.'

'I haven't seen or heard from him since he walked out on Mum and me.'

'I know, and he's been in touch with your mum several times recently.'

'So it's my dad who's sick?' I asked.

'No, I don't think so.'

'Grace, just come out with it. What does my dad want?' I asked, somewhat impatient.

'Okay, I need to start at the beginning. It should be your mum doing this, but like I said, unless you fly back home and talk with her, I have no choice.'

I tried to remain calm. I could see Grace was visibly upset and she was just the messenger, so I sat back down in the chair and listened carefully. 'Go on, it's okay,' I replied, this time with a softer tone.

'Five years after your parents were married your mum found out that your dad was having an affair.'

'That doesn't surprise me,' I replied, nonchalantly. 'I don't know how many affairs he's had, but I wouldn't be shocked whatever the number was.'

'That's the thing, Rob. Your dad got another girl pregnant.'

My heart thumped violently. 'Are you telling me I have a brother or a sister?' I asked.

'No Rob.'

'So the baby died?' I asked.

'No.' Grace looked down at the floor as my eyes welled up. I was scared. 'Rob, you are that baby.'

I froze and remained silent for some time before I walked back into the lounge. Now I was walking in circles and shaking my head.

No Idea

I shouted back at Grace, 'So you're telling me my mum isn't really my mum?'

'I'm so sorry, Rob. She is your mum, just not your biological mum.'

'I don't understand. I've seen my birth certificate, and both of my parent's names are on it?'

'Oh, I can't explain that. You'll need to talk to her.'

'So why tell me now, instead of waiting till we got back to the UK?'

'Your birth mum has been in touch with your dad and she sent him a message to pass on to you.'

'What is it?' I asked.

'She wants to meet you.'

Tears soaked my cheeks and rolled off my chin. 'So why did my mum never tell me,' I sobbed. 'How come I have baby pictures of us both together?'

Grace walked into the lounge and wrapped her arms around me, the tears on her cheeks melding with my own. 'Your mum raised you pretty much from the moment you were born and she told me she loved you from the first time she set eyes upon you. She is your mother, Rob, even if she isn't your biological mother.'

'So my real mother gave me away from birth?'

Grace walked over and tried to comfort me but I pushed her away and headed for the front door.

'Rob, where are you going?' cried Grace. 'Please don't leave. We need to talk.'

'I should be having this conversation with my mum – the one who isn't really my mum – to be precise,' I snapped, approaching the front door.

'I know Rob, but because we might be in Tel Aviv for a while, your mum said time was running out and I had to tell you.'

'But you knew all this time and you kept it to yourself,' I snapped, selfishly. 'And then you saved this bombshell for the day after our engagement.'

'Rob, that's not fair. I didn't want us to have any secrets, but when have I had the chance to tell you?'

'It proves what I've known all along,' I shouted. 'Women can't be trusted.'

I slammed the front door behind me and walked out, who knows where.

***

I'd left my phone in the apartment and walked for several hours before, dehydrated by the sun, I sat under the shade of a large palm tree.

Here was the old Rob again - the one who needed his arse-kicking. Distrustful of people and afraid of getting hurt, the phrase, 'Hurt people, hurt people,' reverberated inside my head. I'd been mulling over who the heck my birth mother could be and wondering why she handed me over from birth, but now I turned my attention to Grace. The girl I shoved away, shouted at and acted like a spoilt brat with. I was overwhelmed with regret. Why had I treated the only girl who loved me, like an extension of myself? I wasn't hitting out at her. I was punishing myself like I always have, like the victim playing for an audience of one, the egotistical self who had just shunned the only woman he had ever loved.

The tweeting of birds and the gentle breeze of the sea pretended everything was fine, but my surroundings belied my self-inflicted wounds. I knew I had to see Grace and apologise and listen to her carefully. 'Rob Wise, you have so much to learn, you muppet!' I screamed.

With a thumping headache from the previous night's alcohol and agitated by Grace's revelation, I'd been walking for several hours in the midday heat. I hadn't a clue where I was, so I flagged down a taxi and made my way back to our apartment, determined to never to treat Grace again like my father had treated his own wife.

***

Grace wasn't inside the apartment when I arrived and I panicked until I read the note on the dining table. 'Rob, I'm out looking for you. If you see this note, please call me on my mobile asap.'

I dialled her number and was relieved to hear her voice. 'Rob, is that you? Are you okay?'

'I am sorry, Grace. Forgive me for the way I acted. Can you come home?'

'I'm pulling up outside now,' she replied.

I ran to the door and waited for her to pay the taxi driver, before embracing her. 'I am so sorry.'

'I understand, Rob. Let's go back inside.'

We held hands as we walked back into the lounge and sat on the sofa together, Grace extending a huge measure of patience and understanding toward me.

'Grace, I want you to tell me everything you know, and I promise I won't throw my dummy out of the pram.'

'I knew this would be painful, Rob, but the reason I had to talk with you and not wait until we got back to the UK was that your birth mother is very sick. She has cancer.'

I didn't know what to think or how to react. I had never twigged that Sally, my mum, wasn't actually my biological mother.

'Does my birth mother have a name?' I asked. 'Sorry, that was rude.'

'All I know is her name is Genevieve and she was only eighteen years old when she met your dad.'

'Why doesn't that surprise me? And Dad was nearly twice her age.'

'So he was about ten years older than your mum?'

I nodded. 'I think I need to phone my mum now,' I replied.

'I agree, but please be gentle with her. She only ever wanted to be a good mother to you. She never wanted to hurt you.'

I thought carefully about her words before replying.

'I've calmed down. And more than that... I've learnt something about my mother. I have more respect for her now than I've ever had before.'

No Idea

Grace wore a puzzled expression. 'Why do you say that?'

'Well, she wasn't the perfect mum by any stretch of the imagination, but she stuck with me through her most difficult times... and I wasn't even her son.'

Chapter 27

Decisions

After a cool shower I had calmed down and was ready to make the telephone call to my mother. I dialled and she answered the phone almost immediately, her tone apprehensive. I figured she must have recognised Grace's number and been waiting for my call.

'Mum, it's me... Grace has told me everything.'

Her silence was replaced by a crescendo of sobbing. 'I love you, son. I am so sorry we haven't talked about this before.'

The lump in my throat brought a stinging sensation. It wasn't going to be easy to control my emotions.

'I don't know what to say, Mum.'

'It means so much to hear you say that.'

'What do you mean?' I asked, puzzled.

'When you call me, Mum.'

I was unable to hold back the tears. She was right. Sally was my mum. Always has been, and importantly – always will be. I heard Vince's voice in the background, asking if she was okay.

'Shall I tell you what happened?' asked Mum.

'Yes... I think so.'

No Idea

'Five years after your dad and I were married, I found out he'd slept with a girl called Genevieve and she was pregnant with his child. My first reaction was to start packing my bags and head for my best friend's place, but after we sat and talked it through, I realised someone else's future was at stake, and not just my own.'

'My future was at stake, you mean?'

Her broken voice laboured amid gentle weeping, carrying a tangible depth to her words that spoke of their authenticity.

'Yes, Rob. The girl was barely eighteen, but the real problem wasn't her age.' I remained silent, waiting for my mother to continue.

'She was a drug user... heroin, cocaine. Whatever she could get her hands on at the time.'

'So how did Dad meet her?' I asked, not quite sure if I wanted to hear the answer.

'Your dad and I had been trying for a baby since we were married, but after years of negative results and tests, the doctors told me I couldn't have children. I was devastated. Your father was always as ever, indifferent, so we slept in separate rooms and soon after I found out he was sleeping around. He even paid for it when he had to.'

I inhaled deeply before asking the inevitable question in my mind: 'So I'm the son of a prostitute? It doesn't get any better, does it?'

Mum cried some more before replying, 'No, Rob, you are not the son of a prostitute. You are my son, my darling boy I nursed and cared for from barely a week old. I never looked at you with anything other than a mother's love. You were my child. You were no mistake. You were God's gift to me.'

I stretched my right arm out toward Grace, inviting her to hug me. She squeezed me tightly, unaware of my mother's precise words, but cognisant of their nature.

I returned to the call. I had no anger for my mother, just admiration and love. I figured despite being someone else's child and living with a serial adulterer, she'd stuck by me, well, at least until I was eighteen.

The sound of Mum's crying caused my chest to tighten with each sob.

'Mum, don't worry. It's okay. I love you,' I said, wanting her to know the depth of my own sincerity.

Now Grace was sobbing. I continued, 'And nothing will change that. I just wish I knew the truth sooner, cos I wouldn't have been so bitter or angry with you.'

'I wanted to confide in you, Rob, so many times. After all, you were often the only male in the house, but I bottled up my feelings. I didn't want you hurt as well.'

'I grew up listening to you both arguing and hearing you cry. Then you turned to drink.'

'Your father was the only one bringing in any money and I didn't want us to end up on the street. I told myself I didn't deserve any better, so I stayed with him even though I knew what he was. Before I moved out and left you the note, I was suicidal, and I knew your granddad, your father's dad, was nothing like his son. I knew he'd take care of you and he was a great support to me, even when I was on the pills and drinking heavily.'

'But Mum, when Granddad died I felt like I had no one.'

I'm sorry I wasn't there for you, Rob. I had no idea he would die just a month after I'd moved out. I know I was being selfish, but I believed you needed a more permanent father in your life, and I hoped by moving in with Granddad, you'd get that.'

'I miss him. I really do.'

'I know, son. I do too, but then after he died, we saw less and less of each other, and I lost contact with you. I know you were angry with me. I'm sorry.'

'I was angry with everyone, even Granddad for dying. I have no one to blame for the bitterness, but myself.'

The line was quiet for a few seconds before I asked about my birth certificate. 'So about my biological mum, what I don't get is, it's yours and Dad's names on my birth certificate. I remember because I saw it again when I applied for my passport.'

'Your father registered the birth. He took our marriage certificate with him and just gave the details over the counter. I know it was wrong, but your biological mother agreed that for your sake it would be best if her name wasn't on the birth certificate.'

'How did you get away with that?' I asked.

'Things were pretty lax in the 80s. Your dad falsified some papers and replaced Genevieve's name with mine. I don't think the registrars even asked for proof.'

'So why did Dad want you both to raise me?'

'Genevieve was only 18 and in no fit state to care for you. No one wanted to see you go into care. I think your dad also thought it would keep me quiet if I had a baby to look after.'

'So why does she want to see me after thirty-three years? Why now?'

'After she got herself clean, she was always asking to see you, but what with the turmoil of our marriage and my desire to keep you away from as much hurt as possible, we decided to keep our secret.'

'So how did she cope with never being able to see her own son?' I asked.

'We came up with a plan so she could see you. In fact, you've already met her, many times.'

'You're kidding me?'

'After I found out your father groomed her and got her into drugs in the first place, we became friends.'

'So who was Genevieve? Was she a dinner lady at school or something?'

'Not exactly, Rob. But I think you should ask her yourself.'

'Mum, I can't explain why, but I can't come back home for a while. I don't even know if I'm ready to meet her yet.'

'The thing is son... she's in hospital.' Mum paused among gentle sobbing. 'Your... your mum has had lung cancer for some time. It's spread to her lymph nodes and other places, and now they think it's in her liver. I think that's the final stage. I'm sorry, Rob.'

'Mum, you've still not told me who she is?'

She hesitated before whispering something to Vincent in the background. I heard her say, 'But he has every right to know who his mother is. I don't want to let him down again.'

'Rob, do you remember my friend who used to bring you home from school when I wasn't well enough to pick you up?'

'You mean Aunty Caroline? Of course I remember her.'

'Of course you do. The lady you called Aunty Caroline is Genevieve, your biological mother.'

I closed my eyes, again, teardrops streaming down my face. I passed the phone to Grace. 'Please tell my mum I'm fine, but I need some space now.'

***

It was three o'clock in the afternoon and I'd slept for a few hours since my life-changing phone call.

'Rob, remember we are meeting my friend, Kaisha, in Jaffa later to go over the story. Do you feel okay to chat?' asked Grace.

'I don't know... I suppose so,' I said.

'How are you feeling? she asked.

'Like my life is perfect material for a soap opera.'

'After you went for a sleep, I spoke to your mum. She's told me everything. So how do you remember your Aunty Caroline, I mean, Genevieve?'

I rubbed my face in the palm of my hands and rested my head and neck back into the sofa before speaking. 'She was quite tall, slim and in her mid-twenties when she used to pick me up from primary school. She worked in a cafe in the high street and was always asking me to pop in for free chips and a glass of coke. I knew it wasn't free though, when I saw her take money out of her purse and put it in the till.'

'So you have fond memories of her?' asked Grace.

'I loved her. She was like a big sister when it was all kicking off at home. I even wished she was my mum, and my mind is blown now I know she's my biological mum. But if I hadn't discovered who she really was, I would still want to visit her in hospital.'

'So when will you take a flight back and go and see her? Would you like me to come with you?'

'I'll talk to her on the phone first and see where we go from there? I don't want to put you in danger. Alexei told us to stay away for a month or two. We've had enough drama to last a lifetime.'

Grace nodded and handed me her phone that was still charging in the wall socket. 'I've added more credit on the phone. And here's the phone number your mum gave me. Genevieve is in Ward 35 and she can take calls.'

No Idea

I dialled immediately. The number rang out for several minutes before it was answered formally by a staff nurse.

'Hi, er, may I speak to Genevieve in ward 35 please?'

'Genevieve who?' She asked, officiously.

'Ah, I don't know her surname.'

'I can only put family members through at the moment.'

'But I am family,' I replied.

'And you don't know her surname?' replied the nurse.

'It's complicated.'

'I'm sorry, but you'll have to speak to her family.'

I sighed loudly before replying forcibly this time. 'Look it's private. Oh what the heck... I've just found out Genevieve is my biological mum! Now will you put me through?'

'Wait a moment.'

After several minutes of holding I was unsure if I'd been cut off, so I used the waiting time to think about what I wanted to say. Like old telephone lines being connected, the synapses in my brain fired all at once, overwhelming me with imaginary conversations and muddled with a plethora of emotions. I decided the best course of action was to listen first and reply accordingly.

'Hello,' said a faint voice at the end of the phone.

'Is this Aunty Caroline, I mean, Genevieve?' I asked.

'Oh my G... Rob? Is that you?' she replied, her voice raised and excited.

'Yes, it's me. Mum told me you were poorly and that you wanted to speak to me.'

'What did Sally tell you?' she asked, her voice wavering between what sounded likes drags from an oxygen mask.

'She told me everything,' I replied in a soft, compassionate tone. 'And it's okay.' The line was quiet so I continued, 'You always felt like a big sister and a mum to me. I've never forgotten you, nor the free chips and coke! And you always made me laugh when I felt depressed about the arguments at home. And now I have two mums - and I'm cool with that.'

I'd never heard her cry before. Now I recalled the occasions where she seemed reluctant to close the cafe, wanting to enquire about my day. I could picture the disappointment on her face when she had to get me home for dinner. We met in the cafe for years, but after it closed down and she ended up working in a school kitchen, we only saw each other when she visited my mum.

'I don't know what to say?' she replied, still sobbing, her breathing laboured. 'You know, everything I did, I did for you, Rob.'

'Mum has explained about my dad and what he did. Truth is I haven't seen him since he left home, about sixteen years ago.'

Genevieve was silent, trying to calm her breathing, so I continued. 'I want you to know I'm not upset with you. And I'm sorry the way things turned out.'

No Idea

'I just wanted to hear your voice again, Rob, and I was kind of hoping I might see you before I'm gone.'

Now it was my turn for silence. I didn't know how to respond, so I opened my mouth and silently prayed the right words would come out. 'We'll see each other soon, and I will always have the most amazing memories of us,' I replied. 'And now they are all the more special to me because you are my mum and not just Aunty Caroline from the cafe.'

Genevieve laughed. 'Yes, we are flesh and blood, Rob. And when I've passed on, I've left some things for you with your mum. I want you to have them.'

'Please don't talk like that,' I said, the weight of her words unintentionally wounding me. 'You can fight this thing.'

'I've been doing that for a long time. I'm tired.'

Grace was stood behind me and threw her arms over my shoulders, the warmth of her body helping me to earth my feelings.

'I'll get a flight back to see you now,' I said, aware I was talking with my heart and not my head.

'It's okay, Rob. Sally told me yesterday that you are away. Let's meet when you get back?' she asked.

It was my turn to cry again. Every tear felt precious and valuable, like they were being stored away in a special bottle or secret place - and just like my 'Pandora's Box' conversation with Grace, my heart was healing even while it was hurting, and love replaced the hurt that had been eating inside of me.

'I will come and see you as soon as I can,' I wept. 'And I want you to meet someone very special. Her name is Grace.'

'I look forward to it, Rob.' I sensed she was smiling and something special was happening to her heart since we began talking. 'Text me your number, will you. I'll call you when I'm a bit better, if that's okay?'

'Sure, I will. But before I go, I want to say something to you,' I replied.

'What is it?'

'I love you, Mum.'

No Idea

Chapter 28

Poetic Licence

As we strolled around Jaffa Old City enjoying the stone-made, whitewash-bricked buildings, I imagined I was in Greece. Not that I had been there before, or anywhere else outside of London for that matter, but technically speaking, it was Western Greece, and seemed unique compared with many of the places we had visited in Tel Aviv.

Grace pointed out the stone-bricked restaurant across the road that we booked for Kaisha's visit. 'Did you know that the name of the Kalamata restaurant originates from a Greek phrase that means, Beautiful Eyes?'

'Ah, that's why this is your dad's favourite restaurant. They named it after you,' I winked playfully, wiggling my eyebrows up and down for comic effect.

'Creep,' she giggled, tickling my waist.

'Don't you mean, handsome rascal?' I replied, grabbing her and laying a kiss on her cheek.

'Rascal, maybe, but I'm not so sure about the handsome bit, what with your sunburnt nose.'

I laughed. 'I don't know why, but I forgot to cream my nose and to be fair, you could have mentioned the white patches around my eyes.'

No Idea

'If you never remove your sunglasses or cream your face properly, then your face might end up looking like a toddler crayoned on it.'

I pocked my tongue out. 'Thanks for the advice.'

An aromatic breeze beckoned us into the restaurant, where we were greeted by joyful Greek music and a warm smile from the waiter. Thanks to a late cancellation, we were led to a table with a perfect view of the Port by the window.

'This is magical, don't you think, Rob?'

'I wish I had the words to describe how I've felt on this trip.'

'Well, you better get that writing muscle going again,' she replied.

I smiled, comfortable amid the warm and engaging chatter of the diners and encouraged by her gentle nudge to start writing again.

'This is how I imagine it when you visit wealthy friends for dinner,' I replied.

'What do you mean?'

'Black and white chequered marble floor, bricked arches. It's like a large kitchen, with plates, bottled sauces, jars of local preserves and condiments on the shelves... a chef's delight.'

'Well observed, Heston Blumenthal,' she mocked.

'I like to think of myself as a Jamie Oliver kinda bloke. Y'know, Cockney accent, cooks naked, sophisticated with simple things,' I teased, pointing at Grace.

'I'd have to be a simple lass to be dating you and anyway, I'm just stooping down to your level to get you into training,' she laughed. 'Don't forget, you're under the thumb my dear,' she laughed, leaning over and pressing her thumb between my eyebrows.

Grace and I enjoyed some Ouzo alcoholic shots before our meal and decided to slow it down before Kaisha arrived and I could line my stomach with more Mediterranean food. We'd arrived forty minutes early, and famished, I'd finished a starter of salted cod served with dill and some fresh bread, but I wanted to remember my manners with Grace and I was happy to wait for our guest.

I'd eyeballed what I wanted to order on the menu - Aubergine Carpaccio followed by the catch of the day, fish kebabs. I'd even talked Grace into choosing the Lamb Souvlaki for her mains (she wasn't a big meat eater and I knew I'd probably end up eating half of it). I had already ordered three Jaffa Breeze drinks - a delightful collection of gin with hibiscus liqueur, red grapefruit juice and raspberry syrup, when Kaisha arrived and joined us by the window.

The girls embraced before I was introduced. 'This is my boyfriend, Rob,' smiled Grace. I had a huge grin, partly from being introduced as her boyfriend, and second, drinking too much Ouzo.

I raised my glass while passing the other drinks to the girls. 'L'chaim... 'To life and well-being'.

Grace giggled. I wasn't sure if it was my pronunciation or attempt at saying anything in Hebrew.

'Rob, where on earth did you learn that?'

'I read it in one of the magazines on the plane. I have a memory like a sieve, apart from some bits of random, interesting stuff. Then of course, I knew Mazel Tov, but I wasn't sure if you only said that at Bar Mitzvahs.'

Grace laughed. 'You might use Mazel Tov for a celebration, Rob, but L'chaim is fine, or you could just say, cheers.'

Kaisha was attractive. In her late 20s and with brown hair tied back to reveal a blemish-free and slim face. Her blue beaded necklace with seashells accentuated the neckline of her white, long-sleeved cotton blouse, and a full length, aqua blue cotton skirt suited local evening dress in Tel Aviv, perfectly.

After ordering food, Kaisha pulled out a Dictaphone and placed it on the table. 'You don't mind if I record our conversation?' she asked. 'Sadly, I'm only here for a day before having to fly back. The paper wants me to follow a lead story. I'm sorry, guys. I hope you aren't too disappointed. I would love to stay longer.'

'Aw, that's a real bummer,' replied Grace. 'Never mind, I think we are safe to talk here.' I nodded in agreement.

Kaisha leaned in. 'Rob, the email you forwarded to me from Alexei gave some clear guidelines for the newspaper article. I need you both to tell me in your own words, everything that's happened in the last few weeks. I'll write it up and email you with it before it goes to press.'

'Thanks Kaisha,' I replied. 'It's gonna take some time, so I suggest we order our starters and mains first. How about I get us a jug of Jaffa Breeze?'

Grace eyeballed me. 'No thank you. And that's your last glass, Rob. We have some important stuff to discuss.'

***

The evening had gone well, and summarising the events for Kaisha had proven okay until we talked about Mortimer and the so-called safe house. Since we'd left the UK, Grace said she didn't want to talk about the attempted rape and that she was fine, but she clearly wasn't and recalling the incident with Kaisha made her tense and understandably upset. Seeing Grace in such a vulnerable position with Mortimer was the very thing that made me propel my forehead at his face like a primed torpedo. But despite our escape and the fact Mrs Popov and her husband were apprehended and highly unlikely to appear on the scene again, thoughts of vengeance and anger filled my mind, fuelled by too much alcohol and only silenced by sleep.

Kaisha came back to the apartment for the night and enjoyed breakfast with us before we lunched in Netanya with Grace joining her for some last minute gift shopping before we said our goodbyes at the airport.

Seeing the Airport Departure sign filled me with anxiety. I wanted to see my biological mother, but we hadn't had the all clear from Alexei to return home, and the story of our adventure and Alexei and his uncle's death in the fire in Sandilands hadn't hit the newspapers.

I filled a jug with orange juice and ice and joined Grace on the veranda of our apartment.

'Honey, I know Alexei said we needed to be away from the UK for a month or two, but why so long?' I asked.

'I reckon it was just in case there are any loose ends with the people who have been looking for him and his uncle,' she replied.

'The thing is, Alexei won't know if we've returned, and if we stay out of London somewhere safe, who else will know we are back home? We don't need to use our cards, and we've got enough cash to last us for ages. If we were in any danger, they wouldn't know about Genevieve, and that's who I want to visit.'

'Rob, whatever you decide, I'll support you. But if we go back, I want to visit my dad as well.'

'Okay, but you'll need to go in disguise then,' I replied. 'I'm thinking big sunglasses, wig or head wrap, or if you want to be totally safe, a full veil like a nun or somethin'?'

'Very funny, just like Marilyn Munroe in the film, 'Some Like it Hot?' she replied. 'I'll do it, if you'll dress up like an Amish with a fake beard and long curls when you visit your mum?'

'Deal,' I joked. 'Book us the first available flights out of here. If Genevieve is really sick, I want to see her straight away.'

Chapter 29

Faith and Mortality

Grace and I arrived at Heathrow airport and were greeted with predictable British winter weather. Our t-shirts were covered with waterproof coats and the mirage of Mediterranean roads was replaced with the shimmer of earnest rain pounding the tarmac and a dark foreboding sky that promised little respite for the day. Thankfully a few weeks of sunshine had banished my SAD symptoms and I felt confident about seeing Genevieve again.

I spent the few hours of our return flight trying to process what lung cancer meant for my relationship with Genevieve, and as an agnostic who was thawing out and warming to the concept of faith, I prayed quietly in my head for her prognosis to improve.

I could still remember Genevieve's face clearly, though I knew her serious illness must have changed her appearance. I'd been reading about lung cancer on my smart phone and tried to prepare myself by understanding her symptoms and treatment. I also hoped I'd done enough crying in the past few weeks to ensure I didn't break down in front of her. I had rehearsed the visit in my head and was determined to hide any shock or disappointment I might have otherwise expressed seeing her in hospital.

No Idea

Most websites said that everyone's experience in the final stages of lung cancer was different. Some experience acute pain and others less so, and while Genevieve needed oxygen to control her shortness of breath, others managed without a mask. I was hoping there wouldn't be a rapid decline in her condition, but common sense suggested I take this trip as soon as possible and prepare for the worst. The fact she was in a hospital and not a hospice, gave me hope that her fight wasn't over yet, but I was under no illusion the prognosis was anything positive.

I avoided any discussions of the 'C' word with Grace, since her mum, Kitty, died last summer from the disease. The internet however, was a safer place for me to learn. But I was keen to talk to Grace about the topic of life after death, so I decided to ask her about it in a taxi en-route to the hospital, about forty minutes' drive from the airport.

'Grace, what do you believe about dying and stuff, y'know, without all the theological fluff?' My question seemed simple, even crude, but I didn't want to get into a debate.

Grace laughed. 'Give me a sec. I'll just de-fluff myself.'

'Sorry, I didn't mean to be insulting. I just wondered what the short answer was. I'm a simple lad.'

'Well, I'm not sure the answer is short or simple, but I had to break it all down when my mum died last year. It all happened so quickly.'

'How did you feel when God didn't answer your prayers?' I replied.

'Not just my prayers, Rob. She was loved by her family and church as well. Lots of people were praying for her.'

'And yet you still believe in God even though your mum died?' I asked, not meaning any offence.

'He didn't answer our prayers the way I wanted. I wanted the cancer out of Mum's body, but I guess He took my Mum out of the cancer instead.'

'Blimey, that's a bit profound. But I suppose it makes sense if you believe in heaven?'

Grace nodded. 'I guess we all just have a short time on earth. That's why I'm grateful for every day. I won't pretend that watching my mum slip away wasn't the most painful experience of my life. I was angry at God, big time. But then I remembered where my mum was, and I felt at peace. The timing of her death was hard to bear, what with my dad's dementia as well, but then life isn't about what's convenient or fair. I had to remind myself what faith and trust in God actually was.'

Grace's eyes filled with tears, so I put my arms around her. 'I'm sorry, Grace. We don't have to talk about this now. I'm an insensitive idiot for asking.'

'No you're not. I'm happy to talk about it with you.'

'I didn't want to make it too personal. I guess my question should have been, 'What do Christians believe about death and the afterlife?''

'Okay. The book of Genesis shows us that in the beginning, we had conditional life, in the sense we were given free will. If we chose the right path and listened to God's warnings, we would be blessed, but if we chose to know evil, then like a virus, sin would affect us all, and death would come as a result.'

I replied, 'So how is it our fault then? Way back in time, a few humans made a mistake and then it was like, boom, and now we all have to die for it?'

'I think that's a bit simplistic, Rob. We all share the same common traits as our ancestors, and despite having the same opportunities to choose what is good, we still sin.'

'I told you I was a simple lad,' I jibed. 'But I've been sitting on the fence for so long, my arse is full of splinters. Maybe you're helping me pull them out, one at a time?'

'Rob, I'm a visual learner.'

'You could do a lot worse than my rear, dear,' I joked.

'If your jeans weren't so saggy, I might see more of it! Anyway, think of it this way. Imagine we're already married-'

I interrupted and wiggled my eyebrows. 'Yep, I can do that.'

'Good lad. Now imagine I say and do things that show you how much I love you, but you take my love for granted and your eyes start wandering. You're flirting with other women and then you screw up, pardon the pun.'

'I'd never be unfaithful to you,' I protested.

'I'd hope not, but maybe my example isn't the best. I think in some way, we've all been unfaithful to God in word, thought and deed.'

'Okay, I get your point. So in one sense, free will is a wonderful thing, but at the same time, it's ruined our relationship with God because we can't help but mess stuff up? Free will isn't all it's cracked up to be, then, is it?' I replied.

'But we wouldn't be human without the ability to make our own choices. For example, when we first met, I didn't put a spell on you and force you to love me.'

'I beg to differ.'

I liked the way I felt when talking with Grace about more mature stuff. It was certainly different from the kind of conversation I had with the lads at the flat. Yet despite her education and Honours Degree, I felt I was involved in dialogue and not monologue and that we understood each other.

'So you believe that God is love, despite the fact that people suffer?' I continued.

'He didn't take my mum's illness away, but like the Footprints in the Sand poem, she wasn't alone, and through it all, she showed real strength and character.'

'I understand. I guess it's an entirely different perspective if you have faith.'

'And maybe the trials we face show what we're really made of?' she replied.

'That's a bit like my theory of the antihero,' I replied. 'If I'd never left the flat, my life would look very different now.'

The taxi driver seemed to be enjoying our conversation as he glanced in his rear view mirror at every opportunity, like he couldn't hear us without watching our lips move.

'Two things people are always arguing about these days - religion and politics,' yelled the cabbie from the front seat. 'We get to talk about everything in our work.'

I whispered in Grace's ear. 'If our cabbie stares at us any longer, we'll be finding out the answer to life after death any minute now.'

The taxi driver blurted out, 'If you ask me, it's religion that's responsible for all the war and suffering in the first place.'

I resisted mouthing, 'Nobody asked you, mate,' but Grace replied courteously. 'Sometimes it is, but look at our world. We still have war, famine, hatred and death, even though most people try to live without God. Look at the last hundred years... Stalin and Hitler murdered millions of people without using religion as an excuse.'

He answered, 'Wasn't it Karl Marx who said, 'religion is the opium of the people?''

'He did, but I don't believe religion cuts it either. That's just our way of trying to please God without dealing with the root problem. The answer is following Jesus, not trying to earn our way into heaven by being religious or ignoring the heart of God's message.'

'Anyway, I thought we weren't doing theology?' I said to Grace.

'You said no fluff and I'm just trying to answer your question as clearly as possible... but I have to confess something. I wasn't completely honest with you earlier.'

'Have you been telling me porkies, Grace Stein? What have you done?'

'I think I might have put a spell on you.'

'I'm quite sure you did, love,' I smiled, thrusting my arms out like a wide-eyed zombie.

'Well, your magic doesn't work on my meter, love. That will be £57.60 please,' said the taxi driver as we stopped outside the hospital.

***

The hospital was bright and surprisingly welcoming with artistic pictures depicting calm scenes on the wall, followed by a few small shops further down the corridor. I was reminded that whatever was left of our beloved NHS, at its heart, it was about a person's dignity and wellbeing. Here any foreboding shadow of pain or suffering was met with warmly-lit ceilings between skylights and cream-coloured walls.

I approached Ward 35 where Genevieve was staying and was greeted by a friendly smile from the nurse sitting at a long desk, surrounded by paperwork. I spotted her name badge, Staff Nurse Debs Mallagh, and thought it might be polite to use her first name if I wanted to fare better than the malarkey when I last telephoned the ward.

'Thank you, Debs. I'm Rob and this is my fiancée, Grace. We are here to see my mum, Genevieve.'

'Ah, yes, we had a long conversation yesterday about you. I've been looking after her, and I tell you, she's been keeping the rest of us in stitches, bless her heart. Would you like me to take you to her bed?' she asked.

'That would be great,' I replied, still smiling at her comment about Genevieve keeping them in stitches. The thought of her friendly smile and banter made me hopeful that cancer hadn't robbed her of the warm and vivacious personality I so fondly remembered.

'Before I take you in to her private room, I need to go over a few things with you. First, she has a compromised immune system. Any colds, coughs or germs can have serious repercussions.'

'We are in good health,' I replied. We both had taken the precaution to shower at the airport and change into some clean clothes.

'Great. Always wash your hands when you arrive in the hospital and also when you leave. You can use the sanitizer on the wall here before you go in. And if you wish to visit Genevieve again, please call the ward first, just in case she's having any treatment or isn't well enough for visitors. We also ask our patients if they'd like visitors and when. It can be a huge drain on them, so please be aware of how long they might want you to stay. The length will vary depending on how tired they are.'

'Thank you for the advice,' said Grace.

'Do you wish to ask me any questions about her care?' asked the nurse.

'I haven't seen Genevieve for a long time, so I don't quite know what to expect when I go in. Is she in pain?'

'She does get significant pain in her chest and back, so please be gentle, I know she's a hugger. Her pain management has been working quite well, but the tumour in her lung has brought on a persistent cough that's left her very tired. She's also been wheezing quite a lot this morning so we've been adjusting her pillows every hour or so to help with the pain.'

Grace squeezed my hand for comfort and reassurance, and then it dawned on me: What a selfish jerk I was to bring Grace into a cancer ward! She might also be clinging on to me, if the memories of visiting her mum were still raw.

The nurse continued, I'll just pop in and tell her you're here. Give me a moment, please.'

We rubbed our hands with sanitizer until they were dry again, while waiting for the nurse. 'I don't know how this is going to go, but thanks for coming with me,' I said to Grace. Her smile hid what I was sure were mixed emotions. Visiting someone with cancer barely a year from her mother passing away from it, couldn't be easy.

Grace's phone rang in her pocket. 'Agh, I forgot to turn it off. Hang on, it's Kaisha. I better take this call quickly.'

I nodded in approval while she walked back out of the corridor toward the exit. The breaking story about the fire in Sandilands and the identity of the bodies was imminent, and Grace and I eagerly awaited its release, knowing the news would travel fast to those who had been trying to find Alexei and his uncle.

I was glad to see Grace scurrying back, because I didn't want to keep Genevieve waiting long.

'It's done, Rob. The story is in today's Daily Telegraph. It's nearly half a page, including photos, and there's confirmation in the article that Alexei and his uncle perished in the fire.'

We hugged before I whispered, 'As one door closes, so another one opens. But first, let's see Genevieve.'

***

I rubbed the back of my neck anxiously, before entering Genevieve's room and tried to form a smile that would hide my shock, but the game was already up. She was unrecognisable. The youthful, plump face I so fondly remember was gone, now replaced with a gaunt, pale reflection and sunken eyes. I'd never really paid attention to the effects of illness before, but now her 51 years hid inside a body that looked ready for leaving this world, my chin began to tremble. I tried to stop myself from crying and squeezed Grace's hand for support, but the sight of seeing her so emaciated took me by surprise.

'Genevieve... Mum,' I cried, leaning over to kiss her softly on the cheek. 'I can't tell you how happy I am to see you again. It's been way too long!'

My emotions had definitely got the better of me, but her upturned face and sparkling eyes showed that my tears were appreciated, even valued.

Genevieve spoke with a raspy voice. 'I've heard you call me Mum so many times,' she said. 'But they were always a dream. Now I've heard it with my own ears, you've made me a happy woman.'

'Now I have two mums, and I'm proud of you both.' My voice wobbled.

'And Rob, you've grown up such a handsome lad. You've definitely got my good looks,' she replied, making light of her appearance. I tried hard not to stare at her bald scalp, but it was a sight too remarkable for me to ignore. I imagined her now with her long curly hair back on, but the only recognisable feature belonged to her large brown eyes that still sparkled with life.

My cheeks reddened as I wiped my eyes with my shaky hand. 'This is my fiancée, Grace.'

She raised her limp and bony hand slowly toward Grace. 'Oh darling, you are beautiful. Rob is a lucky boy. I hope he's taking care of you,' she expressed with a smile.

'I'm so pleased to meet you,' replied Grace. 'Rob has told me some lovely stories about the times you spent together. Chips and Coke wasn't it?'

Mum laughed as she tried to adjust herself among the large cushions that propped her up. 'Those precious memories live with me every day.'

A wave of heat followed by light-headedness overcame me. I needed to be strong, but clearly, recent events and the shock of seeing her in such a poor state were taking their toll, so I pulled a chair up next to the bed and sat down.

'So what's the food like in here,' I asked, keen to make less emotive conversation for now.

She chuckled. 'I haven't met the cooks, but I don't think they trained in a kitchen.'

Grace laughed out loud. 'My uncle worked in a care home and ended up cutting toenails, but it never made him a chiropodist, despite his notoriety and say-so.'

I took hold of my mum's hand, surprised by the affection I was showing. 'You'd laugh your head off if you saw him. His name is Hilary but he has the appearance of a builder and calloused rough hands that are bigger than my head.'

Genevieve coughed hard several times and pointed to her glass of water.

'Are you okay?' I asked. What a stupid question, I thought. Of course she isn't alright, but she nodded and smiled, deflecting the attention away from her illness.

'I'm so sorry what you've been through, Mum.'

'Don't be afraid, Rob. This illness hasn't finished me off yet.'

I recognised her smile and replied, 'I meant what my dad put you through as well.'

'Life's too short to hold on to grudges,' she replied. 'You get to do a lot of thinking when you spend so much time in hospital, and I am at peace with things. Cancer might take my body, but I won't let it ruin me. I try to see each day as a gift, though it's not easy when you're having a crap one.'

I wanted to ask her so many questions about her life and how she managed to find the strength to let me go, let alone, watching someone else raise her own son. But today wasn't about me. I needed to listen to my mum and learn what she was happy to chat about.

We spent the next ten minutes or so talking about her life. I was surprised she'd never had other children, or married, but I was glad she was at peace with her life and being single. In fact, the notion of single people being happy was new to me, but that only reflected the mundane life I had lived and limited company I kept before I met Grace.

'Rob, I'm tired now, love. I hope you don't mind. But will you come and see me again with Grace.'

'I promise. And I will call first to make sure it's okay to visit.'

'Good lad. Just one more thing, though. Your mum asked me to text her if you visited. We've been friends for a long time, and we stay in touch most days. Is it okay if I let her know?'

I looked at Grace. 'Yes, you can tell her I'm back home now.'

'And finally, I want you to know something... both of your mums love you, Rob.'

I burst into tears.

'And I love you both... very much.'

No Idea

Chapter 30

Robots Do It Best

We stayed at a bed and breakfast for the night, before I returned to my Mums and Grace went to see her dad at the dementia home.

I rang the doorbell and was greeted by an excited mother throwing her arms in the air. 'Oh my darling boy, come in, come in! Vince, Vince, it's my Rob!'

I'd only been away a few weeks, but you would have thought it was far longer.

'Welcome, Rob. How are you?' asked Vince from the kitchen. 'Have you been taking good care of my niece?'

'We're both well, thank you,' I replied, surprised at the warmth of his words.

'You'll have to excuse me. I'm just doing some DIY in here.'

Mum's face hadn't stopped gleaming since I'd stepped inside the house. She dragged me through to the kitchen and thrust a scone into my face. 'Fancy one with jam?' I nodded before she continued. 'I see the weather's been amazing in Scotland, then? I've never seen you looking so tanned and healthy.'

Fortunately, I'd rehearsed my answer. 'Been doing lots of exercise and using the local tanning salon as well,' I replied.

No Idea

'Well, just be careful with those tubes. I can't touch a light bulb without burning my fingers, so I don't know how people can lie on them. That's modern technology for you, eh?'

Vince turned around with a screwdriver in his hand and raised his eyes to the ceiling. I'm sure he was well used to her nutty comments and antics, but she was never short of surprises.

I sat down with Mum in the conservatory and enjoyed a crumbling scone with a mug of tea. She looked happy and healthy. Fair dos to Vince. He must be a decent bloke.

'Son, I spoke with Genevieve this morning. I'm so proud of you. It took a lot of courage for you to go and see her.'

'Not half the courage she's had to show,' I replied as my eyes filled with tears without a moment's notice. My emotions had been on tap since I left the flat.

'Do you want to talk about it?' she asked.

'Not now, but I'm glad I went.'

Mum bobbed her head in agreement before putting her feet up on the pouffe and sipping loudly from her mug. 'Oh, you'll never guess who popped by a few days ago.'

'Let me guess: was it Lady Gaga, Dawn French or Joanna Lumley?'

'Oh, wouldn't that be absolutely fabulous,' she said, unaware of the comical connection. She continued, 'It was Ruth Davey, Tom's mum, and she brought a folder over for you. Ruth found it in the loft. I took a peep inside and found some of the stories you and Tom wrote together.'

My eyes blinked rapidly. I remembered the folder well, and thought I'd lost it years ago.

'It's over there, son, on top of the cabinet next to the TV.'

Fascinated, I hurried over to the brown A4 folder and flicked through the pages of notes I had made with Tom, musing over the flood of memories.

My attention was drawn to a dozen or so pages held together with a paper clip. I pulled them out of the folder and was startled to see the title, 'Robots Do It Best,' written across the top of page one. This wasn't my story - it was Tom's winning competition entry that first broke him into publishing, while my entry, 'The Millennium Lover,' earned me my first rejection letter.

'Mum, why do you think Ruth brought this folder over?' I asked.

'Maybe she feels bad that you and Tom don't talk anymore.'

'And there's a good reason why I wouldn't talk to him,' I snapped.

'I know son. We spoke about it when she dropped by.'

'And what excuse is she making for her son this time?'

'None. She said he's always too busy to return her calls, but there is something in the folder she wanted you to see.'

No Idea

I took a deep breath. 'Do you mean his competition entry? It was crap. The competition was about the search for a young romantic novelist. His short story, 'Robots Do It Best,' was basically about an alien invasion that enslaved the world and turned them into sex addicts - with robots. It was tacky in the extreme, and I was amazed when it won.'

'Ruth asked me if you'd give her a ring when you saw the folder. She said it's important.'

'Why would she do that?' I asked.

'No idea, love.'

I stared at Tom's story again, unsure why he'd put a copy of it in my folder, before a rolling wave of nausea swept over me. 'Oh my God,' I shouted.

'What is it, Rob?'

'Ruth knocked his story up on her electric typewriter. I remember... his computer was broken, so he had to hand-write it and she typed it up.'

'I don't understand? What's significant about that?'

I looked carefully at the typed print on the A4 paper. 'Mum, this isn't a photocopy. You can see the letters slightly raised or indented on the paper. Unless she typed two copies, he never sent it off. This one is the original!'

'Maybe he sent a different story in, love?'

'He told me that he won the competition with 'Robots Do It Best'. And how do I know he sent off my story, either? He told me that Ruth went to the Post Office and sent both of our stories together.'

'She must have sent it, because you got a rejection letter in the post.'

'Maybe,' I replied. 'But like I said, this is his original typed copy in my hand, so unless Ruth photocopied it before posting it off, he never won the competition with this story.'

'Rob, maybe you're letting the bitterness of what happened between you and Tom, get to you.'

I sighed. 'You may be right, but Ruth wants to speak to me about the folder? Something's up. Can you give her a call now?'

'Sure.' Mum picked up her mobile and scrolled down the screen before clicking on Ruth Davey and handing me her phone.

The line rang a few times before it was answered.

'Hi Ruth, it's Rob Wise here. Long time no speak, eh. How are you these days?'

'Oh how lovely to speak to you again after all these years, Rob. I am very well, thank you.'

'Fantastic. I'm calling about the folder you gave me.'

'Oh yes, of course.' The line went quiet for a moment until she continued. 'It wasn't an easy thing for me to bring over.'

'Are you talking about Tom's story, Robots Do It Best?' I replied.

'Yes. When I was clearing out the loft, I found some other papers and a letter addressed to Tom from his publisher.'

'Go on,' I replied, eager for her to continue.

No Idea

'It was the letter informing Tom that he'd won the competition you both entered. He hadn't let me see it before, and know I know why.'

I swallowed hard and met her reply with silence, afraid that her answer might cause me to spiral back fifteen years or more.

She continued. 'Rob, the letter said that the winning story was called, The Millennium Lover. I remembered that was the name of your story that I posted off with Tom's.'

'What the...' I paused for a moment, unable to take in the enormity of what Ruth had just told me. 'So what story did Tom send off, if it wasn't Robots Do It Best?'

'After I'd typed it, he changed his mind and swapped it for a different story he'd written with you the year before, I think. I can't remember the name of it, sorry.'

'So are you telling me he swapped our names on the stories?'

'He must have, Rob. I'm sorry. I don't know what's happened to Tom, because ever since he won that competition, he's been a different person. He never wants to speak with me.'

'You're right he's been a different person,' I barked. 'Sorry, I didn't mean to raise my voice at you, Ruth. So why did you decide to tell me?'

'I've always been fiercely protective of my son and I still love him, but I couldn't let the wrong he has done to you, go away. It was your story that was the winner, and you were cheated out of the start you deserved.'

I looked over at my mum, the tears filling both of our eyes. 'Thank you for being so honest, Ruth. When did you last talk to him?'

'Tom hasn't replied to my telephone calls for months, and only last week I finally got through to his agent who relayed a message back, 'Tom said he's busy and he'll call you when he's free.' I was so hurt, so I left a message on Tom's answerphone telling him I knew what he did to you and that he had to make it right.'

'Don't tell me, he called you back straight away? What did he say?' I replied.

Now it was Ruth's turn to cry, as she snivelled and blew her nose. 'He told me he'd make it right by sending me some money and that I should forget all about it.'

I vomited my words. 'I need you to text Tom's telephone number to my mum's phone, please.'

'I don't know if I've done the right thing telling you now,' she sobbed.

'But I have a right to know why my best mate walked out of my life. Thank you for having the courage to tell me. Bye for now.'

My breathing became noisy while my face reddened. I was sweating, enraged at Tom's act of betrayal, compounded by his mother's words. I squeezed the phone and thrust it back at my mum.

'I'm off out. I need to go take care of something. Can you text me her number?'

No Idea

Chapter 31

Too little, too late

Grace returned from visiting her father, only to find me uncommunicative in my bedroom and numb from Ruth's revelation about Tom. Several hours passed before I relayed the entire story to Grace.

She said I should take time to think about my actions and to pray about it, but I was far too angry to pray. I needed to act, and my first reaction after ending the call with Ruth was to phone Tom.

I don't remember a great deal of the message I left on his answerphone, because it was interrupted by my blood vessels almost bursting in my face and a few cuss words that came from the bottom of my gut. There was still some sludge and crap inside of me that bubbled to the surface and poured into my phone.

My recorded message told Tom exactly what I thought of his betrayal and I asked him what he was prepared to do about it. I made it clear I didn't want his money, but that he needed to come clean, and if he didn't I would blow the lid on it all and that was bound to hurt his book sales and reputation.

Unsurprisingly, my mobile phone rang within the hour with the code, 01144.

'Hello,' I answered.

'Is that Rob Wise,' an unfamiliar voice replied.

No Idea

'Who's asking?'

'This is Richard Schneider, Tom Davey's agent.'

'Wow, my message must have made some impression, then. What is it, like 5am there in the States?'

'Let's cut to the bull,' he suggested. 'What do you want from my client?'

'I've no idea, actually,' I replied, deliberately obtuse. 'Anyway, what's up with Tom? Lost his voice? Doesn't have the balls to pick up the phone himself?'

'I've been authorised to deal with this matter. He's a busy man.'

'Wow, you really are full of it, aren't you, Mr Weiner?'

Grace pulled my arm and shot a glare at me, to which I pulled a face of my own.

'The name is Schneider,' he replied.

'I've never heard of you. Oh wait a minute. Didn't you play the police chief, Brody, in the movie, Jaws?'

'No, that was Roy Scheider,' he replied, his manner uptight.

'Ah, that's a coincidence, what with you both working with cold, merciless predators?'

Grace's look of consternation softened as she giggled at my reply.

'Look, Mr Wise, my client doesn't want this kind of negative publicity, so we have two options. 1). We settle this amicably by way of financial remuneration, or 2). I understand you're a struggling writer looking for an agent to represent you. I can look at your work and introduce you to people who can make your book happen.'

'You missed a third option,' I replied. 'My fiancée's bestie is a top reporter with The Daily Telegraph. Your client, being a best-selling fantasist, would make a fantastic story.'

'I can have a lawyer meet you within the hour. You agree that this story disappears, and we wire you fifty thousand dollars. How does that sound?'

I hadn't finished playing with Big Shot just yet.

'What are you, stupid?' I replied. 'I can't spend dollars in the UK. It's called the Great British Pound.'

'Okay, fifty thousand pounds it is,' he replied.

'Mr Weiner, I'm glad we've had this conversation, because I've been able to record it on my mobile. These smartphone apps are wonderful things, aren't they? Your words will make the story so much more fun.'

'Are you threatening us, Mr Wise?'

'Na, I don't do threats, but I do keep my promises, so this is how it's gonna go down, bro,' I mocked with a ridiculous American accent. 'If your client doesn't have the gonads to phone me himself, I want him to go public with the story. He can choose some kind of sob-chat-sicka-show thingy in the States. You have plenty of them, don't you, Mr Weiner?'

'I'll talk to my client and call you back.' The call ended abruptly.

'Rob, I can't believe you,' chuckled Grace. 'I just didn't want you to add any further stress to what's already been a mad month or so.'

'I know, but I just hate all the hypocrisy. First it was the money and then the guy was offering to represent my writing. You couldn't make it up.'

'Do you really want to go to the papers with it?' she asked.

'I don't know really. I just want to hear him own up. And why should he profit from my story in the first place? I know it was fifteen years ago, but it doesn't change the fact that he stole my work. I could have done with that break.'

'Maybe, but then you would have never met Pit Bull, Martin and Rupert, and we may never have met.'

'I know, but I'm just hurt that Tom stole my work and passed it off as his own.'

'Anyone would be hurt,' said Grace. 'But we can't be bitter. We have to look forward to the future.'

'It's hard to be bitter when I'm around you,' I smiled.

Grace snuggled closer to me on the bed and moved her pert lips over mine. 'When you kiss me, it's like nothing else matters,' I said.

'You are a smoothy, Rob Wise. Y'know when we're married I'll expect you to put out the bins and make me breakfast. Will you still want to kiss me then?'

'If you do the ironing, I'll be your bin man. Then we can kiss.'

'Don't forget my waffles,' she winked.

'It's hard to forget your wobbles,' I laughed.

'Waffles, Mr Wise, waffles!'

Our playfulness was interrupted by my mobile ringing. It had the same area code but this time, a different number calling from America.

'Rob, is that you?' asked a faint voice that I recognised was Tom's.

'The very man,' I replied.

'Oh, okay... it's Tom here.'

'I know.'

'Right, well, you've spoken to my agent?'

'If I hadn't, you wouldn't be calling me now.'

'Of course you have. Look, Rob, I think we've got off on the wrong foot.' Tom's voice was weak and soulless, unrecognisable from his famed and charismatic TV celebrity facade.

'Got off on the wrong foot? Are you kidding me? You got off the wrong foot when you stole my story and then treated our friendship like it never existed.'

Grace glanced at me with a tenderness I needed to deal with this call.

He replied, 'I know it was wrong, but when I won the competition, I had no way to backtrack.'

'You mean, when I won the competition but you'd put your name on my entry?'

'Yes.'

'Was it worth it?' I asked.

No Idea

'What do you mean?'

'You know well what I mean, or have you lost your soul as well as your integrity, now?'

My question was met with silence. How could he respond to that? The way I saw it, Tom had already shown his true colours by trying to silence his mother before speaking to me.

'It was the wrong thing to do, Rob, but the truth is, you just got lucky with your short story. I was always the better writer, and you know it, and millions of my readers know it as well. I just fast tracked my career, while putting you out of your misery at the same time. Your ambitions were not realistic. I actually did you a favour.'

A morbid fascination with Tom's words stopped me from ending the call immediately. I replied, 'The only favour you did was showing me what a pile of crap you really are. And I thank you for that, though I doubt your fans will thank me when they get to hear about this.'

'Let's not beat about the bush. I don't want the negative publicity and you feel wronged, so I'll make you an offer. It's non-negotiable, so take it or leave it. Sign something to say you made the story up and you regret ever coming up with the idea, and I will wire you sixty grand. It's as easy as that.'

'So I take it that your agent forgot to tell you that I record my telephone calls. You're being recorded now.'

My words were met with a long and painful silence, so I continued. 'So here is my offer and it's non-negotiable, so take it or leave it. You tell the world what you did to me, and you try and manage the fallout, or I'll tell the world using my tabloid newspaper contacts and produce all the evidence I have, including the testimony of your own mother, and we'll see how you fare then.'

'I need to think about it.'

'Take all the time you want in the next sixty minutes. If I don't hear from you, you know what will happen.'

'So it's sour grapes then? You just want revenge?' replied Tom.

'Not at all - it's about right and wrong. And if you'd been half of the man I'd hoped you might be, we wouldn't be having this conversation, because I don't do grudges and my integrity isn't for sale.'

'I'll call you back,' he yelled before the line went dead.

I turned to Grace. 'Things are about to get VERY interesting.'

'I know Rob, but can you really handle all this drama now? That's why I wanted you to take time out to think about what you want.'

'I don't think I could bottle this stuff up. I needed to get it off my chest and this was the only way I knew how.'

My phone rang again. The app was recording.

'It's Tom. I have an idea that can help us both,' he said.

'Go on,' I replied, wondering what bile he was about to bring up next.

No Idea

'Why don't we co-author a book together? It's what you've always wanted, and I'll give you a cut of the royalties as well. Publishing's a game and you just gotta learn how to play it.'

'That sounds a great idea... as long as it's about two childhood writing buddies who think they are on the same path, until one of them is betrayed.'

'I'm down with that.' Tom's reply was far more animated. 'But I'd want you to sign something to say that the novel is entirely a work of fiction and that any names, characters or incidents portrayed in it are the work of the author's imagination, and any resemblance to actual persons is entirely coincidental.'

'Ah, I have a slight problem with that,' I replied.

'What is it?' replied Tom.

'I was thinking more of a biography. I write about your life and how you turned into such an arsehole, and you get to try and explain yourself when I interview you in the book.'

'You know I can't do that,' he snapped.

'This is the last time we are going to talk together, so listen carefully,' I replied. 'The story is coming out, one way or another. So you can try and manage the fallout by sitting on a couch and facing an audience as you address your adoring fans. Why don't you call one of your TV celebrity buddies to do it for you? How about Jonathan Woss or Pierce Morgan? Otherwise, I'll do it, and it will be far messier for you.'

'Fine, but then I get to tell the world what a terrible writer you were anyway.'

'I don't care! Now get lost. If I don't hear from your agent that there's a public confession on TV in the next 14 days, I'll do it myself.'

'I bet you're enjoying this?' he asked.

'No Tom, I wish I'd never had to do this. I wish I had my old friend back again, the Tom I used to remember, not the one who sold his friend down the river.'

'The Tom you remember would still be living in a terraced house with some crappy office job. I wanted more than that, and I have it now.'

'You may have gained the world, but you lost the most valuable thing.'

'What's that - your friendship?'

'No, it's far worse than that.'

No Idea

Chapter 32

Pierce Morgan It Is

Several weeks had passed since my conversation with Tom and his smarmy agent, and I'd received a text message that the Great Tom Davey would be making a guest appearance on a 'Special' Pierce Morgan Live Exclusive broadcast. Tonight was the night.

I'd moved in to Grace's place (in the spare room, I might add), while Grace returned to her mobile hairdressing work. We felt safe since the story about Alexei and his uncle had gone to press in the Daily Telegraph and that life had returned to some kind of normality. I promised to visit my mother most days and our relationship was pretty good. I also managed to visit Genevieve a few more times, and though her condition hadn't improved, her health was stable and she had returned home to her shared flat in Tottenham, London.

In the past week, Grace had been busy with her hairdressing and I had made a space for writing in my bedroom, complete with a large table by the rear window. I'd started to write a fictional account of my journey, largely focusing on the past month and realised I had enough material for a book. I had no idea for a title, and for the time being I kept the real characters' names which helped me keep it authentic for now.

No Idea

Grace and I sat in front of the TV waiting for the Pierce Morgan Live show to start. My heart beat abnormally fast as Pierce's face filled the screen and addressed the camera:

'Coming up, ladies and gentleman, the amazing story and confession, yes you heard it right, confession of world famous author, Tom Davey. He joins us live for what promises to be an extraordinary revelation for fans across the globe. It's a world exclusive, and it's here on CNN just after the break.'

'You know he's really going to spin this story, don't you Rob?'

'I'm sure he's had plenty of meetings with his agent, publicist, publisher, lawyer and anyone else he thinks can help him, so it'll be interesting to see what he says.'

'And if he spins the story so it's unrecognisable or makes you look bad? What then?'

'He's not that stupid, Grace. Arrogant, proud, boastful and repulsive, yes, but not stupid. He knows if he doesn't tell the truth, he'll be committing suicide on TV.'

'What do you mean?'

'He doesn't want me to counter his argument and expose his version of the truth as a lie.'

'Maybe that's exactly what he wants? People say there's no such thing as bad publicity. It could be the very thing that sees sales of his books rocket?'

'Or plummet,' I replied. 'If he tells the truth, maybe he will be redeemed in the eyes of the world, but I'm banking on the notion that, "if you give someone enough rope they'll hang themselves."'

'I thought you said he wasn't stupid?'

'No, he's not, but I don't think he'll be able to resist falling in love with his own hype. Any decent person will notice the BS that comes out of his mouth. And any readers that aren't bothered will get the author they deserve.'

Grace passed a large bag of Butterkist salted popcorn. 'I thought I'd lighten our evening with some popcorn.'

I laughed. 'What would I do without you?'

'Hopefully you won't need to find out,' she smirked, grabbing the remote control and turning up the volume.

Pierce addressed the camera. 'Ladies and Gentleman, welcome back to our world exclusive interview with Tom Davey. For those who have enjoyed Tom's books, including the worldwide hits, Housewives Come First, Fast Love on The School Run, and Once Bitten, Twice Ravenous, Tom's rise to stardom has been remarkable. Friend to more Stars than light the night sky, His PR boasts an impressive number of clients that include George Clooney, Brad Pitt, Angelina Jolie, Beyoncé, Céline Dion, among countless others.

Now, Tom Davey, you've described your childhood as unremarkable. Tell us more...'

Tom straightened up in his chair and adjusted his shirt collar before replying, 'Thank you for your generous introduction, Pierce. I was born in Wandsworth, South London to loving parents, Ruth and David. We were a family with a modest income and a rented terraced house, and the closest thing we could call a holiday was a day trip to Clacton-on-Sea. Money was always tight, so during the school holidays we spent more time on the bus than we did off it, and if the weather was lousy, Mum still called the bus ride a trip.'

Pierce replied, 'And when you were just 13 years old, your life took a turn for the worse?'

Tom reached for a handkerchief in the top pocket of his tartan jacket. 'Yes, while I was barely a teenager, my father died of a massive heart attack. It was a huge shock to my mother and me, but I knew I had to be strong for her. My father was her world, and now her soul mate and provider had died, we had no income.

'So this is the amazing thing I read about you,' said Pierce. 'Is it true, even at such a young age, you took several part time jobs washing cars and working in a kitchen at weekends?'

'No, it's not right,' I yelled at the TV. 'I took him to wash cars with me a few times, but he didn't like getting his hands wet.'

Tom replied, 'Yes, Pierce, I felt a tremendous burden to support my mother after my dear father passed away.'

'And did you ever feel like, say, "I can't cope with this.'

'I won't pretend it wasn't hard,' replied Tom. 'But when push comes to shove, we weren't going to survive on my mother's newly acquired job as an office cleaner. I needed to pull my sleeves up, and then, I really began to have aspirations.'

'To write?' asked Pierce.

'Yes, or as other writers have said, to bleed on the paper.'

'And now we are getting to the crux of your story and the reason you wanted to appear on this show. You had a writing buddy called Rob. Tell us about him.'

'Rob was a friend who liked to hang around with me after school and weekends.'

'And what did you two get up to?'

'I shared my passion for storytelling with him and I think he caught the bug, so we started writing together.'

'What kind of stuff did you both write?'

'Rob tended to copy whatever I was doing. My interest was in writing romantic fiction and I guess he tagged along.'

'That doesn't sound very magnanimous to me,' said Pierce. 'You make him sound quite subservient?'

'No, not at all. His heart was in the right place, and I enjoyed coaching him and sharing ideas with him.'

Grace looked at me. 'He's spinning, isn't he?'

'Yep, it couldn't be more different. The only talent he had was writing sleaze.'

Pierce leaned closer toward Tom. 'So, what happened to your relationship?'

No Idea

Tom leaned forward to retrieve a glass of water and slowly sipped for dramatic effect. He took a deep breath before uttering the words that would either save or sink his career:

'I betrayed him.'

'And how did you do that?' asked Pierce.

'About fifteen years ago, Rob and I decided to enter a writing competition. The publishers were looking for the next Young Romantic Novelist and asked for short story submissions. I'd written a fun story called, 'Robots Do It Best,' and Rob's story was called, 'The Millennium Lover.' Tom blew his nose and dabbed at a few crocodile tears.

'Who the heck wipes their eyes with a snotty rag?' I yelled.

Tom continued, 'The deadline for entries was only a day away, and I'd spent so much time helping Rob with his story that I hadn't finished my own, so I abandoned 'Robot's Do It Best,' and printed off a short story I'd written earlier that year.'

'Unbelievable,' I snapped. 'I'd spent most of my time trying to help him rewrite his piece of crap, not the other way around!'

'Go on, Tom,' said Pierce.

'I was so frustrated at the time I'd wasted with Tom, that I swapped the names on the competition entries. So Rob got a rejection letter for a story I'd written, while I received a publishing contract for one that should have had some acknowledgment to Rob in it.'

'So let me get this straight,' said Pierce. 'You stole another man's work and passed it off as your own?'

'Like I said, Pierce, I'm not proud of what I've done, and I wanted to make amends by coming on this show. For years I've wanted to unburden myself of this error of judgment.'

Pierce leaned in for the kill. 'Now call me a cynic, but I couldn't help but notice that your books have been reduced today to 99 cents on Amazon. My researchers tell me it's the first time in your career you have ever sold your books for less than $2.99. Are you anticipating that your rankings and readership are about to take a huge dive? Have you reduced the price to counteract a big dip in popularity, or are you desperate for a new audience?'

'Pierce, I don't think that's fair. As part of my spiritual journey, I wanted to cleanse myself of any past mistakes. I believe that if I'm completely transparent, my readers would see my true heart and understand that my confession is a result of my growth as a human being.'

'Some of our viewers might want to ask, 'why now, Tom?' Why has it taken you nearly fifteen years to tell this story? Have Rob's lawyers been in touch with you? Have you compensated him in any way?'

'Because of the guilt I felt, I found it hard to talk to Rob after I'd won the competition.'

'After he'd won, don't you mean?'

'Like I said, Pierce, I helped him write his story.'

No Idea

'But you didn't write it, did you, Tom? And that's the point. Isn't it fair to say the lucky break you received into publishing actually belonged to Rob?'

'Well, I'm not sure I'd go that far. I had a talent and ambition for writing. Rob did it as a hobby. His ambition was to work in retail.'

I was so transfixed by the conversation between Pierce and Tom that I resisted the urge to throw the remote control at the TV. My mouth refused to open as I drew deep breaths with my nostrils to calm myself down.

'I don't buy it, Tom,' replied Pierce, as fierce as I'd ever seen him before. 'So you ditch your friend because you stole his story, his prize and let's face it,' his publishing contract. That's not the kind of start that any writer would be proud of.'

'That's a little harsh,' replied Tom, clearly all out of BS this time.

'Not as harsh as your betrayal,' he replied. 'My question to you again, Tom Davey, is have you tried to make your peace with your old friend, Rob, or compensated him in any way?'

'Yes, we have spoken, and I offered to compensate him significantly, but he refused my money.'

'Well, I like the sound of this Rob, and I think many of the viewers tonight will. Sounds like his integrity isn't for sale, if you ask me? And I for one would like to read one of his books – especially if it was good enough to win a significant prize in the first place.'

'Oh, I don't think Rob has written anything since the competition. The last I heard, he was unemployed and living in a bedsit with a few dossers.'

'Even now, after you've stabbed your best friend in the back, you're happy to belittle Rob on a worldwide TV show. Is that part of your spiritual journey?'

Tom butted in. 'Oh no, I don't mean to be derogatory in any way at all. I wish him all the best. And to answer your question about compensation, I've decided to give Thirty thousand dollars to an educational charity in Burkina Faso,' he said. 'Someone should benefit from my good fortune.'

'thirty thousand dollars doesn't sound a great deal from the millions you've made from your work, though, does it?'

Before Tom could reply, Pierce continued.

'Our viewers have been sending thousands of tweets in. Let's read a few, shall we?'

Tom swallowed hard on screen and nodded. 'Sure.'

'Okay, we have: #whoisRob... sounds a fair question, Tom. What's his surname?'

'Wise, his name is Rob Wise.'

'A few more texts here: Maggie Whittle has texted, 'Tom Davey the humanitarian saves the planet from his writing by having his books pulped by the container load.' And Loo Elton said, 'I hope Davey's readers boycott his books and start reading Rob's!' Here are a few amusing hashtags from our viewers: #RobWiseforPrimeMinister, #RobWiseismyguru.'

No Idea

Tom's neck was reddened either from embarrassment, anger, or both.

'And I'm sure there will be plenty of messages supporting me at this time,' said Tom, unable to hide his emotions.

'I don't expect millions of your readers to disappear overnight,' said Pierce. 'But to be fair, let's read a few from your supporters: Noelle Holten says, 'It would be a crime to stop reading Tom's books!' And Jodie Matthews writes, 'I'm off to buy a few of his books at 99p!'

Pierce continued, 'Tom, I have to ask: Did you come on this show to spin an old story and gain more readers? Isn't this just manipulative marketing on your part?'

'What I have done today, Pierce, is give an example to others that it's never too late to do the right thing.'

'So you want to carry on being a guru to your readers?'

'I still have so much to give,' replied Tom.

'I bet you have, Tom Davey. Thirty thousand dollars is a drop in the ocean for rich guys like you, isn't it.'

'What I give to the world is far greater than what I take from it,' snapped Tom, clearly losing his cool.

'Are you hoping the world will see you, Tom Davey, as a humanitarian, who now uses his wealth for the betterment of society?'

'I'm hoping that people will see that the need for honesty and integrity in one's life far outweighs the desire or pursuit of wealth.'

'It's a bit late for that, isn't it? Anyway, our time is up, Tom Davey. Thank you for coming on to our show and for baring your soul to all. I for one, want to know who Rob Wise is. And if you're watching this, Rob, do get in touch. We'd love to hear your side of the story.

Coming up next: A group of nuns save the day on the Los Angeles Coast.'

I stared at the TV, silent and numb from what I'd just watched.

'Are you going to get in touch with Pierce?' asked Grace.

'No, it's over now.'

'Rob, I think it's only just begun.'

No Idea

Chapter 33

Breaking Good

The world went crazy over the next few days as reporters queued up outside Grace's house. Mail continued to pour through the letterbox from people wanting to represent me, but one particular letter grabbed Grace's attention.

She held it aloft and shouted, 'This is the one, Rob! Let me read it to you.'

Dear Rob,
I hope my letter finds you well.
Forgive me if this feels like an intrusion and just one of many encroachments since Tom Davey's revelation.
I represent several authors who are published under the same label as Tom, so I took the liberty to contact the publisher and request a copy of your winning story, The Millennium Lover. I have to say that I loved it. Your writing was fluent, witty and original, and despite the fact it was penned fifteen years ago, it hasn't aged at all. I urge you to continue your work and would be happy to assist you if you wish to continue writing.
I am also impressed by how you have kept your integrity. The publishing world is more renowned for

cut-throat tactics than its moral high ground. The fact that you have refused to entertain gossip or reply to the barrage of questions put to you from the internet and the media is admirable and refreshing. As an agent, I would normally encourage my clients to use opportunities like this to build upon their author profile, but in this instance I commend you.

Early in my writing career, my work was plagiarised and the experience proved very depressing for me, so I empathise with your predicament. If you are looking for representation in any way, or you would just like a chat on the phone, feel free to contact me anytime.

Please be assured of my best intentions and keen interest in your work.

Kind regards,

Aisha Hussain
Literary Agent

'So what do you think, Rob?' It sounds a good opportunity to me. What will you send her?'

'What will I send? At the moment, I simply have... no idea.'

The End

Thank you

I do hope that you enjoyed No Idea.

I would be delighted if you would consider writing a review on Amazon and/or Goodreads and any other Social Media you consider appropriate.

You can also touch base with me by searching for Si Page Author on Facebook or via my website at www.sipage.co.uk

Thank you so much for investing your time in my work.

My best wishes,

Si Page x

No Idea

Si Page